By Janet Dawson
Published by Fawcett Books:

A
CREDIBLE
THREAT

A Jeri Howard Mystery

Janet Dawson

FAWCETT CREST • NEW YORK

A Fawcett Crest Book
Published by Ballantine Books
Copyright © 1996 by Janet Dawson

All rights reserved under International and Pan-American Copyright Conventions. Published in the United States by Ballantine Books, a division of Random House, Inc., New York, and simultaneously in Canada by Random House of Canada Limited, Toronto.

http://www.randomhouse.com

Library of Congress Catalog Card Number: 97-90550

ISBN 0-449-22357-4

Manufactured in the United States of America

First Hardcover Edition: November 1996
First Mass Market Edition: November 1997

10 9 8 7 6 5 4 3 2

For Spats

Acknowledgments

A WRITER GLEANS INFORMATION FROM MANY people while writing a book. I would like to thank the following people for their assistance:

Andi Shecter; Peter Beall; Kim and Brent McSwain; Lt. Ralph Lacer and Sgt. Dan Mercado, Oakland Police Department; Sgt. Steve Engler and Sgt. Kay Lantow, Berkeley Police Department; Sgt. Marc Mitchell, Mendocino County Sheriff's Department; Kevin Fletcher of Gallery Mendocino; Carolyn Clement of the Cheshire Bookshop, Fort Bragg; Lisa Bryan, Charles Cochran, and Bill Grebe at the Boulder County Courthouse, Boulder, Colorado; Tom and Enid Schantz, The Rue Morgue, Boulder, Colorado; Hank and Bridget Massie of Berkeley, California, for the use of their Doll House; and my parents, Don and Thelma Dawson.

California Penal Code § 646.9 as amended by Stats. 1994, c. 931, § 1:

(a) Any person who willfully, maliciously, and repeatedly follows or harasses another person and who makes a credible threat with the intent to place that person in reasonable fear for his or her safety, or the safety of his or her immediate family, is guilty of the crime of stalking . . .

(e) For the purposes of this section, "credible threat" means a verbal or written threat or a threat implied by a pattern of conduct or a combination of verbal or written statements and conduct made with the intent and the apparent ability to carry out the threat so as to cause the person who is the target of the threat to reasonably fear for his or her safety or the safety of his or her immediate family . . .

One

"WHAT THE HELL HAPPENED TO THE LEMON tree?"

The woman stood in the uncarpeted foyer of the house on Garber Street, hands on her hips and a scowl on her face.

I glanced at Vicki Vernon, pacing like a restless tiger cat back and forth across the worn red and black Turkish kelim. Now she stopped, widening those golden-brown eyes that reminded me of her father.

"Sasha," Vicki said, addressing the newcomer.

Sasha, still scowling, moved toward us. Tall and dark, with short, curly black hair that set off the big gold hoops in her earlobes, she wore loose-fitting blue jeans, a purple turtleneck visible over the collar of her denim jacket. She carried a red nylon backpack slung over her left shoulder. Behind her I saw a little boy, about six, wearing baggy brown cords and a yellow sweater, a bright orange child-sized pack on his back. He stared at me with wide brown eyes, one hand cradling the ripped stem and torn petals of a pink tulip.

Sasha ignored me and fired words at Vicki. "What the hell happened to the lemon tree? And the rest of those plants? There's dirt and leaves and flowers all over the porch and the sidewalk."

"Vandalism," I said. "We think."

Both of them turned to look at me. I'd been sitting at one end of the high-backed persimmon-colored sofa that faced the front windows, its bright upholstery clashing with the dark red of the carpet. Now I stood up. Vicki made the introductions.

"Jeri, this is Sasha Nichols, our landlady. Sasha, this is my . . . this is Jeri Howard. I told you about her."

"The private investigator who used to be married to your father." Sasha slipped the backpack from her shoulder and set it down next to the sofa. "Since when do you call a private eye to report vandalism?"

"Vicki tells me it may not be as simple as that."

Sasha frowned. The fading light of the March afternoon cast her strong features in relief. "Maybe not." She turned and looked at the child behind her, then patted the youngster on his shoulder. "You can play in the backyard until dinner, Martin. Then we have to do our homework."

The little boy, still holding the ruined tulip, opened the door on the opposite side of the hallway. I knew from what Vicki had told me that it led to her landlady's quarters, occupying nearly half the house's lower floor. The room where we were standing had been the formal dining room. It was now the living room, which, along with the large kitchen visible through an open doorway at the rear, was shared by all the residents.

Somehow, when Vicki described her living arrangements, I'd assumed her landlady was older. A professor's widow perhaps, forced by financial circumstances to turn her home into a rooming house. However, Sasha Nichols was in her early thirties at most.

The house was a rambling two-story structure, a brown shingle, one of many similar houses in Berkeley's Elmwood district. Many of these houses had been built in the early part of this century and were prized for their comfort and space. If it were for sale, the down payment on this house would be more than I made in a year. I could only guess at the yearly property taxes and the cost of heat, light, and water.

I was sure my theory about the landlady's tight money was correct. The place was in need of maintenance. Outside I'd noticed the usual things a homeowner has to deal with on a regular basis—the roof, the rain gutters, the exterior shingles that covered the sides of the house. All of these showed signs of neglect, and I'd seen a cracked windowpane downstairs, in Sasha's quarters. Inside there were hairline cracks on the high ceiling. It looked like the walls needed repainting. Patches of wear on the Turkish carpet and the sofa and chairs grouped around the coffee table gave evidence of years of use.

"Anyone going to tell me what happened?" Sasha lowered her voice, already an alto purr, and looked sharply at Vicki.

"Emily and I found the plants when we got home from class," Vicki said. "Emily was really upset."

As if on cue, footsteps sounded behind us as another person crossed the threshold from kitchen to living room. Emily Austen, one of Vicki's housemates, carried a round brass tray with three mugs of coffee, a sugar bowl, and a small pitcher. She stopped when she saw her landlady. "Sasha, I didn't hear you come in. I'll get another mug."

She set the tray on the coffee table and quickly headed back to the kitchen, returning a moment later with a fourth mug. She gave it to Sasha, then sat down on the sofa and picked up her coffee. Vicki perched next to her.

I resumed my seat and reached for one of the steaming mugs. I took a sip and felt a caffeine jolt surge through me as I examined Emily. If Vicki was a vigorous tiger cat, always in motion, Emily was a quiet brown wren, one who never had much to say. Her dark brown hair fell

3

in waves past her shoulders, caught on either side of her temples with matching blue barrettes. She didn't look upset now. I saw a touch of wariness in the blue eyes that looked out from her pale face. Was she wary of me, or of strangers in general? She seemed very much in Vicki's shadow, but something made me think that first impression was erroneous.

Mug in hand, Sasha arranged herself tiredly on the cushions of a wing-back chair and put her feet up on the coffee table.

"It's a lovely house," I said. "How long have you lived here?"

"Most of my life." Sasha sipped her coffee. Now that she was closer to me, I could see lines of fatigue in her dark face. "The house belonged to my parents. My father was a professor at the university. I'm what they call a faculty brat." She looked expectantly at her two tenants. "Let's talk about the plants."

It was the sight of the lemon tree that had upset Emily, according to Vicki. The tree's fate would bother anyone who'd seen the deceased. It pricked at my mind too. But I couldn't recall why. Citrus trees were common enough in the Northern California landscape. In fact, there was one in the courtyard of my apartment complex, near my front porch. I pictured the little tree with its dark, waxy green leaves. We'd had an early spring following a cold rainy winter, and the tree was now loaded with fragrant yellow-white blossoms, harbingers of the hard fruit that would soon appear and ripen from green to yellow.

But the lemon tree Vicki and her housemates had planted would never bear fruit. I'd seen what remained of it when I arrived, fifteen minutes before Sasha. The little tree, about three feet tall, and the other foliage, had been planted in several large clay pots that had then been arranged on both sides of the steps leading up to the

4

porch. When Vicki and Emily returned from classes at U.C. Berkeley earlier that afternoon, they found the plants destroyed, their carcasses littering the sidewalk and porch, a testament of desecration that cast a pall over what had been a pleasantly mild and sunny Friday in March.

I'd had to sidestep potting soil, broken bits of clay, and the smashed remains on my way up the steps. Two azaleas and two hydrangeas had been ripped from their containers and shredded into debris. The pots were smashed against the porch railing. Tulips and daffodils, both bulbs and blooms, had been stomped to a messy pulp under someone's feet.

Pulled from its pot, the lemon tree had been decapitated, its trunk chopped with an ax or a hedge cutter. The dark green top, with its tiny buds, was arranged on the wooden porch, the chopped-off end pointing toward the front door. The lower half sat alone in the middle of the front porch, resting lopsidedly on roots that bled potting soil.

At first, compared to the other plants, the lemon tree looked relatively unscathed. But on further examination I decided that it had been singled out. Tossed, like a gauntlet.

The destruction could have been committed by some random vandal who'd seen the plants as an easy target. Berkeley certainly had its share of crime, no more immune to the underbelly of modern life than its neighbor, Oakland. But I didn't think so. The mess littering the front of the house looked more like a calling card than an impulse.

Who was leaving the message? And why?

As Vicki told Sasha about discovering the plants, I watched Emily's face. She looked troubled. I recalled what Vicki had said earlier, while Emily was in the kitchen making a pot of coffee. She'd described her housemate as an undemonstrative person. But when Emily saw the

5

plants, Vicki said, she got a strange look on her face. Then she clammed up. She still wasn't saying anything. Her blue eyes moved from Vicki to Sasha, as though she were watching a tennis match.

I watched Vicki's face as she talked, thinking how much she looked like Sid. In another lifetime she'd been my stepdaughter. But I never had been able to think of Vicki in those terms, at least not seriously. There were barely fifteen years between us, so during my brief marriage to Sid Vernon, Vicki and I had been friends rather than step-anything. We were still friends. I suppose that's why she'd asked me to come here.

"So why bring Jeri into all of this?" Sasha sounded amused as she shot me a sidelong glance. "Why didn't you just call the cops?"

"Vicki tells me there have been other incidents."

"Well, yes," Sasha said, somewhat reluctantly.

I looked at Vicki again. "Have you mentioned any of this to your father?"

"Are you kidding?" Vicki gave me a knowing glance. "He'd go ballistic."

I had to admit she was right. I pictured Sid's reaction to the possibility that someone, anyone, might even think of bothering his only child. Not a pretty sight. Sid Vernon is a detective sergeant in the Homicide Section at the Oakland Police Department. On a day-to-day basis he deals with the mean streets of Oakland and the ugliness that human beings perpetrate on one another. That would make any father protective of his daughter, particularly if she's barely nineteen years old and on her own for the first time.

It's hard to be alone when you attend the University of California at Berkeley, with more than twenty thousand students swelling the city's population while school is in session. Vicki wasn't a loner either. Gregarious, capable, up to her eyeballs in any number of activities, usually taking the lead, that's how I'd describe her.

But take it from me. The streets of Berkeley can be just as mean as those in Oakland. Murder and violence have visited the U.C. campus on several occasions.

Vicki may have been on her own for the first time, but she was hardly alone. She lived in this house with seven other people, counting Sasha's little boy. She'd met Emily last August, when both of them, brand-new freshmen, moved into this house. There weren't enough residence halls available for Cal undergraduates, so students found off-campus accommodations. Vicki herself had visited Berkeley in May, before starting her summer job, just to find a place to live. She and Emily had quickly become good friends.

Vicki said she liked the house and her housemates. Besides, the neighborhood's proximity to the campus made it popular with faculty and an ideal location for students, who could walk the few blocks north on College Avenue to the campus.

Vicki shifted on the sofa, seeming to be in motion even though she was sitting down. "What do you think, Jeri? Am I overreacting?"

I looked at Emily, thinking that her dark blue eyes reminded me of water, a mountain lake reluctant to give up any secrets. "Vicki says the lemon tree bothered you. Why?"

"It's just that we worked so hard," Emily said finally, setting her mug on the coffee table. "To clean up the front yard and make things look nice. We all pitched in time. And money." She glanced at Vicki. "We went over to the nursery in a group to pick out the plants. For someone to destroy them like that, it's so cruel."

7

"Do you have any theories, Emily? About who might have trashed the plants?"

Emily looked as though she were about to say something, then she kept it back. She shook her head slowly, deliberately, then reached for her coffee mug and raised it to her lips instead.

Sasha sighed and took another hit of coffee before setting her mug on the table. "Well, I'm going to call the cops. I assume that's the recommended course of action. Right, Jeri?"

I nodded. "Before it's dark, so they can take pictures. But they'll probably treat it as a one-time vandalism incident."

"Maybe it is, maybe it isn't. We can talk about the other stuff while we're waiting for the cops to show up."

She got up from the chair and went back to the kitchen. I saw her in the open doorway, with the cordless phone held to one ear, as she gave the Berkeley police dispatcher her address on Garber Street. "That's right. A block above College. On the right, a two-story brown shingle, with a red and yellow kite tied to the porch." Sasha replaced the phone in its cradle and rejoined us. "They're on their way."

I heard a key twisting in the front door lock. The four of us turned to look as a tall young man, all legs and elbows, came clattering into the foyer, bearing a plastic carry sack covered with Chinese characters, its contents exuding a spicy aroma. He stopped and glared at us.

"God damn it, who killed my tulips?"

Two

"TELL ME ABOUT THE ANONYMOUS PHONE calls."

I looked around, but none of the housemates appeared eager to respond to my comment, let alone confirm it.

We were in the kitchen, a big rectangular room that sprawled across the back of the house. Right now it was the hub of activity, warmth contained within its pale yellow walls and high ceiling. As I watched the room's occupants, I thought of planes landing at a crowded airstrip.

Emily, who appeared to be a serious caffeine junkie, was making another pot of coffee, spooning grounds from a bag of Peet's into the basket of a drip coffee maker. Sasha and two women who had been introduced to me as Rachel Steiner and Marisol Gallegos stood at various points along the yellow and white tiled counter, hands busy with varying phases of meal preparation. Emily sidestepped first one, then another of her housemates as she put the bag of coffee back into the refrigerator and filled the carafe with water.

Vicki and I stayed out of the way. We were seated near the back window, at a long oval table with eight matching chairs. This dining room set crowded the kitchen, too large for the space. It was a lovely old piece that looked as though it had seen some hard use, its dark walnut surface dull and scarred between the blue and yellow woven place mats.

At one end of the table, his chair close to the back door, Nelson Lathrop ate his kung pao chicken straight from the take-out container, chopsticks moving methodically to his mouth. Now and then he paused to guzzle soda from a can.

When I'd seen him standing up, expressing indignation about the tulips, I'd guessed he was an inch or two over six feet, with a mobile clown's face and a gangly, bony frame clad in the ubiquitous blue jeans and a green and brown sweater with knit pills all over it. It looked as though he'd had that sweater for years or picked it up in a thrift shop. His hair was brown and untidy, scraggling down to his shoulders. He appeared to comb it with his fingers, as he did now, shoving a couple of strands behind his ears. He poked the chopsticks into the container in search of another morsel. Then he glanced to his left with sly twinkly blue eyes and grinned, raising his thin brown eyebrows several times in some sort of greeting.

I turned my head. Through the window at my back I glimpsed Sasha's little boy, Martin. He was on the wooden deck at the back of the house, peering through the window at the grown-ups and wriggling his own eyebrows at Nelson. Then he saw me watching him. His face became wary, as if to say, I don't know you. The boy turned from the window and went down the steps into the backyard, its vegetation dim and leafy in the twilight.

Emily retreated to the end of the table opposite Nelson, where she'd stacked her books on returning from class. The book on the top was a trade paperback of *Sense and Sensibility*. Judging from it and the other books on the stack, I guessed at Emily's field of study.

"Emily Austen. Good name for an English major," I said.

Everyone laughed at my friendly jest. Except Emily. Maybe she'd heard the joke once too often. Or perhaps there was another reason for the guarded flash in her blue eyes.

"The anonymous phone calls," I said. "Tell me more than you told the officer."

"What's to tell? The caller hasn't said anything."

Sasha had been chopping vegetables on a big wooden cutting board. Now she set aside the knife and used both hands to scoop the vegetables into a cast-iron skillet that rested on one of the front burners of the stove. She opened the cabinet next to the stove and took out several spice jars, shaking a dash of this and that over the skillet, then pulled a wooden spoon from a chipped crock on the counter and gave the mixture a stir.

Rachel and Marisol had arrived home within minutes of one another, while the Berkeley police officer was surveying the damage. As I had predicted, the officer treated the destruction of the plants as a routine vandalism call, taking a report and a couple of photographs. When Sasha, almost reluctantly, mentioned the phone calls the residents had been getting, he promised to contact the phone company and have a tap put on the line, to see if the anonymous caller's location could be determined.

The residents of the house seemed chary about talking with the officer, all except Vicki, the daughter of a cop. Sasha was right. There wasn't much the housemates could tell the Berkeley cop. None of them had been there when the plants were destroyed. Nelson didn't seem to have a clue about who'd stomped his tulips, and once he'd gotten over his initial outrage, his focus shifted rapidly to dinner.

But the reactions of the other housemates made me

11

curious. Sasha and Emily both seemed guarded, as though they had suspicions of their own about the vandal. Rachel, a tall blonde in a Guatemalan blouse and dangling beaded earrings that caught in the loose strands of her braided hair, mourned the demise of the azaleas she had picked out, wondering aloud what kind of low-life scumbag had done such a thing. But she'd been subdued when the officer questioned her.

Marisol's reaction had been to the presence of the cop, as though the very sight of a uniform triggered unpleasant memories. Her mouth thinned, her dark brown eyes narrowed, and she was barely civil when responding to his queries. She acted as though he, not the vandal, was the lowlife scumbag. It made me wonder what reason she had to dislike cops.

Marisol was a good foot shorter than Rachel. Her long black hair was wound into a knot at the nape of her neck, wound as tight as Marisol herself. Right now she seemed full of contained energy in gray slacks and a red sweater as she and Rachel bumped elbows between the refrigerator and the microwave oven that rested on the counter next to it. The kitchen cabinets in this old house were high on the walls, and Marisol couldn't reach past the second shelf. Instead of asking Rachel for help, she grabbed a sturdy-looking wooden step stool resting to one side of the refrigerator, flipped it open, and climbed up, resting one knee on the counter as her hands probed the third shelf and drew out a jar. That done, she clambered down and replaced the stool, then twisted her mouth as she twisted the lid off the jar.

The microwave oven beeped and Rachel stepped up to open its door. Her dinner appeared to be reheated pasta, tiny shells decorated with a splash of bright red sauce from a jar in the refrigerator and a sprinkling of Parmesan cheese from the same source. Now she set the shallow

12

bowl she held on a place mat, fetched a spoon from a nearby drawer and a paper napkin from a container in the middle of the table.

"First I've heard of phone calls," Nelson declared. "Nobody ever said anything to me about it."

"The reason you haven't gotten any phone calls is because you have your own phone," Rachel said.

"Nelson and Ben live in the garage apartment." Sasha waved the wooden spoon vaguely in the direction of the backyard, now barely visible through the windows as afternoon gave way to evening.

"We're segregated from the female population of the house," Nelson told me with a wicked grin. "Which suits certain members of the female population of the house."

He shot a pointed look at the smallest of the three women at the counter. She glared back at him. Marisol evidently didn't think much of Nelson. He glanced at me and combed his untidy brown hair off his forehead. "Two rooms, a tiny bath, an even tinier kitchenette. I'm just as happy not to share a bath with all these women. Believe me, I have sisters. I know. But I take my meals here in the bosom of the household. I enjoy the camaraderie."

"Where is Ben?" I asked.

"He works nights," Rachel told me. "Waiting tables at a restaurant downtown."

Nelson finished his Chinese takeout. He turned in his chair and tossed the container and the chopsticks into the trash. Then he angled the chair so he had a better view of the kitchen and its occupants.

"So how come I didn't get any phone calls?" he said, leaning back, soda can in his hand.

"Because you're a man," Marisol said, her words sharp as she took her turn at the microwave, sliding a plate inside, then shutting the door. She punched buttons and the oven began its cycle. While her dinner cooked she

13

stared across the kitchen at Nelson, a challenge in her dark brown eyes.

"Yeah, sure." Nelson rolled his blue eyes upward as he finished his soda. He got up from the chair. In a few long strides he crossed the faded linoleum floor to the sink, where he pointedly ignored Marisol and rinsed the can. With an underhanded throw, he tossed it into one of the cardboard recycling bins sitting next to the trash can. Then he resumed his place at the table, stretching his long legs out in front of him.

"I resent the implication," he said, "that I might have had something to do with whatever is going on, simply because I'm male."

Marisol made a derisive little noise, then the microwave beeped. She opened the door and took out her plate, which held what looked like rice and leftover stew. After grabbing a spoon from a drawer, she carried the plate to the other end of the table, sat down, and began eating.

"The phone calls?" I prompted, feeling a bit exasperated at all this byplay that, so far, hadn't told me anything.

"We need to talk about this before Martin comes in," Sasha said, turning down the gas burner under her skillet. She gave the contents another stir, then set the spoon aside. Then she leaned back against the counter and stared at me with solemn brown eyes.

"I'm not sure when the phone calls started. I think it was about the same time as that hate mail incident at Boalt."

As Sasha spoke I nodded slowly, recalling what I'd read in the newspapers. Earlier that year an anonymous— aren't they always?—flyer replete with racial epithets had circulated at Boalt Hall, the University of California law school, fuel to the current political fire raging in California, a sometimes uncivilized debate about affirmative action and whether it benefited women and minorities to the detriment of white males. There had been a demonstration in support of affirmative action at Sproul Plaza, site of so many other protests in the sixties.

"I'm the president of the African American Law Students organization," Sasha continued. "I'm visible. And outspoken. I had a hand in organizing several protest demonstrations. And I've had run-ins with some of the anti-affirmative action crowd. So I thought the phone calls were directed at me."

"Heavy breathing and hang-ups?" I asked.

Sasha's mouth tightened. "Nobody called me names, if that's what you mean."

I'd wondered whether the racial epithets on the flyer had been whispered into a phone receiver. Evidently not. At least not yet. Sasha forestalled my next question.

"After a couple of weeks I had the phone number changed. The calls stopped for a week or two, then they started again. I don't know how. I'm careful about giving out my phone number. So are all the residents."

"I don't give the number to anybody," Marisol chimed in, as Rachel nodded in agreement.

"As a private investigator," I said, "I can tell you it's very easy to obtain someone's number. All it takes is persistence and luck. What about that cracked pane I saw in the front window? How did that happen? And when?"

"That?" Sasha looked at me as though she hadn't considered that the cracked window could be connected with the nuisance calls. "I came home from class, a week or so ago, and found it like that. I assumed it was one of the neighborhood kids, but when I asked around, none of them would cop to it. I need to replace it, just haven't gotten around to it yet." She frowned. "You'd think if someone was going to toss a rock at my window for a reason, they'd wrap a note around it."

"It could be nothing but an accident," I said. "I doubt

15

the neighborhood kids would cop to it if they had broken the window."

Next to me Vicki was shaking her head. "The phone calls started earlier, Sasha. Right after New Year's, I think. So it couldn't have been the hate mail thing. That was in the middle of January. There's this guy, Jeri. He kept asking me for a date. Emily too. He called here a couple of times. I don't know how he got the number. I certainly didn't give it to him. Anyway, I really didn't want to go out with him and he refused to take no for an answer." She looked at Emily, as if prompting her to say something.

"I didn't want to go out with him either. He came on awfully strong." The coffee was ready by now. Emily got up from the table to pour herself another cup. "More coffee, Jeri?"

"Yes, thanks." While she filled my mug I digested what Vicki had said about the guy who wanted to go out with her. Last December I'd worked on a case with some disturbing similarities, involving a young woman who wound up dead because of someone who wanted to control her life. These days the suitor who wouldn't take no for an answer could be more dangerous than benign.

"This guy was upset because neither of you would go out with him?"

My question was directed at both of them. Emily didn't respond as she replaced the coffee carafe on its warmer, but Vicki answered with a shrug. "He called us dykes," she said.

"Typical," Marisol growled, banging her spoon against her plate as she ate. "You won't date the creep so you must be lesbians."

Unfortunately, I knew the term was thrown around quite frequently. I'd been on the receiving end myself,

16

simply because I was walking through a San Francisco BART station with a female friend.

"Emily, is there anything else that's happened recently to make you think someone might be directing these phone calls at you?" Once again I saw that distant look in her blue eyes and felt as though she were keeping something back.

"I'm not sure, Jeri. I'll have to think about it."

Now I looked at Marisol and Rachel. "What about the two of you? Any reason to think the calls are aimed at you?"

Rachel poked at her pasta with her spoon before she answered. "I do escort duty at a local abortion clinic. I have encountered some truly frightening people. They've certainly targeted the doctors and other clinic employees, finding out where they live, passing out flyers in their neighborhoods. So I suppose getting my phone number isn't out of the question. But none of the other people I escort with have gotten any calls. And these anti-abortion protesters are usually right up front about calling us baby killers, right there at the clinic. They certainly wouldn't hesitate to spew venom over the phone. Whoever's making these calls doesn't talk. That's why the calls are so disconcerting."

I agreed. If the phone caller had said anything, he or she might be more readily identified by the content of that speech. But to say nothing increased the menace. Not only was the caller anonymous, so was the target.

Rachel looked at Marisol, passing a figurative baton. One that Marisol didn't appear to want. She'd finished her dinner by now and she got up from the table and carried her plate and spoon to the sink, where she rinsed them and put them into the dishwasher.

"Come on, Marisol," Sasha said wearily. "Don't be so tight-assed."

"I am not being tight-assed." Marisol whirled and stared furiously at her housemates. "Confidentiality is very important in what I do."

"Obdurate, then," Rachel said. "Give Jeri a break. She's here to help."

"I don't see how she can help. We'd probably be better off just changing the phone number again."

"And how long would it be before whoever is calling gets that number?" Emily asked. "Just because you have a problem with authority doesn't mean Jeri can't help."

Marisol glared at her. Then she looked at me and folded her arms across her chest, words coming reluctantly. "I'm a volunteer too. At a counseling center for battered women. We've had trouble before, with husbands who want to get another crack at their wives."

"And sometimes the anger gets directed at the counselors instead," I said.

"At anybody who's convenient." Marisol's mouth had a bitter twist as she said the words. Given her obvious distrust of men and cops, I wondered how close to the bone this issue cut.

"Any recent incidents, directed at you?"

"The creeps I see, they're not interested in stomping a bunch of plants. They like beating up on the women in their lives. Or the kids."

She hadn't really answered my question. "But has anything been directed at you, Marisol?"

She hesitated, but Rachel shot her a pointed look. "All right, all right," she snapped. "There is this one creep. We've had trouble with him before. Every time his wife leaves him and goes to a shelter, he comes to the center and makes threats. Then she goes home and the whole damn cycle starts over. The wife came in looking for help again. I got her and the kids into a shelter. I hope to God she stays put this time."

"When was this?"

"Last Friday, a week ago." She looked at me with opaque brown eyes. "Monday after class I went over to the counseling center. He was there, royally pissed, wanting to know where she was, threatening all the counselors." Marisol squared her jaw. "I don't intimidate easily. I threw the bastard out. Haven't seen him since."

"Have any of you had the feeling that you're being watched or followed?" I saw the women look at each other. I'd experienced that feeling before. It started as a prickly sense of awareness between my shoulder blades, followed by a quick glance over my shoulder that revealed nothing, or perhaps a shadow in my peripheral vision. From the unspoken looks that were moving like electric currents around the kitchen, I knew that someone else in this room had felt that too. But no one said anything.

Now I looked at Nelson, the only adult left, except for the absent Ben. "What about you? You said you hadn't gotten any phone calls. Ever see anyone out of the corner of your eye?"

"Me?" He shrugged and flashed his wide grin. "If someone were following me, they'd have to hit me with a book bag before I'd notice. I just hustle my butt, study, try to keep my grade point up so my folks will keep paying for my exceedingly expensive education. I do work, by the way. I tutor." I smiled at the image of this gangly-looking kid tutoring other students. But he wouldn't be enrolled at U.C. Berkeley if he weren't intelligent and at the top of his high school class.

Nelson raked a hand through his untidy hair. "The women I date all want to go out with me because I'm such a sensitive twenty-first-century guy," he continued, to the accompaniment of a derisive snort from Marisol. "In other words I do know how to take no for an answer. I would never hit anyone, male or female. And I fully support a whole range of issues from abortion rights to affirmative action." He placed his hand on his chest, then his smile disappeared.

"I guess I'm blissfully unaware too. I didn't know about any crank calls. Hell, I didn't know anything was wrong until I saw the damn plants. None of my roomies here told me."

Nelson's blue eyes moved around the room and settled on Sasha. "I don't like the idea of somebody hassling my roomies." His grin returned, this time wry. "It makes them all tense and snappish, and they take it out on me."

Three

As I WAITED FOR THE SIGNAL TO CHANGE at the corner of College and Ashby, I watched the neighborhood residents going in and out of the shops and cafés. The sidewalks of the Elmwood district's main shopping area were crowded this Friday evening in March. Café Roma was filled with people talking and sipping espresso. A few doors beyond that, the marquee of the old Elmwood Theatre announced a double bill of two of my favorite Audrey Hepburn movies, *Roman Holiday* and *Sabrina*. I'd have to call my friend Kaz to see if he wanted to join me at the movies tomorrow night.

The traffic light changed from red to green and I continued past Ashby, driving down College Avenue toward Oakland. I watched the taillights of the car in front of me as I sifted through my impressions of the place Vicki Vernon now called home.

The household seemed chaotic to my eyes, but I was an outsider. I was sure that once I looked past my initial impression of disorganization, it had a rhythm all its own. I recalled what Vicki had told me about the living arrangements in the Garber Street house.

Rachel had the longest tenure as a tenant. She was older than the others, in her mid-twenties, a political science graduate student who was also a teaching assistant. She'd lived in Sasha's house for three years. Her seniority had earned her the master bedroom upstairs, the one with its own bath. Marisol, a sociology major, had lived there about eighteen months. She, Vicki, and Emily had the other three second-floor bedrooms and shared the big bathroom. As Nelson had told me earlier, he and Ben shared the single-car garage, which had been converted into a tiny apartment, with a living room, kitchenette, and bath on the first floor, and one large bedroom on the second.

Sasha Nichols had taken over half of the house's first floor. She'd expanded the first-floor bathroom, adding a shower, and turned the former living room, her father's old office, and the enclosed back porch into an apartment for herself and her son. According to Vicki, Sasha's parents had died about five years ago, within a year of each other, her father of a heart attack and her mother of cancer. In order to keep the house where she'd grown up, Sasha began taking in roomers.

No one had said anything about Martin's father, I realized. Was he in the picture at all?

Living in the Berkeley brown shingle with all its occupants was not the sort of living arrangement I would enjoy. Except for the time I lived with Sid, first as lovers and later as husband and wife, I'd never had a roommate. Unless you could count Abigail, the fat brown tabby who'd been with me through it all, and Black Bart, the half-wild kitten who'd joined the household in December.

I prefer living alone, not having to check in with someone every day, making my own rules. I understood the necessity of roommates, though. Living anywhere in the Bay Area was expensive, and Cal students often had a difficult time finding housing. Sasha's house was in a great location, with its proximity to the campus and AC Transit line 51. It appeared that most of the people who lived there had found their own congenial rhythm, though I was sure Marisol would be just as happy if Nelson would go away.

Farther down College Avenue I crossed the boundary that divided Berkeley from Oakland and continued on past the Rockridge BART station, bustling with commuters who'd gotten off the trains on the elevated platform and were streaming down the stairs and escalators to the parking lot and the sidewalks outside the station. Many of them stopped at the Rockridge Market Hall shops, to buy bread or produce or fish for the evening meal, or to have coffee or a drink with friends.

Someone in the Garber Street house was being harassed, maybe even stalked. The events the housemates had described didn't seem random. If the phone calls represented the start of that harassment, the destruction of the plants was definitely an escalation of hostilities. Who was behind this? I wondered. And for what reason? I had a range of possibilities to choose from, all very good possibilities. Before leaving the house, I told the residents I'd do what I could to find out who was responsible. For Vicki's sake, I told myself. It might as well be for Vicki. That's why she'd turned to me for help. From the others, I sensed varying degrees of reluctance.

Stalkers are a frightening feature of the modern landscape, I thought, as I turned right from College onto Broadway. Maybe they were always out there, like sexual harassment and environmental damage, and we are more aware of them because of the huge amount of information that gets thrown at us every day. Stalking is an insidious, scary crime, and sometimes there doesn't seem to be any defense.

I recalled the most recent case I'd read about in the newspapers, unfortunately all too familiar in its similarity to other such cases. It involved a woman who lived in Oakland, not far from my own apartment in the Adams

Point area. She'd ended her marriage three years before, but her ex-husband continued to harass her. She got phone calls, complete with heavy breathing and silence, like the ones the occupants of the house on Garber Street were receiving, only the ex-husband would call fifty or sixty times a night. She got an unlisted number, but it only slowed the ex-husband down for about a week. He followed her, her friends, anyone she dated. He drove up and down her street, parked outside her apartment building. Then his phone calls changed, from heavy breathing to whispered death threats, and he violated the restraining order she'd obtained.

But even restraining orders could be merely paper shields. There was a woman several years ago in Richmond, north of Berkeley. She'd obtained a restraining order, more than once. In fact, she'd done everything the experts recommended. She'd gone through counseling with her husband. When that failed, she divorced him. He kept invading her home and beating her, so she went to a women's shelter and got restraining orders to protect herself and her children. She even had him jailed after a violent episode, but it didn't work. He broke into her home with a semiautomatic rifle. She and her teenage son were gunned down but survived. The two local cops who came to assist were shot and killed.

Right now the Oakland case was in the newspapers because the ex-husband was being prosecuted under California's antistalking law. It was the first one in the nation, passed in 1990 after an actress was stalked and murdered, and it became the model for laws in other states. Some people felt it didn't go far enough, though, and the law was amended to give it more bite, to allow the prosecution of stalkers who intend to instill fear.

Penal Code Section 646.9 calls it "a credible threat,"

24

meaning a verbal or written threat, or one implied by a pattern of conduct, with the intent and ability to carry out the threat to cause the target to reasonably fear for his or her safety. The language wasn't supposed to be gender specific, but the statistics showed overwhelmingly that most victims of stalkers were women, harassed by ex-husbands or ex-boyfriends. Sometimes the problem was to get police and judges to take the crimes more seriously. But sometimes the cops did respond strongly, and in the Richmond case, two of them died.

The actress who was murdered was tracked through state motor vehicle files. Access to those had since been tightened, which made my job of finding information more difficult, but not so difficult that I couldn't get what I looked for. Privacy and anonymity are hard to come by in this technological age. At the urging of George, the computer consultant down the hall, I'd recently upgraded my office computer to include a modem, and I could now dial into all sorts of databases and do the sort of electronic information gathering he used to do for me. The computer just made it easier, though. Information is out there, public record, for all to find if they know where to look. If I want to know how much Sasha Nichols paid in property taxes, all I had to do was walk over to the Alameda County Assessor's Office and look through the microfiches available to the public.

I'd worked on a stalking case several years ago, when I first became an operative for the Errol Seville agency. Errol was my mentor, a private investigator I'd met while I was working as a paralegal for a downtown Oakland firm. I was bored with legal research, and when Errol told me he needed a female operative, I jumped at the chance. I'd worked for Errol for over five years, until he retired, sidelined by ill health. That's when I set up my own shop. It was about the time Sid and I broke up.

Come to think of it, I'd met Sid while working on that stalking case. I smiled at the memory, a bittersweet smile, thinking of all that had happened since.

Broadway to Twenty-seventh, then to Vernon and up the hill to Adams Street, and my one-bedroom apartment. As I crossed the courtyard I noted the cream-colored blossoms on the lemon tree, planted in the small square of dirt under my front window. Through the slats of the vertical blinds I saw Abigail sprawled on the back of the sofa. At the sound of the key in the lock, she leaped down and came to meet me, tail up, imperious meows in greeting.

I looked around for Black Bart, the interloper who had joined us in December. He was nowhere in sight, but the door to the hallway linen closet was open. There was something wrong with the latch, something I never seemed to get around to fixing. As a result, Black Bart had discovered that a paw hooked underneath the door opened it with ease. As I went through the hall on my way to the bedroom, I looked into the linen closet and saw him crammed into a crevice between two stacks of towels, an inky black spot on a background of green and yellow terry cloth. His head was tucked under his paws, but when he heard my approach he brought it up and I saw the white mask over his wide yellow eyes. He stared at me warily, still wild despite my attempts at domestication.

Black Bart, named for a famous California outlaw, was a feral kitten who'd showed up on my patio before Christmas, hungry enough to gobble the cat food I left out for him, and scared enough so that it took me days to catch him. Once I had, he'd spent a lot of time hiding from Abigail, who, after ten years as a solo cat, was not thrilled at the prospect of sharing quarters and human. They'd warmed up to each other sufficiently to romp now and then, but Black Bart still wasn't sure about me. I was the person who put the cat food in the bowls morning and evening, and my feet were nice to sleep on at night, but whenever I moved to stroke the kitten's jet fur or pick him up, he shied away.

I didn't think Black Bart was going to be a lap cat.

Four

I WENT BACK TO THE GARBER STREET HOUSE Saturday morning. I wanted to meet Ben, the resident who had been working the evening before, when I first encountered the housemates. And I wanted to ask Sasha Nichols the question that had occurred to me after I left.

It was about eleven when I parked my Toyota in a tight space about half a block from the brown shingle house. The sun was bright today, a welcome sight after two days of off-and-on rain that turned the East Bay hillsides a fresh green enlivened with the yellow of wild mustard. As I walked toward the house, I saw Martin, a small figure in red and blue, playing alone near the curb. He held an orange plastic contraption that on closer examination turned out to be a toy spaceship. The little boy was carrying on an intense conversation with himself, until he saw me. Then he stopped and stared at me as though I were an alien descended from another planet.

"Is your mother home, Martin?" I asked.

I thought I saw him shake his head, then he bolted for the walk leading to the front porch, which by now had been swept clean of yesterday's debris. In fact, there were new additions, a couple of bright red geraniums bravely ensconced in clean clay pots, set on either side of the bottom step. Emily Austen knelt in a patch of dirt to the right of the front steps, transferring purple and yellow pansies from their plastic nursery containers into a long redwood planter box.

"Can't let the vandals get the best of us," she said with a smile when she saw me. "I went to the nursery first thing this morning."

Her long brown hair was pulled back from her face and tied with a scarf. The tiny gold earrings in her lobes caught the sun as she moved. She mounded potting soil around the last pansy, then stood up and brushed soil from the formerly white gardening gloves she wore, then from the knees of her faded blue jeans.

"Vicki's not here. She's studying over at the library. I don't know when she'll be back."

"It's not Vicki I came to see. I want to talk with Sasha. And Ben."

"Ben's probably still asleep." Emily nodded toward the driveway that led back to the garage apartment. "He works nights and doesn't usually get in until past eleven. It may be noon before he surfaces. As for Sasha, she had a ten o'clock meeting over at Boalt. I told her I'd keep an eye on Martin till she got back. I expect her soon, though. She and Martin have plans this afternoon. Don't you, Martin?"

The little boy had been hovering on the other side of the porch, his wide eyes taking it all in. He didn't respond to Emily's question. Emily smiled at him, then turned to me. "He's shy. Could you help me with this box, Jeri? It's heavy."

"Sure." I grabbed one end of the redwood planter and together Emily and I carried it up the steps. "Where do you want it?"

"Along the railing, to the left of the front door. That way it will get the afternoon sun." We set the box down where Emily indicated. "Thanks," she told me as she removed the gardening gloves. She stepped back to examine the newly planted flowers, head tilted to one side. "Perfect. I like pansies. They're so cheerful." She turned and went back down the steps, picked up the trowel she'd been using to repot the flowers, and put it and the gloves into a large basket that held other gardening tools. Then she rejoined me on the porch. "Would you like some coffee? I've got a pot going in the kitchen."

"I'd love some." I'd already had plenty of coffee that morning, but sharing a cup with Emily would give me a chance to learn more about her. At least that's what I hoped.

"I'd like you to play in the backyard," Emily told the little boy, "so I can watch you." Martin nodded and trudged up the stairs to join us as Emily pulled a key from the pocket of her jeans and unlocked the front door. Once inside, Martin ran ahead, through the living room to the kitchen. By the time Emily and I entered the sunny room with its oversized table, he was outside, on the back deck, running his plastic spaceship along the top of the railing.

"You really do keep an eye on him," I said. "Most people would let him play in the front yard. It looks like a nice safe neighborhood."

"Not these days, with all those stories about strangers snatching children off the streets." Emily opened a cupboard, took out two mugs, and poured coffee into both. "And not with all this stuff happening. It's got us all edgy."

"Have there been any more phone calls?" I pulled out a chair and sat down.

"Yes." Emily joined me at the table, her fingers tracing the design carved into the back of one of the chairs. "Last night. After you left. Rachel answered the phone."

"Why didn't you call me?" I asked, leaning forward.

She gave me a look with those deep blue eyes of hers, and I saw that wariness I'd seen earlier, which made me wonder whether Emily was keeping something back. She glanced outside to make sure Martin was still in view, then arranged the chair at an angle so she could keep one eye on the child and still see my face. She sat down and put the mug on the place mat in front of her.

"I don't know what good it would do," she said finally.

"If the people in this house don't tell me what's going on, I can't find out who's making those phone calls."

"That's a tall order, isn't it?" Emily sipped her coffee. "I'm sure you're a good detective, but there are five of us living here in the main house. How can you find out which of us is the target? Or maybe we all are. Maybe it's just some random idiot dialing a random number. He never says anything. He's just . . . there."

"I don't think it's random. And neither do you. Not after he took the trouble to find out the new phone number after Sasha had it changed." I noticed we were both referring to the anonymous caller by using the male pronoun. The caller could just as easily be female.

"What happened to all those potted plants yesterday makes it look very personal," I continued. "Don't you agree?"

Emily didn't say anything. Her eyes moved from my face to Martin, still playing on the back deck. "Chopping the top off that lemon tree was a particularly malicious touch," I continued. "I'm sure the call last night wasn't random. He wanted a reaction to the plants."

"No one has given him the satisfaction," Emily said. "We just hang up."

"But it's wearing thin, isn't it?" She nodded, a brief up-and-down movement. "Then help me out, Emily. I'll

31

ask you again. Is there anything going on in your life that makes you think you might be the target?"

She frowned, then we both looked up as footsteps thudded on the back steps. I glanced outside and saw Martin smile as the newcomer brushed a hand across his curly head. Then the back door opened and a young man entered the kitchen. He was short and barrel-chested, his torso straining the white T-shirt he wore. Khaki pants and a pair of sneakers completed his ensemble.

"Is that fresh coffee I smell? I hope?" he boomed as he made a beeline for the coffee maker on the counter. He helped himself to a mug of coffee and leaned against the counter, savoring the first mouthful. He smiled at Emily and looked inquiringly at me.

"Jeri, this is Ben Winslow."

"So you're Vicki's friend, the private eye." Ben's brown eyes looked at me appraisingly from his dark face, then he crossed the linoleum and held out his hand for a shake that was quick and firm. "Nice to meet you. I didn't know about all these phone calls, not until Nelson told me. Gonna have to get on Sasha's case for not telling me. How long has this been going on?"

"Since right after the Christmas holidays, it appears. I'm trying to find out why. Sasha thought it might have something to do with the hate mail incident at Boalt."

Ben scowled over the rim of his coffee mug. "Yeah, that. Well, I've been called an affirmative action baby too, and worse. I'm here to tell you, black or not, I earned my way to U.C. And I'm working my butt off to stay." That challenge delivered, he turned and set the mug down on the counter, then opened one of the lower cabinets and pulled out a box of cornflakes. He poured what looked like half the box into a big bowl and added sugar and milk, then sat down at the table and dug a spoon into his breakfast.

"There's no way to be sure Sasha's the target," I said. "It could be any of the women here in the main house. Emily, Vicki, Rachel, or Marisol."

"Marisol," Ben said, shaking his head, a spoonful of cornflakes in midair. "That woman's got a problem with men."

Based on what I'd seen and heard yesterday, I was more than willing to concede that point. But perhaps Marisol had good reason for her antipathy toward men.

"Where is Marisol?" I asked. "And Rachel?"

"Rachel went up to Calistoga for the weekend," Emily said. "She's got friends up there. And Marisol was gone when I got up. She may be at that counseling center where she volunteers. She spends a lot of time there."

"Do you know where it is?"

Emily shook her head. "Just that it's in Oakland, in the Fruitvale district. Near East Fourteenth and the BART station."

"That's her old neighborhood." Ben spoke up from his end of the table, where he'd finished off his cornflakes. "I think she once said something about growing up in Jingletown."

I nodded. The area Ben referred to was a small community sandwiched between East Fourteenth and the Nimitz Freeway, with a large Hispanic population.

I heard the front door slam shut, the report reverberating through the old house. Footsteps came through the living room toward the kitchen. Vicki Vernon walked quickly into the kitchen, a frown on her normally cheerful face. She was dressed casually in jeans and a heavy knit sweater over a blue chambray shirt, with a gray nylon pack on her back. So many Cal students used backpacks to carry books and other belongings that sometimes it seemed that everyone on Telegraph Avenue had sprouted a hump.

33

"Jeri, I'm so glad you're here." Vicki set the pack on a chair and folded her arms across her chest, as though protecting herself. "Something happened over at the library."

The alarm in her voice set me on my guard.

"That guy I told you about. The one who asked both me and Emily for dates. And when neither of us would go out with him, he called us dykes."

"Not him again," Emily said, a shadow passing over her face.

"When he saw me at the library, he started in on me again, asking where my girlfriend was. People kept shushing him, but he wouldn't shut up. Finally I left." Vicki gave a little shudder. "But he followed me. All the way to Sproul Plaza. I lost him on Telegraph and dodged over to Durant just in time to hop on a 51 bus."

"You want me to go pound this creep?" Ben offered.

"That wouldn't solve anything," Emily said.

"Yeah, but it sounds like he's got it coming." Ben got up and carried his bowl and spoon to the sink, where he rinsed them, then pulled open the dishwasher. "Looks like this baby's full," he said, more to himself than anyone else. He grabbed a box of dishwashing detergent from under the sink, filled the receptacles, and started the cycle.

"Maybe Jeri should talk with him," Vicki said over the hum of the appliance. She looked at me with troubled brown eyes, asking for help. "His name's Ted Macauley."

I wanted to pound this Ted Macauley too, whether or not he was the one responsible for the phone calls and the destruction of the plants. Where the hell did he get off calling Vicki names simply because she chose not to go out with him? As I looked at the frown marring her young face, I didn't like the effect his harassment was

34

having on her. If I had to put a name on it, I guessed I was feeling motherly.

Emily's eyes were concerned too, but she was looking out the window, not at Vicki. She moved quickly to the back door and pulled it open.

"Where's Martin?" Her voice was suddenly shrill with alarm. "He's not in the backyard. Where did he go?"

Five

MARTIN WASN'T ON THE DECK. HE WASN'T hiding in or around the garage apartment shared by Ben and Nelson. In fact, he didn't appear to be in the back-yard, or the front.

"He can't have gone far," I told Emily as the four of us stood on the sidewalk near the front porch. "It hasn't been that long since we saw him."

My words had little effect. Her blue eyes, usually calm and wary, were frightened. Her voice thinned like a tightly stretched wire. "We have to find him. Right now."

"We will." I kept my voice calm. "Emily, you and Ben go up the street." I pointed to my right, toward the Berkeley hills. "Vicki and I will go down toward College. Let's split up, one person on each side of the street. Ask everyone you see. Go up driveways and look between houses. Call Martin's name while you do it."

"Got it," Ben said. "There's a park up that way. Maybe he's gone up there."

He grabbed Emily's shoulder and gave it a supportive shake, then they set off, Emily on this side, Ben jogging across Garber Street to the opposite sidewalk. I nodded at Vicki and crossed to the other side. We were headed toward College Avenue, little more than a block west.

Three or four blocks to the south, Ashby Avenue paralleled Garber. Both were busy thoroughfares, no place for a little boy on his own.

Maybe it was different now, but when I was that age, my mother wouldn't let me cross a busy street like that on my own. And that was in quiet, staid Alameda, not bustling Berkeley with its many charms and dangers. We now live in a world where strangers snatch children off front lawns, or even from their bedrooms, and the lost little faces look out at us from flyers plastering windows and papering walls.

In that world, Emily's reaction to Martin's vanishing act was prudent and normal. But I was curious. Emily, the few times I'd met her, always seemed so calm and self-contained, despite the occasional hints of some inner turmoil. Now she was so upset she was vibrating. Was it because Sasha had entrusted Martin to her care and she'd lost sight of the little boy? Was something else going on? Had Martin wandered off before? Once again I wondered about Martin's father. Was there some sort of custody dispute? Or was it the residue of some experience in Emily's past that had her shaking with tension?

I stopped to talk to a man who was edging a flower bed. No, he hadn't noticed a little boy in red and blue. Nor had the woman a few doors down, washing the plate-glass window at the front of her house. I went up several driveways, calling Martin's name, hearing that name echoed across the street as Vicki did the same thing.

At the corner of Garber and Piedmont I stopped a young man with a backpack. He looked like another U.C. student. When I asked the question, he pointed back up Piedmont.

"I saw a bunch of kids up there," he told me. "Half a block or so. Playing in a driveway. I don't know if one of them is the kid you're looking for."

"Thanks." I headed in the direction he'd pointed, scanning both sides of the street. I heard the children before I saw them. Then I spotted a boy standing on the hood of a car as four or five other boys, shouting and laughing, milled around the front end of the vehicle. The youngster on the hood jumped off, with the others hollering as he landed on something. Crossing the street and heading up the driveway, I saw a pair of blue pants and a red shirt. Martin lay on the gravel drive, the other boy on top of him. Martin's orange spaceship lay about three feet to the left, smashed and broken.

"What the hell do you think you're doing?"

Anger roughened my voice as I strode to Martin and turned to face the boys. There were six of them, a mixed bag of colors and sizes, all bigger than Martin. Older too. Eight or nine, most of them, except the one on top of Martin. As he scrambled to his feet I guessed he was about ten. They stood in a semicircle around me, watching me with wild eyes as I knelt and pulled Martin to a sitting position. His clothing was covered with mud and he had a scrape on his chin.

"You okay?" I asked him. He nodded, tears welling in his dark brown eyes.

I helped him to his feet and surveyed his tormentors. "What's your name?" I asked the oldest. He appeared to be the pack leader.

He sneered at me. I fought down the urge to smack him. I wasn't used to that kind of behavior from a ten-year-old, but I'm not around kids much, unless you count my niece and nephew. They're younger, with better manners.

"What's your name?" I demanded again.

"None of your damn business," he shot back.

I took Martin's hand, walked around the house to the front door, and pounded on it. "Are any of these kids yours?" I asked the woman who answered. She was about my age, with tired eyes, a toddler whining crankily at her side.

"What's the matter?" she said, looking past me.

"These kids were beating up on Martin." I glanced over my shoulder and saw a couple of the kids peel off, abandoning the field. The mouthy ten-year-old stood on the front lawn, still looking belligerent. "They broke his toy."

"They're just playing," she said distractedly as the toddler at her heels wailed. "Who are you? What do you care? He doesn't look like he's yours anyway."

"It doesn't matter whether he's mine or not," I argued.

She glared at me, then at the big kid behind me. "Get in here, Tommy."

Tommy wasn't having any of it. He ran instead, up the street, shouting with derision as he ran, with his remaining cohorts for company. The woman gave a helpless shrug and shut the door in my face.

"Come on, Martin."

I trudged back to the driveway, still holding Martin's hand. The orange spaceship looked as though it had been stomped good and hard. Its shiny surface was pitted from the gravel on the drive, and the plastic was split and broken in a couple of places.

I picked up the toy and looked down at the little boy. "Let's get out of here."

We set off in the direction I'd come, with me slowing my steps to account for the child's smaller stride. He didn't say anything, but right before we got to the corner I heard what sounded like a choked sob. I looked down and saw tears trickling from Martin's eyes, cutting a path through the dust on his face. I stopped and used the tail of my T-shirt to mop the flow. Then I stuck my hand into the pocket of my jeans, coming up with a tissue that looked unused.

"Here, blow your nose."

He did as I directed. I spotted a low retaining wall in front of the house on the corner and sat down on the uneven stone, pulling Martin to sit next to me.

"Those guys pick on you all the time?" I asked.

"Yes." It was the first word I'd heard him utter. "They go to my school."

"What do they do?"

"Push me around on the playground. Trip me. Call me names." He emitted a long forlorn sigh. "They take my stuff."

"Like today? They took your spaceship?"

"Yeah. Brandon took it." He sniffed and wiped his nose again. "He's in second grade like me." I'd been figuring Martin for a first grader, like my nephew Todd, but he must have been small for his age. "I was in front of our house and Brandon took my spaceship and ran away. I went after him," Martin continued. "And Tommy and the other guys jumped on me."

"Ambush, huh?" He nodded. "Emily asked you to stay in the backyard."

"I know. But I was looking to see if my mom was home yet."

"Have you talked with your mother about these kids picking on you? Or your teacher?" Now he shook his head. "Maybe you should."

"Don't want to tattle."

Only seven, I thought, and already the peer pressure exerted its strong pull. "I understand, but it's not fair for them to gang up on you like that. Especially if they do it all the time. There's six of them and one of you. Those are not good odds."

Particularly if one of the boys was that hooligan who'd sneered at me. He was a candidate for the California

40

Youth Authority if I'd ever seen one. "You'll have to decide for yourself whether you want to tell your mom or your teacher. But just between you and me," I said, looking at the broken toy, "this seems to be pretty serious. I think your mom should know."

Martin gazed at me as though he were considering whether it was safe to confide in me further. "The crack in the window," he whispered. "That was Tommy. They were throwing pinecones at the house."

That answered one question. Maybe it answered another. "Do you think those boys trashed the plants yesterday?"

He thought about it for a moment. "I don't think so. That must have happened while we were in school. How could Tommy chop the lemon tree?"

I was willing to bet that Tommy could lay his hands on an ax if he wanted to bad enough. Stomping the tulips to pulp was on a par with stomping Martin's toy. On the other hand, I couldn't escape the feeling that the decapitated tree and the phone calls were the work of a more adult malevolence.

I heard someone calling my name and looked up to see Vicki jogging across Garber Street. "Oh, I'm so glad you found him. I looked all up and down College." She sat down next to us on the retaining wall, running a hand through her blond hair. "Where'd you go, Martin? We were worried about you." She peered at him and saw the evidence of his tears and the broken toy I held. "Uh-oh. What happened?"

"It's a kid thing," I said. "You go find Ben and Emily. Martin and I will go back to the house. We might make a little detour first, though." I nodded in the direction of College Avenue.

"Got you." Vicki stood up, dug a hand into her pocket,

and pulled out her key ring, selecting a brass key. "Here's the key to the front door. See you in a bit."

I watched her lope up Garber Street. Then I looked at Martin.

"You like Nabolum's Bakery?" I asked him. The bakery was only a block away, on Russell Street, just off College. He nodded. "So do I. Let's go get us a nosh."

Six

"MARTIN'S FATHER IS NOT AN ISSUE," SASHA said.

He also appeared to be a subject Sasha did not want to discuss. She sat very still on the green and blue flowered sofa set under the front window of her quarters, framed by the ivory damask drapes on either side.

I looked at her steadily from the armchair where I sat. The afternoon sun played with the crack in the upper pane of the window above her, fingers of light making the fissure glitter. Most people are uncomfortable with silence. Too much of it makes them want to fill the void. But Sasha was training to be a lawyer. She was as well versed in the uses of silence as I was. Finally we came to a draw. Just as I opened my mouth to break the silence, Sasha did it for me.

"We were never married. I don't even know where he is."

"Is there a chance he might be in California?"

She shrugged. "Possibly. Although I can't imagine that seven years after the fact he would take any interest in me. Or my son. He certainly ran the other way when I announced I was pregnant."

"We both know what I'm driving at, Sasha. Is he a possible candidate for harasser?"

She thought about it, fingering the beaded earrings she

43

wore. "I don't think so," she said. "That would imply he cared enough to hate me."

I looked back on the events of the past couple of hours. Martin and I had made a run to Nabolum's Bakery, where we'd wolfed down a couple of cookies in our new-found camaraderie. At my suggestion, he had picked out cookies to take home to each of the housemates. We walked back to the house on Garber Street, Martin carrying the white bakery sack and me with the broken toy, neither of us saying much. Vicki, Emily, and Ben sat together on the front steps.

"Martin, your chin," Emily began, her blue eyes no less worried now that Martin had been located. I shot her a look that said, Don't fuss, so she didn't.

"We brought stuff to eat," Martin announced, brandishing his bakery sack.

"Hey, I'm all for that." Ben stood up. "Let's see what you got in there, buddy."

Just as Ben opened the sack and began inspecting the contents, an old blue Volvo drove up Garber Street and pulled into the driveway. Sasha got out and pulled a battered soft leather briefcase from behind the seat. She headed for the front porch.

"What is this, a block party?" She stopped on the sidewalk and looked at her son with a mother's practiced eye, missing neither the scrape on his chin nor the residue of dried tears edging his eyes. "What happened?"

Now we were in Sasha's rooms, her half of the house's lower floor. Martin had been fussed over, his abrasion doctored with antiseptic and his mother's kiss. He appeared to have gotten over his bad experience. He was in the kitchen having lunch with the others. I could hear his high voice. I found that I could now distinguish the voices. Vicki's was throaty, like her father's. Ben had a rumbling chuckle, while Emily's voice was quiet and mellow. The goofy laughter belonged to Nelson, who had shown up late in the drama carrying, as seemed to be his pattern, a fast-food sack containing takeout.

Sasha's quarters reminded me of a shotgun apartment. We were in the house's original living room, which also served this purpose for Sasha and her son. It was crowded with furniture, some of the pieces expensive antiques. The back corner of the living room was Sasha's office, with a big wooden desk, an ergonomic office chair, and several tall bookshelves. This room opened onto another, half the size of the first, square, with one window and built-in bookshelves on two walls. This had been the office used by Sasha's father, the U.C. Berkeley professor. Now it was Sasha's bedroom, with a double bed under the window and a dresser opposite. Another door led to a narrow hallway. Off this was the downstairs bath in which Sasha had installed a shower, then the small enclosed back porch where Martin slept in a brightly painted daybed. It had once been larger, but when Sasha changed her living arrangements, she had the room split into two, with the smaller area used for the washer and dryer as well as additional storage.

"Tell me about Martin's father."

"What's to tell?" She got up from the sofa and moved restlessly around the room, stopping at the double windows on the side wall. She stared through the glass, not really seeing the sunny spring afternoon. Then she turned to face me. "He's Haitian. I met him at U.C. Not all Haitian immigrants are poor boat people. His family is rich and light-skinned. They're the ones who've spent the last fifty years sucking up to the Duvaliers and oppressing the poor boat people. I think they're living a luxurious exile in Paris. If I had to describe Etienne, I'd say he is Eurotrash. Just a few shades darker than the usual."

"So he was a student."

45

"Until he got bored with it."

"Did you love him?"

Sasha laughed, but there was little humor in the sound. Bitterness, definitely, tinged with regret. "I prefer to think of it as being infatuated with him. Maybe it was the accent or his elegant looks. It certainly wasn't his politics. He was such a charming reactionary, so sure of his place in the world. He liked American people of color, but he thought the Haitian peasants were one step above mules. So much cattle to be controlled by the ruling class."

She returned to the sofa and sat, head back, her profile highlighted by the sun streaming in the front window. "Martin wasn't supposed to be born. He was an accident, but I love him dearly. So did my parents."

"Does he look like his father?" I asked.

"A little bit. Not enough to make me feel uncomfortable. He's dark, like me. Actually, he looks a lot like my grandfather on my mother's side." She gathered her legs under her and sat cross-legged on the upholstered cushions of the sofa. "From what you say, I'd better have a talk with Martin's teacher and principal. About these kids who are harassing him. Kids can be so damned cruel."

"Maybe you'd better ask Martin first," I said. "He might not want you to get involved."

"If they were kids his own age, perhaps I wouldn't. But you said several of them were older than he is. And much bigger. He's small for his age."

She looked over my shoulder and smiled. I turned my head and saw Martin standing in the doorway leading to the back of their quarters. "Mama, you better come eat your cookie, or Nelson's gonna."

"Oh, no." Sasha laughed as she stood up. "He wouldn't dare."

"Yes, he would," Martin assured her. "Nelson's hungry all the time."

"It seems I'd best go defend my cookie," she told me.

"From what I've seen of Nelson, that sounds like a good idea." I got to my feet. "You've taken quite a risk, haven't you? Opening your house to these roomers."

"I prefer to think of it as a leap of faith," she said, smiling. "I haven't had any problems. Until now."

I followed Sasha and Martin back to the kitchen. Three of the housemates were grouped around the big table, Nelson's hands swooping toward the white bakery sack as Ben blocked one arm. Vicki swatted Nelson's other arm and chuckled. Emily was at the counter, making another pot of coffee.

"All right," Sasha said in a firm no-nonsense mother voice as she stood with her hands on her hips. A smile twitched her full lips. "What's this I heard about a stated intent to consume my cookie? In the legal biz we call that conversion."

The phone hanging on the wall next to the refrigerator rang. Sasha reached for it with her right hand and held it to her ear. "Hello."

Then her face froze. The smile congealed into a frown. Without a word she handed me the receiver.

Seven

NOW HE WAS TALKING.

The anonymous caller was definitely a man. An adult voice, not that of a child. Even though I'd heard children using those words, this was not one of the young hooligans who had been tormenting Martin. There was laughter amid the words, but it was ugly and menacing, as threatening as the words themselves.

I tried to disassociate myself from the chill I felt at hearing this invective, from the urge to respond with words of my own or by banging the receiver back in its cradle. I'd had anonymous phone calls before. Who hadn't? There had probably been crank calls ever since the invention of the telephone. Receiving one always filled me with a sense of outrage, violation, invasion. The same emotions I felt now, even though this wasn't my phone and the venom wasn't directed at me. Coming as it did on the heels of the destroyed plants, this call represented yet another escalation of hostilities.

Concentrate on the voice, I ordered myself, wishing I had a tape recorder. I moved the receiver quickly from my right ear to my left, reaching for a pencil and a pad of paper from the plastic holder affixed to the side of the refrigerator. I forced myself to listen, asking myself questions.

Is there anything identifiable about this voice, such as

range, tone, timbre? A speech impediment? Is there any background noise that would give a clue as to the caller's location? Any static that might mark the use of a cellular phone? And what exactly was he saying? Did it have a pattern, substance, meaning?

The man at the other end of the phone must have been used to the house's residents hanging up on him. He didn't expect to be listened to, at least not as long as I held the receiver. Finally, with a crescendo of obscenities, he hung up. I stood with the phone against my right ear until I heard a dial tone. Then I slowly moved the receiver to the cradle.

I looked at the words I'd scrawled on the pad of paper, my own notes and the ugly epithets the voice had spewed forth, about black people, Hispanics, Jews, women, and gays. He'd covered most of the hot-button hate speech bases, presumably with a wide enough spread to encompass all the residents of the Garber Street house. His voice was somewhere between tenor and bass, sounding like thousands of other men. There was no sibilance, no discernible accent. Not much background noise either. The caller could have been shut up in a room or a phone booth. Or in a car, with a cellular phone. I'd heard just a bit of static, the kind I'd heard before when people called me from cars.

These days, millions of people had cellular phones. So did I, a Christmas gift from my father. However, I didn't much care for the possibility that the harasser had one of the gadgets. That meant the creep could be parked outside on Garber Street, on the curb right in front of this house, getting his jollies while he terrorized the occupants.

I looked up from the paper at the assembled housemates.

"He's never talked before," Sasha whispered.

"What did he say?" Ben scowled and moved toward

me for a look at the notepad. His frown deepened as he read what I'd written.

Nelson got up and looked over Ben's shoulder. "Articulate, isn't he? Should we sit up all night with baseball bats?"

"I don't think baseball bats would do the job." I surveyed the housemates, noting the look of uncomprehending alarm on Martin's face as the little boy picked up on the mood of the grown-ups. He moved closer to Sasha and crowded against her hip, seeking comfort in his mother's touch. "First thing you do is call that Berkeley cop, the one who was here yesterday. Tell him what time you received the call and ask him to contact the phone company, to see if the tap picked up the location of the call. Make sure the doors are locked all the time. You've got to keep up your guard. This guy sounds dangerous."

"This is so frustrating," Sasha said, suddenly furious. "There's nothing to go on. It's like grasping at shadows."

"Yes, it is. But you've given me some shadows to investigate. Such as this guy Macauley who's been hassling Vicki and Emily because neither of them will go out with him."

Vicki nodded, looking preoccupied. I didn't know whether she was thinking of this morning's encounter with Ted Macauley in the library or debating whether to tell her father the Oakland cop. We both knew how Sid would react.

I looked at Sasha. Since the caller didn't seem to have an accent, that presumably ruled out her ex-lover, Etienne, Martin's father. Still . . . I shook my head and moved on.

"I know Rachel's out of town this weekend," I said. "She'll have to wait till Monday. Tell me where I can find Marisol."

The corner of Fruitvale Avenue and East Fourteenth Street is one of the busiest intersections in what is known as East Oakland. As I stood waiting for the light to change I heard a BART train go by on the elevated tracks two blocks to my right and glanced that way, seeing the end of the silvery line of cars as the train slowed on its approach to the Fruitvale BART station. Just beyond that a freight train on the tracks that paralleled San Leandro Street had traffic stopped, temporarily blocking access to Interstate 880, the freeway all the locals call the Nimitz.

The light changed and the walk signal flashed. I stepped off the curb and joined the pedestrians in the crosswalk. Many of the people around me were Hispanic, and the signs in the windows of the shops reflected the demographics of the neighborhood. This part of Oakland frequently spoke Spanish first and English second, shopped in the many bodegas that lined the neighborhood's business section, and ate at the *tacquerias* that drew people from all over the East Bay to sample the authentic Mexican cuisine.

On the other side of Fruitvale I turned left, sidestepping a group of teenagers holding signs advertising their high school fund-raiser car wash at a nearby vacant lot. My destination was Farnam Street, one block up. It paralleled East Fourteenth for a couple of blocks, and the counseling center where Marisol volunteered was in the middle of the first block. It was a plain storefront with glass windows that were partially obscured by plain unpainted shutters. A sign over the entrance bore words in Spanish and English. LAS HERMANAS, I read. THE SISTERS.

I opened the door and walked inside, my shoes whispering across linoleum that had once been white but was now faded to gray, speckled with bits of color that looked like spent confetti, forgotten and now adhering to the floor. The front part of the center was open, with the rest of the long narrow space walled off with framing and Sheetrock that looked a good deal newer than the building itself. Directly in front of me a hallway led to the rear of the building, with doors at intervals down this passage, most of them closed, from what I could see.

To my left I saw an old wooden office desk decorated with a phone and a bouquet of colorful freesias, their spicy scent tickling my nose. An older woman sat behind the desk, presiding over a mug of coffee and a stack of pamphlets. She appraised me carefully. I didn't look like I belonged here. But neither did she. Her short gray-blond hair didn't go with the neighborhood clientele and she wore laugh lines on her wrinkled face, instead of makeup. She was wearing a flowered peasant blouse, and I was willing to bet that behind the desk the rest of her was clad in a long skirt and Birkenstocks.

"May I help you?" she offered tentatively.

"I'm looking for Marisol Gallegos."

"Marisol isn't available right now." She gestured toward a long bench against the opposite wall. It looked as though it had spent its previous life as a church pew. An older woman huddled by herself at one end, head down as her hands busied themselves with some needlework. "Would you care to wait? There's coffee over there."

In the corner next to the bench a rickety-looking table held one of those institutional-sized stainless steel coffee makers and a mismatched collection of mugs and cups. I thought about it, then decided against it. After drinking Peet's finest earlier at the Garber Street house, I didn't want to chance my taste buds on coffee that had no doubt come from a can.

I took a seat at the unoccupied end of the bench and

surreptitiously examined my companion. She appeared to have a short sturdy figure, clad in a plain blue house-dress and a black cardigan sweater. She was in her fifties, I guessed, with black hair, copper skin, and a profile one might see in a museum display of pre-Columbian art. She held a small round frame in her left hand as the fingers of her right hand punched a needle back and forth through the snowy white material stretched tightly in the frame. Bright red embroidery floss moved in the wake of the needle, sketching some intricate design.

She saw me watching her and glared at me, eyes full of affront at this intrusion. I looked away as the phone rang. The woman at the desk picked it up, answering, "Las Hermanas." She listened, then spoke again in Spanish, with the accent of someone at ease in the language.

I heard voices echoing in the hallway leading to the back and turned to look in that direction. Marisol and another woman appeared at the head of the passage. The woman could have been anywhere between twenty-five and thirty-five. She was visibly pregnant, her high round belly pushing against the oversize shirt she wore over her brown maternity slacks. She looked enough like the woman on the bench for me to guess that they were mother and daughter, but the younger woman had two features the older lacked. Her left eye was discolored with a fading bruise and she had a cut on her lip.

Marisol walked a few steps behind the other woman. She was doing all the talking, in quick and crackling Spanish. I could only pick up a few words here and there, enough to guess that Marisol was exhorting the other woman to do something she wasn't planning to do. The pregnant woman jerked her head toward the woman who sat on the bench. Now my companion put away her embroidery, tucking the frame into a big canvas purse at her side. She got to her feet as the pregnant woman put her hand on Marisol's arm, stopping Marisol's flow of words. She said something in a low voice, then she and the older woman moved away, toward the door.

As Marisol watched them go through the door to the sidewalk outside, she threw up her hands and spat out some Spanish epithets I understood all too well.

The receptionist sighed and stood up. "I need to go to the bathroom, Marisol. Would you listen for the phone?" Marisol gave a curt nod and the receptionist moved away from the desk, her long skirt swirling around her legs and the sandals on her feet. I was right. Birkenstocks.

"She wouldn't take your advice," I said as I stood up.

"She won't take anyone's advice." Marisol radiated anger and frustration. "He beats her up, she goes to her mother's. She comes here to talk to one of the counselors. All the time she's at her mother's, he's oh-so-sweet and apologetic. He pleads with her to give him another chance. Then she decides it must be her fault because she hasn't been a good wife. So she goes back to him, and a few months later he beats the shit out of her again." She shook her head, as if trying to dispel the bitterness of her words. "One of these days he's going to kill her."

"You've been there, haven't you?"

Marisol folded her hands across her chest and narrowed her wary brown eyes. Then she favored me with a tight reluctant smile. "How did you know?"

"It was a good guess," I said. "We need to talk."

Eight

WHEN THE RECEPTIONIST RETURNED FROM THE bathroom, Marisol helped herself to a mug of coffee from the urn in the corner. Then she motioned me to follow her through the doorway, to one of the cubicles that had been constructed at the rear of the storefront.

It was a stark windowless square, one wall enlivened by a poster, its bright colors and lettering advertising Oakland's Festival at the Lake, held in June at Lake Merritt. The desk was a twin of the one the receptionist was using, scarred brown wood decorated with nicks and dings. It, and the swivel office chair, looked as though they were donations or had recently spent time in a surplus furniture store.

There were a couple of other chairs in the room. One was the hard plastic kind with the seat supposedly molded to fit the human posterior. Whose posterior? I wondered. Not mine. Since I'd never found them comfortable on my rear end, I sat down in the other chair, a plain wood ladder-back with a thin pad on the seat. It looked like a refugee from someone's dining room.

Marisol set the mug on the desk and grabbed the arm of the swivel chair. It moved on casters across the dingy linoleum floor as she positioned it so it was facing me. She sat down, slumped in her blue jeans and sweater, and crossed one leg over the other. "What do you want?"

I wanted to talk about Marisol. Maybe this counseling center environment would loosen her tongue. Confession is good for the soul, and all that. Provided I could push the right buttons.

"Have you had any more trouble?" I asked. "With the angry husband you told me about?"

She shook her head. "No. He seems to have backed off for now."

I looked at her, with her small regular features and the coil of dark hair at the nape of her neck. Vicki had told me that Marisol was a junior at U. C. That meant she was in her early twenties at most.

"You're young," I said, "to have been in an abusive relationship."

"Get real," Marisol scoffed. "It happens all the time. As soon as the kids hit puberty. Elementary school these days." She reached for her coffee, drank a mouthful, and grimaced, confirming my theory about the quality of the brew. "Mostly it starts in junior high. I've seen it. Girls just barely into puberty. They think they're women because they've started their periods. They think they have to have boyfriends, because all their friends do."

Her brown eyes, usually so wary, took on a different cast, softened, became vulnerable. She looked as though she were remembering.

I remembered those days too. My brother once described them as the days of hormones and acne. I felt gawky and awkward because I was taller than most of the kids in my class. My hair wouldn't behave, I had spots on my face, I was unsure of myself. And more than anything in the world I wanted one of those coltish adolescent males to pay attention to me. I pushed away the thought of the girl I once was and focused on Marisol, whose experiences were more recent than mine.

"Is that what happened to you?"

56

Marisol cradled the coffee mug in her hands. "I grew up in this neighborhood, in Jingletown." She nodded in the direction of the freeway. "Went to Catholic schools. What a crock that was. Sister Mary Holy Water, teaching algebra and telling us how to act. What the hell did she know about it?"

"Can't help you there," I said. "I went to public schools. Though I often wondered myself what those nuns knew about life."

"Yeah. All they knew was training us to be good little Catholic wives and mothers." She set the mug on the desk and clawed one hand through her tangled dark hair. "My parents bought into all that stuff. Still do. I was one of six kids, three girls, three boys. The dutiful daughter, and all that shit. My father couldn't understand why I wanted to go to college. College was for the boys. I was supposed to graduate from high school, work for a couple of years, find some nice man to marry, and settle down and have babies." She shook her head. "Both my sisters are doing that. They've got five babies between them."

I shifted on the ladder-back chair, which was getting more uncomfortable with the passage of time. "What about the boyfriend?"

"Ah, the boyfriend." Marisol looked at the coffee, instead of me, as though she were trying to decide which was worse, the oily black liquid or the memory I was dredging out of her. "I was in the ninth grade, fourteen. I had just started menstruating, later than all the girls I knew, and my sisters too. I thought there was something wrong with me." She stopped, opting for another sip of coffee. "Peter was older than me. Nineteen."

I raised an eyebrow. A five-year age difference didn't matter as much when both parties were adults, but for teenagers, at that age and level of maturity, it was a wide gulf.

"He likes them young," Marisol said, her words sardonic, as though she knew what I was thinking. "And stupid, as I found out later."

"You weren't stupid, just young."

"Naive, stupid, young, what's the difference." Now her mouth curved in another one of her tight reluctant smiles that never seemed to reach her eyes. "He's probably still at it. Hanging around playgrounds looking for little girls to fuck."

"Is that where you met him?"

She shook her head. "At a friend's house. Me, tagging along, as usual. The odd one out. The only one who wasn't paired up." She sighed. I understood. I had memories like that too. "One of his buddies was dating one of my girlfriends. I thought Peter was so cool. I guess it was because he was different from anyone else I knew. He was Anglo, from Hayward. My whole life I'd been around people who spoke Spanish better than they spoke English. He was in his first year of college, down at Chabot. I wanted to go to college, so I was impressed. He dressed really cool. He smoked. He had his own car. His own apartment, just a room, really, above a store. And he was paying attention to me. Little Marisol, who barely had breasts."

Given what she'd told me so far, that was probably part of the attraction. I looked at the young woman before me, with her hard-won tough veneer, and saw the little girl she must have been at fourteen. Shark bait, for the predators that swim in the always complicated sea of male-female relationships. It probably hadn't taken him too long to nail his prey.

We must be in sync this afternoon. Marisol was reading my mind again.

"Oh, he had me in bed in the blink of an eye," she said

with an offhand shrug, as though it didn't matter. "A week or two after we met. He took me for a ride in his car, then he brought me back to his apartment and popped my cherry. With me saying, oh, no, we shouldn't do this. But we kept doing it. It's a wonder I didn't get pregnant. Because, of course, there was no question of him using a condom. Him? Worry about birth control? Forget it. One of my girlfriends, she figured it out. That I was getting laid, I mean. Got me some pills. They probably screwed up my body chemistry royally, but I didn't get pregnant. So many of these girls do. And then they marry the guy. And they're trapped. Like my sisters."

"When did Peter start hitting you?" I asked. We'd danced toward the subject long enough.

Marisol compressed her lips into a line and crossed her arms protectively over her chest. She had breasts now, but at that moment she looked very much like a child. "Almost from the start. At first it was playful, you know. A little slap here, a little shove there. I didn't think anything about it. I saw the same thing happening to the other girls and women around me. It crept up on me. He didn't really hurt me until a year or so later. We had an argument and he punched me, so hard I had a bruise for days. I thought it was my fault for doing something to annoy him."

I'd heard this tale, or one like it, before. Recently, in fact, while working on the Raynor case. In that instance, the abusive husband wound up dead, his wife a suspect in his murder. When she'd described the evolution of their relationship, it sounded similar to what I was now hearing from Marisol. What she no doubt heard every day when she volunteered here at this counseling center.

Whether it was my earlier client, with her WASP background and middle-class upbringing, or Marisol, here in the East Oakland barrio, battering cut across all socio-economic, cultural, and racial boundaries. And, from what Marisol said, all ages.

Suddenly I remembered something I hadn't thought about for years, the woman who lived next door to us, when I was growing up and my parents were still a couple. Sherman Street in Alameda was worlds away from the corner of East Fourteenth and Fruitvale in Oakland, a neighborhood of trees and well-kept Victorian houses. I could see my mother in our backyard, a basket handle over one arm and a pair of scissors in her hand, talking to her neighbor as she snipped oregano, sage, and rosemary from her herb garden.

"Why do you put up with it?" my mother asked the woman. "I certainly wouldn't. Why don't you leave?"

In my memory the woman didn't have a face. All I could see was her hair escaping from its loose knot, falling on her slumped shoulders. "Where would I go?" she countered. "How would I support my kids?"

I shook my head and the memory dissolved. I was back in the utilitarian counseling center for battered women, sitting on an uncomfortable chair and scrutinizing a survivor. "How did you get out?" I asked her.

Marisol compressed her lips. "All along, I wanted to go to college. That's been my dream. And in spite of me dissing Sister Mary Holy Water, I was an honor student. I had a chance at a scholarship. In the fall of my senior year, my grades started slipping. Peter didn't like me being such a bookworm. That meant I wasn't paying enough attention to him. Finally, we fought about it and he beat me up real bad."

She ducked her head. "I told my family I'd been in a car accident. They bought it. I'll tell you why. They've been buying it for years. One of my brothers, he slaps his wife around. And nobody in the family thinks it's wrong. Except me. Isn't that crazy?"

When I didn't answer, she continued. "So about the time I've got all these bruises from my bogus car accident, my sister-in-law shows up one Sunday with a black eye. I told her she should talk to someone about my brother. She looks at me and says, you're one to talk."

Marisol laughed and shook her head. "Earth to Marisol. Finally. I realized she was right. I was involved in the same kind of relationship. Except I could get out, because I wasn't married to the guy. I decided I'd better do something about it. So I came to this counseling center, right here in one of these offices, and spilled my guts to one of these volunteers. Then I told Peter to go fuck himself for a change."

She flashed a triumphant smile, then frowned. "My sister-in-law is still married to my brother. And he still beats her up."

"What about Peter?" I asked. "Was that the end of it for him?"

It couldn't have been that easy for Marisol to break off this abusive relationship. There were too many men who wouldn't let go or take no for an answer.

She shook her head. "Not for him. He couldn't believe I'd told him to get lost. For months, he kept calling, coming around the house. By that time I'd graduated and started school at Berkeley. I shared an apartment with some other women."

"Did he ever stalk you?" I asked. "Or call you at that apartment?"

"For a while," Marisol said slowly. "He'd call my folks. They must have given him the number. And the address. There were a couple of times that first year, I'd look over my shoulder and catch a glimpse of him. Or someone who looked a lot like him. But the Berkeley campus is a big place. I couldn't be sure it was him. Maybe it was just paranoia, making me see Peter in the shadows. Anyway, I moved from that apartment into Sasha's house, about a year and a half ago. No more phone calls. No glimpses of Peter out of the corner of my eye. Nothing."

Both of us were silent for a moment.

"Do you think Peter's still carrying a grudge?" I asked.

"Enough to trash the plants and make those phone calls, you mean?"

"Yes. It is a man, by the way. He called this afternoon while I was at the house." I gave her a brief rundown of the morning's events.

"I don't know, Jeri." She shook her head. "It's been a long time since I broke up with Peter. I have no idea where he is. Yes, he hassled me after I ended our relationship, but to start up again after all this time. Finding out where I live, and my phone number, particularly after Sasha changed it. On the one hand, I wouldn't put it past him. But on the other, why would he bother now?"

Nine

I DIDN'T HAVE AN ANSWER TO MARISOL'S QUES-
tion. But I intended to find one.

Before leaving the counseling center, I obtained from
her as much information about Peter as she could dredge
from her memory. Maybe Peter was a wild goose chase.
But he'd stalked her in the past. I couldn't discount the
possibility that he was stalking her now.

I went home to feed the cats and get ready for my
Saturday evening date. Kaz and I were going to see *Sabrina* and *Roman Holiday* at the Elmwood. We had dinner
first; nothing fancy, just burritos at a *tacqueria* across the
street from the theater. Kaz is a vegetarian, and he'd
opted for black beans and rice in his burrito, eating it
with a knife and fork because it was so messy. No such
niceties for me. I was a hands-on person when it came to
Mexican food. As I wrapped both my hands around my
chicken mole burrito, I cast aspersions on Audrey Hepburn's choices in men, at least during the first show.

"Why would any woman dally with William Holden
when she could have Humphrey Bogart?"

Kaz grinned at me, a twinkle in those incredibly blue
eyes of his. "Holden was easy on the eyes. Besides, not
everyone shares your passion for Bogart." He'd seen my
vast collection of Bogart videotapes, everything from
The Petrified Forest to *The Harder They Fall*.

"And I suppose you don't have a thing for Ingrid Bergman," I said, dipping a tortilla chip into some guacamole. I'd been to Kaz's apartment a time or two. I knew about the *Anastasia* poster in the bedroom.

"That's different."

"Yeah, sure."

"Humphrey Bogart was way too old for Audrey," Kaz pointed out.

"So were William Holden and Gregory Peck," I admitted. "But this is fantasy, not real life."

And we both needed some fantasy now and then. We had jobs that brought us into contact with the bleaker side of life. I'd met Kaz back in December while working on a case involving a missing child named Dyese Smith. Her mother, a murder victim, had been HIV positive and I needed more information on how the disease was passed from mother to child. So I visited Children's Hospital in Oakland, where Dr. Kazimir Pellegrino worked in the Pediatric AIDS/HIV program.

I'd found Dyese later that month and taken her to Children's. Mercifully, she had tested negative for the virus. She was in foster care now because her grandmother had turned her back on the child. Kaz gave me periodic updates on her progress.

Kaz had looked me up a few days after my visit to the hospital, and we'd spent New Year's Eve together. Since then, we'd dated several times during the intervening months, sharing an interest in jazz, old movies, and good food. I had a feeling our interests were going to move toward something physical too, but we hadn't gotten there yet. I had to admit that his deep blue eyes had been playing a part in some of my fantasies. So had his curly black, silver-streaked hair, which he wore clubbed back into a short ponytail. I wanted to run my fingers through that hair. Soon, I thought.

But the man was so busy. I brought up the subject of a play opening in San Francisco next weekend and proposed a night at the theater. He shook his head.

"Can't do it. I'm going to an AIDS conference in London. I leave Wednesday."

"Too bad. The play has a short run. I'll cook dinner for us Tuesday, then. How long will you be gone?"

"Ten days, including travel time. The conference is five days. After it's over, I'm going to take the Chunnel to Paris and look up some of my Doctors Without Borders colleagues."

Kaz had been involved with the physicians' relief organization for three years, in Somalia and Rwanda. Then he'd experienced burnout and returned to the States, where he'd joined the staff of Children's Hospital.

Who knew how long he'd be there? When I looked at him and heard his past history of moving from job to job, I had to wonder how long he'd find a challenge in working with his kids.

The sooner I ran my fingers through his hair, the better, I decided.

"I went to Paris a couple of years ago. After Sid and I broke up. It was a wonderful trip, far too short. I'd like to go back."

"My favorite city." Kaz smiled. "Maybe someday I'll show you the Paris I know."

His words left me contemplating walks in the Jardin des Tuileries with the good doctor. The picture in my mind was so pleasant I almost didn't hear him ask after my father.

"Dad? He's going to a conference too. In Albuquerque, at the University of New Mexico. Something about western history." My father, Dr. Timothy Howard, taught history at California State University in Hayward. "In fact, I'm taking him to the airport tomorrow."

We finished our dinner, while I brought him up to date on the rest of my family, as well as my friend Cassie's wedding plans. Which wouldn't get very far until she found the perfect wedding gown. Then Kaz and I strolled across the street, holding hands.

Yes, I liked the touch of his hands and the way he smiled. I'd have to do something about that when he returned from Paris. Just as we got to the box office of the Elmwood Theatre, I reached up and tweaked the curly hair at the end of his ponytail.

"What's that all about?" he asked, with a grin and a sidelong glance from his blue eyes.

I answered him with a grin of my own. "Just thinking."

Ten

"I DON'T HAVE A PROBLEM WITH MEN," RACHEL Steiner told me. "Men in the abstract, men in general, or men on an individual basis. I guess I've been lucky. Now, Marisol . . ." She waved her fork for emphasis. "Marisol's got a problem with men."

She looked relaxed this Monday morning, after her weekend in Calistoga. We were seated at a small table for two in the front corner of Rick and Ann's on Domingo Avenue. Her back was to the plate-glass window, but I had a view of the sidewalk and the street. Beyond these I glimpsed the stately white sprawl of the Claremont Hotel, the resort where firefighters had made a stand against the devastating East Bay hills fire in 1991. The hotel survived, but in the hills behind it homes went up like so much tinder.

On weekends there was a long wait to get a table at Rick and Ann's, but now, on a weekday, we'd been able to walk right in. Rachel, with unabashed enjoyment, dug into a stack of buttermilk pancakes. My omelet, with layers of eggplant, tomatoes, and feta cheese, was so large as to be daunting, but I was making a concerted effort to reduce its dimensions.

I reached for my coffee and examined the woman who sat opposite me. I am five feet eight. Rachel was probably an inch or two taller. Her blond hair was pulled back from her face, its length twisted into a thick braid that fell halfway down her back. This morning she wore blue jeans and an oversize sweater, patterned in shades of blue and pink. Tiny silver stars dangled from her pierced ears.

"So what do you want to talk about, Jeri?" Rachel reached for the syrup and poured another dollop on her pancakes. "Besides men."

I polished off a forkful of my omelet before answering. "About what's happening at the house."

"Yeah. Sasha told me about the phone call on Saturday. They got another one last night, before I got home."

I made a mental note to call Sasha, to see if she or the Berkeley Police Department had received any information about the tap on the line. Perhaps the phone company had been able to trace where the calls had originated.

"Strange," Rachel continued. "This is the first time whoever is doing this has talked. Always before it was—" She stopped, fork in midair. "Menacing presence. But no words."

"Everyone else seems certain the calls started in January. Are you?"

"Oh, yes. Just after New Year's, I think." Both of us fell silent as our server replenished our coffee cups. Rachel's hazel eyes turned thoughtful as she sifted back through the calendar.

"Most of us were gone during Christmas break. Sasha and Martin were there, of course. Marisol stayed. She's not too keen on spending a lot of time with her family. From what she's said about them, I don't blame her. Me, I was in and out. Went skiing with some friends up at Tahoe. They have a cabin, so I stayed with them for several days over the holiday itself. I came back the week between Christmas and New Year's. Ben's got

68

family over in San Francisco and Nelson's parents live on the Peninsula."

I knew that Vicki and her father went up to Sacramento to spend Christmas with Sid's sister Doreen. "What about Emily?"

"Emily's parents are dead," Rachel said. "She was raised by an aunt who lives up north. They went to Hawaii for Christmas."

"So everyone was back by the first week in January."

Rachel nodded. "All of us getting geared up for the next term, and Martin back in school. The phone calls started about then. But I couldn't tell you exactly when." Rachel took another bite of her pancakes. "But we told you all of this when you were over at the house last Friday. Now you've been to see Marisol at the counseling center and you want to talk with me. Digging a little deeper?"

I looked at her steadily. "Whoever is making those calls has some connection with one of the people who lives in that house. I'm trying to figure out what that connection is, and who it's with. According to Nelson, he and Ben weren't even aware of the calls until Friday, when the plants were destroyed."

"You don't believe them?" Rachel asked.

"I'm a private investigator," I said, a smile twitching on my lips. "I'm suspicious of everyone and everything."

"But why do such a thing?" Rachel countered. "Though I've considered that one of my housemates might be responsible, I haven't been able to cast any one of them in the role, at least not for long. Let's face it, we've all got a pretty good place to live. Sasha doesn't charge us an exorbitant amount to live in her house. And she could. It's hard to find accommodations so close to campus. We're a fairly congenial bunch. Even if Marisol snipes at the guys." She shrugged. "Marisol snipes at everyone, me included. She's always got a mad on about something. That's just Marisol."

Rachel lifted another forkful of pancakes to her mouth. I wasn't as quick as she to dismiss the possibility that one of the housemates was behind the calls. What she said was correct. As near as I could tell from my investigation thus far, the calls had come at times when not all the residents of the house were there. Should I believe Nelson and Ben when they denied knowledge of the calls?

But as Rachel pointed out, a motive for one or both of them to do such a thing was unclear. It appeared that the only time Nelson and Ben were routinely in the main house was mealtime. Their apartment had a tiny, barely adequate kitchen, which allowed them to at least prepare coffee in the mornings. As far as partaking of meals, even though Nelson seemed to live on takeout, both claimed they preferred the interaction with the other residents of the house in the big kitchen.

My next line of investigation, the one I was pursuing now, was that the caller was someone known to one of the housemates. "Have you been able to cast anyone you know in the role of anonymous caller?" I asked Rachel.

"Back to men," she said. "Marisol said she told you about the guy she was involved with in high school. But that's hardly recent."

"Maybe not." I'd already put the wheels in motion, trying to find Peter Dace. If he'd stalked Marisol before, that made him a good candidate for the current role of stalker. But there was another possibility. It could be someone she encountered at the counseling center, a disgruntled boyfriend or husband. Marisol and I had discussed that prospect before I left Las Hermanas on Saturday afternoon. Other than that man she'd mentioned Friday night, she had not been immediately able to think of anyone who'd hassled center volunteers because of their work with battered women. Marisol told me they were all on a first name basis, clients and counselors alike, and last names rarely came into play. Still, there was a chance that a man whose wife had left him because she got some counseling would track down one of the counselors. Marisol said she'd think about it and write down any names that occurred to her.

"There's that guy who's been hassling Vicki and Emily," Rachel said. "He's called the house several times. If you ask me, he's the one. Vicki said he accosted her Saturday when she was at the library."

"Mr. Macauley is definitely on my list. What about you, Rachel?"

"Me?" Rachel smiled. "I don't have any men in my life, Jeri. At least not right now. And I haven't had a relationship that ended badly enough for the guy to want to harass me."

"What about men you don't know? You said earlier that you volunteer for escort duty at a local abortion clinic. And that anti-abortion pickets had targeted the doctors and some of the other employees. Let's consider that possibility."

It was, however, fraught with the same drawbacks as Marisol's counseling center. A doctor was an easier target than a volunteer, as Rachel had pointed out earlier. Doctors were in the phone book, with first and last names. With that information, I could find out where my target lived. Anyone could. But the volunteers at the battered women's center tried to keep communication between themselves and their clients on a first name basis. It was safe that way. I was sure it was the same way with Rachel's clinic escort duty. Why go to all the trouble to pick one volunteer, find out her name, then find out where she lived? But there were some seriously obsessed people in the anti-abortion movement, as Rachel's next words pointed out.

"It's worth checking," she said. "A doctor in Dallas got a civil judgment against a bunch of anti-abortion protesters last year because they were stalking him. And that guy in Boston, who shot and killed the receptionist, just because she was there." She shook her head. "Some of these people are quite sincere in their opposition to abortion, for religious or whatever reasons. However, my impression is that a lot of the men who show up at these protests simply hate women. They're using the anti-abortion movement as a vehicle to express that hatred. Usually they target the clinic staff, not the escorts. But it's possible someone could fixate on me. . . ."

"You thought of something," I said as Rachel frowned.

"Yes, I did." She looked thoughtful. "The last time I was at the clinic, I'm sure I heard one of the protesters call my first name. I think it was a man. What if he found out my last name, where I live, my phone number? Particularly after Sasha had the number changed. Now, that's creepy, isn't it?"

"I'll look into it," I said.

Rachel now looked troubled. She finished her pancakes and wiped her mouth with a napkin. "I'm on escort duty tomorrow morning. You could come to the clinic, do a little surveillance. But I'll have to clear it with Tate. He's my escort partner. I'll talk with him and call you."

Our server appeared at the table and I asked her to box up the rest of the omelet, which had defeated me. When she brought that, and the check, I examined the total and pulled some bills from my wallet.

"Thanks for breakfast," Rachel told me as we stood. "Hope our conversation was helpful."

Not as helpful as I would have liked, I thought, as we parted on the corner of Domingo and Ashby. I watched

Rachel stride briskly down Ashby and felt as though I'd barely scratched her surface. I still didn't know much about her, or any of the people who shared the house on Garber Street. I headed for downtown Oakland and my Franklin Street office, where I was about to remedy that lack of knowledge.

Eleven

MUCH AS I ENJOYED USING MY MODEM TO SURF the Internet, I was of the opinion that there were still aspects of investigation that required old-fashioned legwork, such as tracking down and interviewing witnesses. And surveillance, or as I sometimes called it, hanging out on street corners. I was sure my mentor and former employer, retired investigator Errol Seville, would agree.

I stuck the box containing the remains of the omelet into the little refrigerator tucked under a worktable at the back of my long narrow office. Then I wrote myself a note that read, "Take leftovers home." Otherwise the box would sit there, forgotten, contents growing mold, until I began to wonder what was causing the smell.

I made a pot of coffee. While the water dripped through the grounds, I checked my answering machine for messages and returned calls, setting up several appointments. A fellow P.I. in Eureka had completed some work I'd asked him to do and faxed me his report. I poured myself a mugful of coffee and sipped as I read through his information, then called him with a few questions. Once satisfied, I wrote out a check to pay him, stuck it into an envelope, and tossed it into the basket that held my outgoing mail.

These tasks completed, I moved to my filing cabinet and dug out the folder I'd started on this case. Then I switched on my computer and cruised onto the information superhighway. I had a brief twinge of regret that I was about to infringe on the privacy of the people who lived in the Garber Street house. Especially since Vicki Vernon was one of those people. But I told myself it was a necessary step. The need to track down the harasser outweighed the privacy issue.

Besides, I had the feeling something bad would happen if I didn't find this guy.

I was looking for signposts, something the housemates had in common that might point to the person in their lives who was making those phone calls and who had taken what appeared to be such pleasure in destroying the lemon tree and the rest of the plants. But so far in my talks with them, I hadn't found what I sought. They all came from different backgrounds, different places, different interests. The only thing they shared was their status as students at U.C. Berkeley and the house on Garber Street.

The first person to go under the microscope was Sasha Nichols. My assets check, and an earlier trip to the Alameda County Courthouse, confirmed that she did indeed own the house on Garber Street. Free and clear, as a matter of fact. The mortgage insurance held by her parents had, on their deaths, paid the outstanding balance owed on the house. It was worth quite a bit in the current real estate market, despite its somewhat lived-in condition. That was no doubt due to what real estate agents call "location, location, location." Close to the U.C. Berkeley campus and in the Elmwood district, the assessed value was enough to impress me, particularly since I couldn't scrape together enough for a down payment on a condo.

Professor and Mrs. Nichols had bought the place after California's Proposition 13 went into effect, so the property taxes on the place were higher than they would have been had they owned the house for a longer time. Since Sasha was a full-time student with a young son to support and a household to maintain, I could see why she felt the need to take in roomers.

The Volvo she'd been driving on Saturday must have belonged to her parents as well, since my credit check didn't yield any information about outstanding loans to any financial institutions. She had a credit card that she managed to keep paid down, although it showed an upward surge at Christmas. So had mine, I reminded myself as I reached for the coffee mug at my elbow.

Just to satisfy my curiosity, I ran a check on Sasha's former lover, the Haitian émigré who was Martin's father, to see if there was any indication that Etienne was currently in the Bay Area. Eight years ago he was driving a BMW that had collected quite a few unpaid parking tickets, in locations ranging from San Francisco to Carmel. Then he'd unloaded the BMW, gotten himself a Porsche, and moved to Southern California, where he'd taken to speeding through West L.A. He hadn't netted any tickets lately, though. After being cited for driving 100 miles an hour on the road to Palm Springs, Etienne had either left California or he'd cleaned up his act. This avenue of my investigation appeared to be a dead end, but I wasn't yet ready to discount him entirely.

Sasha had an undergraduate degree in sociology from Berkeley, obtained as a part-time student over a period of about seven years. After her parents died, she decided that what she wanted to be when she grew up was a lawyer. She took the LSATs, scored high, according to Vicki, and won entrance to the university's law school. She was now in her third and final year of study.

I'd done some actual legwork on Sunday, after taking Dad to the airport. That research included a trip to the Oakland Public Library. There, I'd scanned microfilmed issues of the Oakland and San Francisco papers. I made copies of articles about the January hate mail incident at Boalt Hall and the subsequent demonstrations in favor of affirmative action. Now I opened the folder on my desk and reviewed the articles.

A flyer had circulated at the law school, lauding the recent conservative turn in national politics as well as the current anti-affirmative action mood in state politics. Sasha had given me a copy of the flyer itself, and what I read made me want to hold the sheet of paper carefully between finger and thumb before depositing it in some garbage heap where it belonged. With crude racist and sexist epithets, the flyer denigrated women and minority students at the law school. A pro-affirmative action demonstration was quickly organized by the African-American law students' organization. As president of the organization, Sasha Nichols was quoted prominently in several of these accounts.

But the incident occurred in mid-January. All the housemates seemed to agree that the phone calls had started the first week in January. Could they be connected with the Boalt Hall business? When the anonymous caller finally spewed forth words on Saturday, he'd used the same ugly language printed on the flyer, and more.

I recalled the old rhyme I'd heard so many times in my childhood: "Sticks and stones can break my bones but words can never hurt me."

Not true, I thought, shaking my head. Words can be painful and brutal, carving their power viciously on one's psyche. Particularly words full of venom, which deliberately underscore the fact that people are different. I thought of all the things that make people different—skin color, ethnicity, immigration status, or the shape of one's eyes, religious beliefs, sex and sexual orientation, even age and youth. These days people seemed to be focused on differences rather than similarities, looking at the things that separate us rather than concentrating on the ways we are all alike. I hope we don't destroy ourselves before we realize that we're all in this together.

Destroy. I tapped a pencil restlessly against a notepad. Words, while they can hurt, are often a precursor to action. Instead of my computer screen I saw an image of the firebombed interior of a Sacramento city councilman's house, a cross burned on the lawn of a family in San Leandro. I recalled the gay man who was beaten to death a few years ago on a San Francisco street. The baseball bats and epithets were wielded by a couple of young punks who, according to the mother of one of them, just didn't like homosexuals. As though that excused murder.

The angry white male is as much of a stereotype as the affirmative action baby. Nelson Lathrop certainly didn't fit the stereotype. He appeared too laid-back to be angry at anyone. When I'd interviewed him over the weekend, Nelson seemed quite open. He told me he grew up in Menlo Park, the oldest of three children, in what he described as "your basic intact upper-middle-class nuclear family." His father worked in the computer industry and his mother was an elementary school teacher. Nelson was a sophomore at Cal, studying engineering. Despite the goofy demeanor, he had a brain and knew how to use it. Getting into U. C. Berkeley, the flagship of the state university system, wasn't easy. Nelson confessed he'd graduated first in his high school class. From what I could see, or couldn't see from my empty computer net, he hadn't been in any trouble since he turned eighteen.

The fact that Nelson's parents were comfortably well-off and had put money away for his college education meant that he didn't have to get a job to make ends meet, like his roommate in the garage apartment. Ben Winslow, a history major, was attending Cal on a scholarship, but even with the addition of a student loan, he was still stretched for money. He'd told me his widowed mother in San Francisco's Potrero Hill district couldn't give him any financial help. In fact, he was trying to assist her any way he could. She had his younger brothers and sisters to look after. He'd lived at home and commuted to Berkeley the first year he was in school, just to save money. But the time spent commuting and the boisterous and noisy atmosphere at home had taken a toll on his grades.

The garage apartment was a godsend for that reason, but in order to pay his share of the rent and other expenses, he'd taken a job as a server at Marquessa, a restaurant on Oxford Street. The tips were great, he said, but working four nights a week cut into his study time.

"I do what I have to," he'd told me with a shrug. "Besides, this lets me give my mother a little something, to help her out."

My computer queries on Marisol Gallegos netted me little information. Marisol had stayed out of trouble and she paid her bills. After our conversation at the counseling center, she'd told me she was the first of her family to attend college. All her sisters and brothers had married and gone to work as soon as they got out of high school. In her opinion, she was considered the family oddity because she hadn't taken that path.

Marisol also had a scholarship, her focus sociology. Her mother was born in Los Angeles, her father in Mexico, though he came to this country as a child with his farmworker parents. He'd worked for years in a factory in an industrial part of East Oakland, between Hegenberger Road and Ninety-eighth Avenue, until the corporation that owned the place shut it down in one of the "restructuring" waves that had swept over the workforce in the past decade. He hadn't been able to find another job so he set himself up in business as a handyman, repairing whatever machinery and small appliances came his way. Marisol's mother waited tables at an Oakland restaurant.

My fishing expedition on Peter Dace, Marisol's old boyfriend, netted me an address and phone number in San Jose. Now I punched in the digits. An answering machine confirmed that there was someone named Pete living at the address. I hung up without leaving a message.

Dace had been attending Chabot College in Hayward when Marisol Gallegos met him seven years ago. The relationship ended three years after that, but Dace had apparently hassled her for nearly a year afterward. Marisol said she didn't think he'd graduated from the two-year college, and a phone call to the administrative office at Chabot confirmed that Dace hadn't obtained any sort of degree or certificate. The last address they had for him was in San Jose.

I picked up the phone and called Norm Gerrity, an investigator colleague with an office in San Jose and plenty of contacts in that police department. When he called me back he had what I needed.

"Peter Dace was busted on an assault charge a couple of years ago." Norm's voice was a familiar South Boston rasp. "The complainant was a woman, Dace's girlfriend."

"Why am I not surprised?" I commented, as I picked up my pencil and jotted notes on a lined legal pad. "Is he in jail?"

"Nah. She dropped the charges. Same old song and dance."

Norm gave me the details. The woman's name was Cathy Mason. She and Dace had shared an apartment near San Jose State University, where she was a sophomore and Dace was a part-time student. Evidently he'd continued his educational pursuits after leaving Chabot. Mason had called the police one night and told the responding officers that Peter had knocked her around. But she'd subsequently decided she was mistaken, that she'd fallen down the stairs leading to the second-floor unit.

Although she wouldn't press charges, she did have the good sense to split up with him. She'd moved out. Norm's contact at the San Jose Police Department said she'd transferred to San Francisco State. But Dace still lived in the same apartment, still taking a few classes. Most of the time, however, he worked at an auto parts store near downtown San Jose. Norm gave me the address.

"Thanks. I owe you one."

"Any time, Jeri."

I hung up the phone and turned back to my computer. Rachel, my breakfast companion, had been arrested three times, first at the Concord Naval Weapons Station out in Contra Costa County, a recurring magnet for demonstrations. She'd been picked up a second time at the Lawrence Livermore Lab, which did nuclear weapons research. Most recently she'd been arrested during the protests that rippled through Berkeley and the rest of the Bay Area when the Persian Gulf War began. Evidently, any arrests at the abortion clinic where she did escort duty had been aimed at the anti-abortion protesters.

In between her activist pursuits, Rachel was doing graduate work in political science. Her choice of study didn't surprise me, nor did her long tenure at Berkeley. Rachel appeared to be like many other residents who'd come to U.C. as freshmen and simply stayed to become part of the community. My friend Levi Zotowska, who owned an electronics store on Telegraph Avenue, was that way. He'd originally come from the coal mining country of eastern Pennsylvania. Rachel was from upstate

New York, she told me over breakfast earlier, but she hadn't been back since her mother died.

I knew quite a bit about Vicki Vernon, after having been married to her father. She was born in Oakland, but Sid and his first wife Linda divorced when Vicki was five. Linda moved to San Diego, where, several years after the divorce, she married a dentist. So Vicki spent her childhood and adolescence in the pleasant middle-class surroundings of sunny San Diego. She was close to her father, though.

I knew how Sid would react if he found out about the harassment of Vicki and her housemates. Which is why she'd come to me first. Sid wouldn't like that either. I doubted we could keep any secrets from him long.

I warmed up my coffee, then turned the computer microscope on Emily Austen. And found nothing.

It was as though she didn't exist.

Twelve

THAT WAS AN OVERSIMPLIFICATION, I SUPPOSE.
Of course Emily existed. I had talked with her, seen
her brush the dark brown hair away from her face, looked
into her dark blue eyes. I'd watched her move around the
kitchen of the Garber Street house.

But I've discovered that most people in this life, even
those as young as Emily, leave a trail, whether in paper
or computer bytes. Emily didn't have much of a trail.
She was a freshman at the University of California. She
didn't own property but she did own a Chevy sub-
compact that she'd bought at a Berkeley used car lot just
prior to starting classes at Cal. She had a driver's license
to go with the car, a sizable bank account at a Berkeley
Wells Fargo branch, and a credit card that she paid off
every month. It was as though she had no life before she
arrived in Berkeley the past August. Since then she'd led
a very careful and circumspect life, which was not unusual for a quiet and studious nineteen-year-old.

Rachel told me that morning over breakfast that
Emily's parents were dead and she was raised by an aunt
who lived up north. Northern California? Or farther, in
Oregon or Washington? I tried to recall anything else
Vicki had told me about this new friend of hers, but came
up empty.

Something pricked at me. Emily's panicky reaction to Martin's sudden disappearance Saturday morning. Initially I thought she'd gone overboard. The kid had just wandered off, we'd find him. Then all the residue kicked in, left by those news reports about children snatched from their front yards. I'd started feeling it too.

Now I wondered if there was a more personal reason why Emily had been so upset. Had something similar happened to her? Perhaps someone had tried to snatch her in the past. Was she a missing child?

My office door opened, interrupting my speculation. My best friend Cassie Taylor walked in, resplendent in a tailored gray suit with a lilac blouse. The elegant effect of what I called her lawyer clothes was somewhat tempered by the high-topped running shoes and thick white socks. Cassie was a recent convert to comfort, after having sprained her ankle last January while trekking on high-heeled shoes between her office and the courthouse. Cassie was a partner in the law firm of Alwin, Taylor and Chao, which occupied the front suite of offices on the third floor of our Franklin Street building.

A big diamond sparkled on Cassie's left hand, a reminder of why she was there. She and I had a date to go over to San Francisco. The great wedding dress hunt was on, and so far she hadn't found anything she liked. But she was early, wasn't she? A glance at the clock on my wall showed the reverse was true. I was late. The whole morning had whizzed by while I was sleuthing on the information superhighway.

"You are staring at that computer screen," she declared, "as though you expect it to reveal all the secrets of the world."

I sighed and cruised off the Net. "At the moment, I'm not finding out anything, let alone the secrets of the world."

"Tough case?"

"Perplexing," I said, not going into details. "I hope we're going to have lunch before we trek through every store in the city." You wouldn't think I'd be hungry after that omelet at breakfast, but suddenly I was ravenous.

"Of course. As soon as we get to the city. It'll have to be a quickie, though. We've got several stops to make."

I locked my office and we headed for the Twelfth Street BART station, where we caught the next train to San Francisco. As the silver cars hurtled into the tunnel, I barely suppressed a shudder. Someone had pushed me in front of a train last December while I was working on a case. Now I couldn't look at a BART train without thinking about it, though I'd ridden them several times since. Taking public transportation to San Francisco was preferable to driving. Besides, there was something about that old adage of getting back on the horse after I'd been bucked off.

On the way over to the city Cassie and I talked about her wedding plans. She was marrying Eric Lindholm, the accountant she'd met last year when she deposed him during a civil suit. The wedding was planned for July and I was going to be maid of honor, a role that rested uneasily on my shoulders. I hadn't been in anyone's wedding since I was in college and stood up by the altar as a bridesmaid at the wedding of one of my Howard cousins.

My own wedding to Sid had been an informal ceremony, performed by a justice of the peace in the living room of my parents' Victorian house in Alameda. I'd worn a pale green silk dress and I carried a bouquet of roses clipped from Mother's garden. My mother, the gourmet chef, had taken charge of the small reception that spilled from the dining room into the backyard.

We were a small group that included my grandma Jerusha, who was my father's mother, my brother Brian and his wife Sheila, themselves not long married. My employer and private investigator mentor Errol Seville and his wife Minna had been there, along with my cousin Donna Doyle, a Fish and Game biologist who made the trip down from Humboldt County with her lover Kay, who made jewelry. And Cassie, who'd been my only attendant. Sid's sister Doreen was there, along with her husband, and Sid's partner at the time, Joe Kelso, had been his best man.

There was a lot of water under that bridge, I reflected. Grandma Jerusha had been diagnosed with cancer and she was gone now, leaving a hole in the lives of her family. Not long after my own marriage commenced, my mother decided to end hers. She walked out on my father, after thirty years of marriage, and went back to Monterey, where she'd grown up, to open her own restaurant. My father had rebounded fairly well from this double whammy, the death of his mother and the loss of his wife. Brian and Sheila now had two children, Todd and Amy. Donna had transferred to Monterey County, and she and Kay lived in Pacific Grove. Errol had retired, sidelined by a bad ticker, and I'd set out on my own. Sid had moved from Homicide to Felony Assault after Joe Kelso retired, then back to Homicide. And our marriage ended, almost as soon as it had begun. I'd ended it, figuring it wasn't a good idea to stay when the spark was no longer there. Sid had been more willing than I to work at what I considered a lost cause. He'd taken it hard when I moved out of his apartment and found my own. We'd been divorced more than two years now, and our relationship was still rather prickly.

Now Cassie was getting married. That meant our relationship would change. It already had, ever since she'd met Eric. Those spontaneous single woman outings had taken a backseat to her growing relationship with this man who would soon become her husband. Intellectually I understood it, of course, having been through it myself. Still, it made me feel a little sad.

We came up out of the BART station at Powell Street and headed into the lower level of San Francisco Centre, where our first stop was Nordstrom, on the upper five levels.

"No, you may not wear jeans and a T-shirt." Cassie rolled her eyes upward at my suggestion for maid of honor attire.

"Nobody's gonna look at me. You're supposed to be the star, right? I think a nice clean pair of Levi's and maybe a green and yellow Oakland A's shirt—"

"This is a church wedding, Jeri. I'll get you into a dress yet." We sidestepped a couple of shoppers and made our way toward the curving escalator.

"No high heels," I warned. "I don't do high heels."

"How about hats?"

I glared at her, aghast, as we stepped onto the moving silver stairs that would carry us upward. "Hats? Cassie, are you on drugs?"

"It's my wedding," Cassie declared. "I get to do what I want."

"Yes, but that's not a license to get carried away. You have my blessing to deck yourself with all sorts of frills. But be merciful to your maid of honor, please."

Cassie's response was a wicked laugh, followed by a thoughtful expression. She looked as though she were a partisan getting ready to storm the barricades. "Don't worry. I have something in mind. I just haven't found it yet. But I'll know it when I see it."

I sighed. "Battle stations, then. On to Nordie's."

Thirteen

WHATEVER CASSIE HAD IN MIND FOR A WEDding dress was not to be found at any of the downtown
San Francisco department stores, at least not that afternoon and evening. After we stormed the barricades at
Nordstrom, Macy's, and several downtown bridal shops,
we had dinner at the City of Paris on Geary Street. Thus
refreshed, we tramped the city sidewalks to Neiman-
Marcus and Saks before running out of steam around
eight-thirty. Empty-handed, we took BART back to the
quieter side of the bay, with Cassie plotting our next
outing and me thinking fondly of my own bed.

But I went to my office first, to check messages. There
was one from Rachel Steiner. She'd checked with her
escort partner and it was okay by him if I showed up
Tuesday morning. According to their information, the
clinic was expecting an organized protest. This would be
a good opportunity for me to observe the anti-abortion
protesters.

Early Tuesday morning I stopped at Peet's on Piedmont Avenue for a large container of strong black coffee.
Then I headed for the address Rachel had given me. It
was a one-story building on a side street that intersected a
major North Oakland thoroughfare. The clinic performed
abortions on Tuesdays and Saturdays, and the escorts
were supposed to show up early, hoping to get a jump on

the protesters who had been targeting the clinic for the past year.

I drove slowly past the clinic and didn't see anyone outside. Rachel had told me to be there by nine. It was just now eight-thirty.

Don't park near the clinic, Rachel had cautioned. Sometimes the protesters follow people to their cars. They'll take down your license number and follow you home. Sometimes they put sugar in the gas tank, she added. That's why I have a locking cap on mine.

Mindful of Rachel's warning, I left my locked Toyota in a residential neighborhood some four blocks away and took a circuitous route back to the clinic. On the steps in front of the clinic I saw three people, two women and a young man, all three casually dressed. Rachel wasn't among them. I turned and scanned the street, both directions, to see if I could spot her. No sign of her yet. I raised the container to my mouth, sipping coffee through a hole in the lid.

"Do I know you?" a voice said behind me.

I turned and saw the young man, in his twenties, I guessed. He'd left the group at the door and walked over to check me out, assessing me with narrowed blue eyes. Hair and mustache were an ashy brown. His T-shirt featured a coat hanger graphic and a message that left no doubt which side of the abortion battle he chose.

"Jeri Howard," I said. "Rachel Steiner asked me to meet her here."

"Oh, yeah. I'm Tate."

Rachel hadn't mentioned anything about Tate, other than he was her escort partner. I could only surmise that he was a friend who shared some of her activist interests. We shook hands. "Sorry to be so suspicious," Tate said. "But these days we never know whether someone's going to toss a bomb or pull out a gun."

"I know." I smiled grimly. "I read the newspapers."

Rachel and I had touched on that subject during breakfast on Monday. The tally nationwide in recent years included two doctors, one escort, and two clinic workers murdered, numerous clinics firebombed or shut down, many doctors and clinic workers harassed by protesters.

Which brought me to the reason I was here. If some anti-abortion zealot with a gun thought a clinic receptionist in Boston was fair game, it was just as likely that some protester could focus on an escort like Rachel, to the point of finding out where she lived. Especially since she thought one of the protesters knew her name. But as she had pointed out Monday, until Saturday the anonymous caller had been silent. And in the spewing of venom I'd listened to during that call, I hadn't heard the usual epithets the anti-abortion crowd was so fond of flinging at everyone who disagreed with their narrow view of the issue.

"They usually show up by ten," Tate said as we walked toward the door of the clinic. "Though the past couple of weeks they've been early."

It looked like someone else had made a Peet's run before coming over. I saw a row of four large steaming coffee containers lined up on the clinic's cement porch.

Tate introduced me to the two women. The younger of the two, Sarah, was in her twenties, curly black hair pushed back from her face by a headband. She told me she was a part-time student at Laney College here in Oakland, and also temped as a legal secretary. Since I'd done that sort of work before becoming a paralegal and later a private investigator, I felt some kinship with her.

Edna, the other escort, was older, past sixty, with a stocky build in tailored blue slacks and a flowered shirt. Her carefully coiffed gray hair and a layer of makeup made her look like any prosperous middle-class East Bay matron, but her words were gruff and to the point.

"I had an abortion, back when I was in college and it was illegal," she told me. "It was a horrible experience. I almost died. Believe me, abortion's got to stay legal. We can't let these zealots change the law."

"That's the way I feel," Sarah said, brushing a few escaped strands of hair off her face. "Women my age have grown up in a country where abortion is legal. I don't think they realize what it means to go back to the back alley coat hanger days."

"I can tell them what it's like." Edna shook her head, mouth grim. "If they'll listen."

"I wouldn't count on it." Tate's thin lips moved into a tight humorless smile. His eyes were moving restlessly as he scanned the street for Rachel. "The protesters you'll see here this morning aren't interested in listening, Jeri. Their ears and their minds are blocked."

Edna snorted. "It's worse than that. These people are fixated on fetuses. They don't give a damn what happens to mothers and babies after the kids are born. Not when it comes to funding day care, education, or WIC programs. Forget it. They live in some dreamworld that never existed, where some unreal mother stays home and raises flocks of perfect children and never has to worry about paying the rent or putting food on the table. Well, I was a single mom. I'm here to tell you that world doesn't exist."

"I'm inclined to agree with our former Surgeon General, the one who wasn't afraid to speak her mind," Tate said. "She said the anti-abortion movement is just a ploy for right-wingers. They're not interested in people, but in political power."

Sarah nodded. "The first thing I noticed when I started doing escort duty is how many men are in charge of the

91

anti-abortion groups. They run the show. The women do the dirty work. I think it has less to do with fetuses than some sort of need to control women."

"You mean hatred of women," Edna said bluntly.

"Surely some of the protesters are sincere," I said. "Religious people who view abortion as a sin."

"I used to think that too," Edna said. "But things have gotten really ugly over the past few years. The protests have escalated from peaceful to confrontational, and the nutcases started bombing clinics. I knew it was only a matter of time before someone got killed, and I was right. It's got more to do with politics than spiritual beliefs."

"I'm always suspicious of people who claim to have a direct line to God," Tate said. Then his voice took on a note of relief. "Here's Rachel. I was afraid something had happened to her."

We turned and saw Rachel walking quickly toward us, dressed in blue jeans and a sweatshirt, a sturdy pair of walking shoes on her feet.

"Sorry to be late. I had a little trouble with my car this morning. It's that alternator again." She looked at Tate. "Maybe you can take a look at it after we're done here."

"Sure thing." Tate handed her one of the coffee containers and nodded toward the clinic door. "The rest of us have already checked in."

Rachel took a swallow of coffee, then opened the door and went inside. She returned a moment later. "Have you talked with Vicki?" she asked. "About the call we got last night?"

"No." Vicki had left a message on my home answering machine saying they'd received another call, but leaving no details. I hadn't called her back. "Was there something different about this one?"

Rachel shrugged. "Vicki answered the phone this time.

She thought she recognized the voice. That it was some-one she'd heard before. Ted Macauley, I'll bet. The worst part was, Vicki's dad called right after. He asked why she sounded upset and she told him everything that's been going on."

I grimaced, speculating as to my ex-husband's reaction to the news. Ballistic, Vicki had predicted. "What about the tap on the phone line?"

"Sasha talked with that Berkeley cop. He said the calls have been made from pay phones in Berkeley and Oakland."

So the caller was moving around. I had guessed as much.

"Here they come," Tate said, drawing us back to the current situation.

A car and a van pulled up at the curb in front of the clinic. A group of about twenty people piled out of both vehicles, carrying signs. As Sarah had pointed out earlier, it seemed to be the men who were directing things, telling the mostly female protesters where to stand. I glanced past the group and saw an Oakland police cruiser drive slowly by on the opposite side of the street. The black and white parked at the curb, and the driver looked across the street at the assemblage.

"Who have we got this morning?" Edna asked, peering at the cop.

"Looks like Delgado," Tate said. "He's okay. He's fairly quick about calling for reinforcements if things get out of hand."

Rachel took another swallow of coffee and touched my arm. "What we do, Jeri, is take up a position on the perimeter. We don't talk to any of them. You can't even say good morning without getting a sermon."

"Looks like a few of them have rosaries." I scanned the group that had arrayed itself on the sidewalk in front of the clinic. The sentiments on the signs the protesters carried ran the gamut from reasoned to venomous.

"They can keep their rosaries," Rachel said, hands on her hips. "I'm Jewish. I don't appreciate anyone saying prayers over me. Their religion doesn't give them the right to confront sixteen-year-old girls and tell them how to live their lives. Just watch them. They'll target any women near the clinic."

"What do you do if that happens?" I asked.

Tate answered my question. "We deal only with what happens on clinic property. Our job is to help the clients get inside. If the protesters hassle people on the street, that's Officer Delgado's job."

Rachel's words were borne out a few minutes later when a woman who looked about twenty-five appeared, walking down the street in the direction of the clinic. But she wasn't planning on having an abortion that day. She had what looked like a bundle of clothing tucked under one arm and her destination appeared to be the dry-cleaning shop a few doors down. Two of the protesters swooped down on her and tried to hand her some litera-ture. She stared at them in alarm and backed away. The cop got out of his cruiser and headed across the street toward the protesters, who backed off, only to circle again as a car pulled into the clinic's lot.

The escorts moved into position, flanking the young woman who got out of the passenger seat. She was about eighteen, I guessed, and the older woman who'd been driving looked like her mother. Tate and Rachel quickly shepherded the two women toward the clinic door, ignoring the voices of the pack behind them.

That's how it went for the next hour or so. I hung around the edges, observing, trying to decide if any of these people had fixated on Rachel Steiner. It looked as though this group of protesters had been here before, since they were as organized as the escorts. I noted the license plates of the two vehicles, thinking that both sides could play this game. This got me a suspicious look from Officer Delgado, who had so far limited his activities to herding protesters away from passersby.

Finally I heard someone saying Rachel's name. It wasn't Tate or any of the other escorts. I zeroed in on one of the protesters, a tall man in his mid-thirties, with brown hair, blue suit, and a tie. "Rachel, Rachel, Rachel," he said in a monotone, his eyes on her as she and Tate escorted another client from the parking lot to the clinic. It wasn't as overt as saying, "I know where you live." But there was something menacing in the way he said it over and over, like a litany. I don't think she heard him.

I watched him for a while, watching his lips move as he said, "Rachel, Rachel, Rachel." Then he saw me watching him and he faded back toward the van.

"Know that guy?" I asked Edna, who was the only one of the escorts within range.

"The face is certainly familiar. He's been here before."

"I need a name."

I faded too, toward the side of the clinic. Then I circled, as I had earlier when I'd written down the license numbers. I had a feeling Officer Delgado was watching me, instead of the protesters, but he didn't make a move toward me. Then I started walking toward the clinic, as though I had an appointment. The protesters circled me, first exhorting me not to kill my baby today, then damning me as a murderer because I didn't break my stride. I got a good look at the tall man who'd used Rachel's name. As I reached the sidewalk leading up to the clinic, Rachel and Tate moved into escort position and hurried me up the sidewalk.

"What the hell was that about?" Rachel asked when we reached the front door.

I took her arm and pulled her into the foyer. "That tall lanky guy in the blue suit. He's the one who knows your name. Do you know his?"

Rachel stared outside at the blue-suited man. "He's a regular, one of the leaders. Bill or Bob. Don't know his last name. Do you think—" She stopped.

"I don't know, but I'm going to check him out. I think I've seen enough for now. Is there a back door to this place?"

Fourteen

THE AUTO PARTS STORE WHERE PETER DACE
worked was just off Guadalupe Parkway, close enough to
San Jose International Airport that the roar of the jets
taking off and landing at the nearby runways drowned
out all other ambient sounds. After driving the forty-odd
miles from Oakland Tuesday afternoon, I parked in the
asphalt-covered lot and got out to have a look around.
The retail outlet was to my right, selling everything from
tires to air freshener promising "that new car smell." To
my left three oversize doorways punched through the
concrete walls, leading from the lot into the mechanics'
bays of the garage.

Finally I spotted Dace, based on the description Marisol
had given me and helped by the fact that, like the other
employees of the store, he wore a red and blue shirt with
the store's logo on the left front breast pocket and the
name "Pete" on the right.

Some women might find Peter Dace attractive. I didn't.
In fact, given what Marisol and Norman Gerrity had told
me about him, he made my skin crawl.

He was twenty-six now, medium height and build, with
ruddy skin and shaggy blond hair. At the moment, my
view was partially obscured because Dace was in the
center bay of the garage, talking with the casually dressed
older man who went with the late model American car

parked there. Dace had the hood of the car up, leaning in as his hands probed the engine. I couldn't tell what he was doing, but he kept up a constant line of chatter with the customer.

Dace moved to this side of the car, leaned forward, and lifted a grease- and acid-stained battery from the car and set his burden on the concrete floor of the bay. He picked up a new battery, as yet pristine, and hoisted it into position. As he replaced the connection he turned his head toward the customer, and I heard both men laugh.

When Dace had finished, he shut the hood and the customer backed his car out of the bay. Dace watched him go, then moved in my direction, with a preening, cock-of-the-walk stroll. Had he spotted me watching him? No, he was headed for the soda machine on the outer wall between the garage and the retail store. He dropped some coins into the slot and reached for the can that the machine thunked into the receptacle at the bottom. He walked back to the fence at the rear of the parking lot before popping the can open and swallowing several large gulps. Then he took out the pack of cigarettes that distended the breast pocket of his shirt, shook out a butt, and lit a match to the end. I watched him suck in the smoke.

Dace looked at me appraisingly as I approached him. His blue eyes raked over my body as he assessed my figure, my age, my attractiveness. Just as quickly, he dismissed me. According to Marisol, he liked young flesh. At thirty-four I was far too old to interest him.

"You want something?" he asked, a challenge behind his disinterest. If I were a customer I'd have a work requisition in my hands, but I didn't. Besides, he was on his break, dosing himself with nicotine, sugar, and caffeine. He didn't want to be bothered.

"Are you Peter Dace?" I took a position a few feet in front of him, invading his space. He was a bit shorter

98

than my five feet eight inches, so I drew myself up to my full height and looked intimidating.

"Who wants to know?" He growled the words and glared at me with hostility.

"I'm a friend of Marisol's." I took a step forward. I was making Dace feel uncomfortable, which was exactly what I wanted.

"Marisol." He frowned, then shrugged, all dismissive bravado. "That bitch. What about her?"

"You used to beat her up."

"Who says?" He was all innocence. "Did she say that? She's lying. I never beat on her." I looked at him steadily, not buying it. "Yeah, well, Marisol had a mouth on her. So maybe I slapped her once or twice, when she got out of line."

"What about Cathy Mason? Does she have a mouth on her too?"

His eyes flashed at me as though I fit into the category of mouthy female. His fingers twitched on the can, perhaps itching to slap me into line. Instead he gulped down the rest of his soda, then crushed the can with his strong grease-stained hand and hurled it in the direction of an overflowing garbage can. He missed. Zero points.

"What is this?" His mouth tightened, his eyes narrowed with suspicion. "You a cop?"

"I told you. I'm a friend of Marisol's. Talked to her lately?"

"Why would I do that?" He snorted, took another hit from his cigarette, then tossed the butt on the asphalt. "Not gonna waste my time on that little bitch."

"Do you call all the women you know bitches?" I asked, keeping my voice pleasant. "Even your mother?"

"Hey, you leave my mother out of this." He came away from the fence, looking for a fight or an exit. I didn't give him either. "What do you want?" he snarled.

I leaned toward him and spoke with icy calm. "I want to know if you've been hassling Marisol."

"Hassling her?" He laughed as though the idea was absurd. "Hassle Marisol? I haven't seen her since she split. Four years ago."

"That's not what she tells me."

"Oh, yeah? What did she tell you?"

"That you wouldn't leave her alone. You used to call the house. Maybe even followed her a time or two when she moved up to Berkeley."

"She's dreaming," he said derisively. "Why would I bother?"

"You tell me."

"I'm not interested in telling you anything." His voice filled with scorn. "If Marisol says I've been hassling her, she's lying. I got other fish to fry. Now get out of my face."

He looked over my shoulder as a car pulled up, salvation in the purr of its engine and the music blasting from its radio. I moved so that I could keep an eye on Dace and check out the vehicle, which, as it turned out, contained the other fish.

It was a flashy red Camaro. The little girl at the wheel didn't look as though she was old enough to drive it. She looked no more than thirteen or fourteen, her heart-shaped face surrounded by a swirling cloud of black hair that had been streaked with different colors, fuchsia and green predominating. The blaring music stopped as she cut the engine, opened the door, and got out, teetering toward us on high spike heels. She wore a fuzzy short-sleeved sweater and skintight black leggings that showed off her childlike figure. When she reached Dace, she put her right arm around his waist and dangled the keys in front of him with her left hand. All the while her big brown eyes stared at me, wide with curiosity. She'd done

100

a fairly good job of covering the purple bruise with makeup, but I knew a black eye when I saw one.

Dace grabbed the keys. "Wait for me in the car," he barked. His latest child-woman scuttled away and got into the Camaro's passenger seat.

"Hey, Pete!" The voice came from the garage, aimed at him by a beefy-looking man wearing coveralls. He had supervisor written all over him, waving a work requisition and jerking a thumb toward a station wagon parked in one of the bays. Dace stepped around me, glad of the chance to escape me and my questions.

"I hope you're not lying about hassling Marisol," I told him. "If you are, I'll be talking to someone at the San Jose Police Department."

He froze in mid-step and I moved into his path, facing him once again. "About things like assault and battery," I continued. "And statutory rape. You are familiar with the laws concerning statutory rape, aren't you? If you're not, you should be."

I shot a sidelong glance at his underage inamorata. In denial about the mouse under her eye, she waited patiently in the fiery red chariot, presumably for Prince Charming to take a break. Dace followed my eyes, and my drift. For once he didn't have a tough-guy comeback.

"Just so we understand each other, Peter."

Fifteen

I HAD TO AGREE WITH MARISOL. WHY WOULD he bother her, after all these years?

I headed back up Interstate 880 toward Oakland. Was Peter Dace hassling the residents of the house on Garber Street? The guy was a sleazeball, certainly, with his brain lodged firmly in his crotch, and his own sick need to wield power over the women in his life, with his fists, more often than not.

True, he'd hassled Marisol after their breakup. But then he'd moved on to greener pastures. After the incident with Cathy Mason, no doubt there had been others, like Marisol and the baby-faced girl in the red Camaro. Why, after a time lapse of more than a year, would he track down Marisol and harass her and her housemates with anonymous phone calls? Whoever was making those calls had gone to the trouble to find out the new phone number after it had been changed. Somehow I didn't think that person was Dace.

That left Ted Macauley. I'd figured him as a good bet ever since Vicki and Emily described his unwanted attentions. He, at least, was a more current jerk. Had he made last night's phone call? Vicki wasn't sure. I talked with her after leaving the clinic, before driving to San Jose. All she could say was that the voice sounded familiar.

It was slow going back to Oakland. The afternoon traffic

rush seemed to start earlier these days. Or did it ever go away? The sky darkened and it began to rain. As my windshield wipers whisked back and forth, smearing drops into transient visibility, I reviewed what Vicki had told me about Macauley.

She and Emily met him sometime in October. They had gone to a movie at the Pacific Film Archive, then stopped at a coffeehouse near the campus. There they encountered a group of students, some of whom they knew from classes. Macauley was part of the group, one of several people clustered around a big table. They found out later he was a senior, studying chemistry. At the time, both women thought he was rather loud and brash. Each in her own way dismissed him.

Then he turned up more often. They encountered him, sometimes separately and sometimes when they were together, as they walked to class or strolled through Sproul Plaza near the university's South Gate. When they attended a concert at Zellerbach Hall, he was in the lobby at intermission. He was at a party given by a graduate student. No matter where they saw Macauley, he always paid a lot of attention to both young women. He came on strong, Vicki said, polite at first, then more aggressive. Emily's version was that he was overbearing from the start.

Macauley first asked Vicki for a date in November, around the time of midterm exams at the university. Vicki wasn't interested. She told him no. He persisted, and she kept saying no. When Vicki mentioned this to Emily, with some irritation, she was surprised to learn that Macauley had been pulling the same routine on her friend, at the same time. They compared notes, decided the guy was more of a jerk than they already thought he was, and tried to ignore him.

Macauley didn't like being ignored. They weren't sure

how he got their phone number, but Vicki said he kept calling, ignoring polite brush-offs from Sasha and Rachel. Finally, one night Marisol answered the phone. She wasn't one to mince words and had instead minced Macauley.

But Macauley retaliated, a few days later. He encountered them on Telegraph Avenue on a Saturday afternoon as they meandered along, checking out the wares of the street merchants who crowded the sidewalks.

All Vicki could remember was that Macauley suddenly appeared in front of them, a sneer on his face, and in a loud voice began to shower them with vituperative words. He called them bitches and dykes, saying they wouldn't go out with him because they were obviously involved with each other.

They walked away from him, Vicki said, shaking her head at the memory, but he followed them across the street. They finally escaped by dodging into the quiet confines of Cody's Books. They waited a half hour or more, lurking warily in the aisles, surrounded by tall bookshelves and watching to make sure they hadn't been followed. Then they left the bookstore and caught the 51 bus home. Since then, every time they'd encountered Macauley, he'd trotted out the lesbian accusation and thrown it at them. Most recently, it was Vicki he'd attacked, Saturday morning at the library.

Vicki didn't know where Ted Macauley lived, but I'd found out quickly enough. Like most of us, he was in the phone book, at an address on Regent Street. I consulted my *Thomas Guide* and located the block, in an area bordered by Ashby and Alcatraz avenues on the north and south, between College and Telegraph avenues on the east and west, on the Oakland side of the red dotted line on the map that separated the two cities.

It wasn't that far from the house where Vicki and Emily

lived. Close enough to make me wonder if Macauley had made a little plant-destroying excursion on his way home from classes the past Wednesday. Could I pull a few strings and get his phone records, to see if there were any calls to the Garber Street house?

I parked on Regent Street just after six that evening. By now it was raining. Macauley's apartment was in an older house that had been turned into flats. According to the mailboxes, he and someone named David Walker lived in unit C, on the left at the top of the stairs.

I knocked. Music played loudly on the other side of the door. The volume came down a notch and the door opened, revealing a young man who was trying with limited success to cultivate a mustache. Judging from the scraggly growth on his upper lip, he would have been better off marching straight to the bathroom to mow it down to skin. As it was, he rubbed it unconsciously, as though contact with his fingers would make it grow.

He gazed at me with polite interest. "Hello."

"Ted Macauley?" I asked.

I didn't think so. Vicki and Emily had both described Macauley as tall with a stocky build, short sandy hair, and blue eyes. This young man was tall and slender, and his eyes and hair were brown. He had to be Macauley's roommate.

"I'm Dave. I'll get Ted." He opened the door wider, smiled, and waved me into the apartment. "C'mon in."

Dave's friendly, I thought. Or he thought I was someone else.

I stepped into the living room. I'd been in plenty of similar apartments, enough to guess what the interior of this one looked like. If the occupants were young and didn't have much money, the flats were furnished with castoffs from home, sofas and chairs that Mom and Dad didn't need anymore.

The apartment shared by Macauley and the young man with the nascent mustache was no exception. They never would have chosen the flowered fabric on the sofa themselves. We were past the era of brick-and-board shelves. The bookcases that lined one wall were particle board, inexpensive, easy to assemble, and readily available at stores all over the Bay Area.

The roommate disappeared into a hallway that led to a bathroom and a couple of bedrooms. I looked around. The living room to my left was long and narrow, with the sofa along one wall. At the end of the room, near the front window, stood a disreputable looking wing-back chair upholstered in some shiny blue fabric. To my right a round table with four chairs denoted the dining area. Beyond this a door led back to the kitchen, crowded with a small refrigerator, a four-burner stove, and a counter not much larger than the sink itself, just long enough to hold the drainer piled with dishes.

Back in the living room, I noted that the TV and stereo equipment were new and high tech. They always were. I didn't recognize the music emanating from the CD player on top of a waist-high bookcase. Presumably it was from one of those rock groups I'd never heard of, a fact I confirmed by fingering the CD cases piled haphazardly next to the player. I was more into jazz myself.

"Ted'll be right out." Dave came up behind me. "He was in the shower. He's getting dressed now."

"Thanks," I said.

Ted had a date this evening, and the roommate assumed I was it. "Can I get you something to drink, while you wait?" he inquired, altering course for the kitchen.

I shook my head. "No, thanks. That won't be necessary."

I set the CD case I'd been examining on the shelf and turned, my knee coming in contact with the edge of an oversize book on a lower shelf. I knocked several books askew. Two of them tumbled to the floor. I knelt and retrieved them. The paperback was a copy of *The Anarchist Cookbook*. Interesting, I thought, riffling the pages. Ted Macauley's name was scribbled on the inside front cover.

I put the book back on the shelf. The other volume was quite different, a high school annual. I had a few like it tucked into a box in my hall closet, only the dates on those were far older than this one.

"Did you go to Menlo Park High School?" I asked.

"What did you say?" Dave came out of the kitchen carrying a bottle of beer.

"Menlo Park." I held up the annual. "Is that where you're from?"

"Me?" He smiled politely. "No, I'm from out of state. Illinois. Ted's from Menlo Park. That's his." The CD in the player reached the end of its appointed rounds and the music stopped.

"Is that a fact?"

My voice seemed loud in the sudden and welcome silence. I leafed quickly through the pages, to the alphabetical listing of seniors who'd graduated from Menlo Park High School that year. I found Macauley's photo, then quickly turned the pages until I found another name and photograph. I was looking at it just as Ted Macauley walked into the living room, sandy blond hair still damp from the shower. He looked clean, pressed, and collegiate, a bit older and more sophisticated than his high school picture. His stocky frame was clad in a green and gold shirt, khaki slacks, and loafers. He looked surprised to find me in his living room, especially since he had no idea who I was.

"I thought you said Lisa was here." He fired the words at his roommate in an irritated tenor that made me guess he wasn't the easiest person in the world to live with. His tone was matched by a scowl that brought his eyebrows to a V above his eyes.

"You're not Lisa?" Dave looked from Ted to me, genuinely perplexed.

Macauley fired the next salvo at me. "Who are you? What are you doing here?"

Was he this grumpy all the time? I set the annual on the shelf.

"My name is Jeri Howard, Ted. I'm a private investigator. You and I need to have a talk."

Dave looked at me with even greater interest, as though he'd read everything Raymond Chandler ever wrote and he'd love to ask me a million questions. Lisa be damned; a private eye was so much more fascinating.

Ted Macauley, however, only looked irked. "I don't have time to talk. I'm expecting someone. Besides, I don't know you."

"Aren't you even curious why I'm here?"

He put his hands on his hips and tried to tower over me, which didn't have the effect he'd hoped. "All right. I'll bite," he said with exaggerated patience, as though he were humoring me. "Why are you here?"

"It has to do with your harassment of Victoria Vernon and Emily Austen."

He looked at me, incredulous. "What harassment?"

"You accosted Vicki Saturday morning in the library. When she left, you followed her."

"Oh, this is rich," Macauley said with a derisive snort. "She doesn't like me talking to her so she sends a private investigator after me. I've never heard anything more ludicrous in my life."

A familiar refrain, one I was so tired of hearing. He doesn't think it's harassment. But she does. So it turns into a he said/she said situation. Who is believed, and who isn't? Eye of the beholder. I knew all the neat, legal definitions of harassment. From where I stood it looked clear-cut. If Vicki and Emily felt threatened by Ted Macauley's actions, he should cease and desist. Pronto.

"Why did you follow her?"

He shrugged and spread his hands wide in exaggerated supplication. "Oh, for God's sake. It was nothing. I said hello and she ducked into the stacks like I was Count Dracula. So I followed her, for the hell of it. Hey, it was a joke. What's the matter, can't she and her girlfriend take a joke?"

"You think it's amusing to follow two women down Telegraph Avenue and call them dykes? I don't. I think it's offensive."

"What a bunch of politically correct bullshit," he exploded. "God, you can't talk about anything anymore. Blacks, Hispanics, Asians, or even women. Those two girls are joined at the hip. I was just expressing an opinion that they might be more than friends. Free speech. You ever hear of that?"

"Spare me the P.C. tag line, Macauley. It's overused and it's an excuse. It sounds like you think you're God's gift to women and you were pissed that neither one of them would go out with you. As far as free speech is concerned, I was always taught that my right to swing my arm ended at the other guy's nose."

He glared at me and I couldn't help feeling I'd hit the nail squarely on its head. Pompous, arrogant, and opinionated—that was my take on Macauley. He was physically attractive, no doubt used to having all the girls swoon over him. Maybe he just couldn't deal with the fact that Vicki and Emily didn't. Even if Vicki had exaggerated Macauley's behavior, his following her, first on Telegraph and that weekend at the library, was stepping over the line.

"Fine, fine." Macauley shrugged again. His roommate

was at the far end of the living room standing next to the ugly wing-back chair. "They don't want me to talk to them, they could just say so."

"I believe they already have. On more than one occasion."

"So they went out and hired some private eye to lean on me," Macauley was saying, warming to his persecution routine. "Ludicrous, just ludicrous."

"It's not ludicrous when someone makes threatening phone calls," I said, nailing him with a look. "And trashes all the plants on the front porch."

"Wait a minute, wait a minute, hold the phone." He scowled at me, alarm in his blue eyes. "They told you I did that? That's bullshit."

"You knew the phone number. You called the house several times before one of the housemates told you to stop."

"So I stopped calling," he sputtered, stumbling over the words in his haste to disassociate himself from the anonymous calls. "I haven't called for months."

"You didn't vandalize their porch Friday afternoon?"

"No." His voice was outraged. "I never went to the house. Hell, I don't even know where they live."

So he claimed. But if he was in such a following mode earlier this year, he could have followed Vicki or Emily home.

"No obscene phone calls, such as the one they got last night?"

"No," he bellowed. "And if they say so, they're lying."

I looked at him steadily, trying to decide whether he was telling the truth. Then my eyes were drawn over Macauley's shoulder, to his roommate Dave. He stared at Macauley's back, frowning, as though Ted were a strange new life-form and Dave wasn't sure he wanted to

110

live with it. There was something there, in his expression, that made me want to talk with Dave later. Had he overheard or observed some behavior in his roommate that had some bearing on why I was there?

Someone knocked on the door, so hard it rattled. "That must be Lisa," Macauley said, moving quickly to answer it.

But it wasn't Ted Macauley's date. It was Vicki Vernon's father.

Sixteen

SID WAS TALLER THAN MACAULEY BY A COUPLE of inches. He loomed in the open doorway of the apartment, looking mad as an alley cat who'd had his tail tweaked.

"Are you Ted Macauley?" he asked. The growl in his voice didn't bode well for whoever answered that question in the affirmative.

Macauley growled right back and took a step forward, out into the hall. "What if I am? Who the hell are you?"

"My name's Sid Vernon." Only someone who knew him as well as I did would recognize the edge that meant danger. "I understand you've been harassing my daughter."

Macauley got belligerent. Bad choice. I could have told him that, but he wasn't interested in listening to my version of reason. Neither was Sid.

"Jesus, I don't believe this. All I did was ask her for a date."

"That's not the way I heard it," Sid said. "You've followed her twice, verbally abused her, and there's evidence that you've made some obscene phone calls. That sounds like harassment to me."

That last bit about the phone calls was stretching it, I thought. Sid sounded as though he were reading a formal complaint. Macauley picked up on his language.

"Evidence, harassment. What are you, some kind of cop?" Macauley's face reddened, as though he were just warming up. His eyes blazed and his mouth twitched into a sneer, trying to goad Sid. By this time several of his neighbors had opened their doors and were poking their heads out into the hallway.

"What a crock. First a private dick with no dick, then the daddy police." Macauley laughed, the sound at odds with his jeer. "Where the hell does she get off, sending her storm troopers to hassle me. The little bitch—"

The pejorative was barely out of Macauley's mouth when Sid moved forward, six feet two inches of deadly fury. One of Sid's hands shot out. I caught it before it grazed Macauley's shoulder, interjecting myself between the two men.

"Back off, Sid." He didn't want to, but he did. I turned to Macauley. He looked cocky and red in the face. He opened his mouth. I spoke before he did. "Don't even think about it. Get back to your apartment."

He was ready to argue with me. But Dave, the roommate with the scraggly mustache, was right behind him. He grabbed Macauley's arm, hauling him backward as he shut the door.

I turned and stared at the neighbors in the hall, and they too retreated.

"Let's go outside," I told Sid.

He withered me with a glare and stomped down the stairs. I caught up with him in the front yard. It was still raining, the drops hanging like bits of crystal on his curly gold head. There seemed to be a lot more silver there than there was before, but maybe that was just the light from the streetlamp.

"That was a real bone-head move, Sid Vernon," I said, keeping my voice level.

His jaw worked. I watched the muscle pulse. "I know."

I took a deep breath, feeling the chill rain. "If you knew it, why did you do it?"

"When I talked with Vicki last night," he said slowly, "and she told me about the calls . . . Then she said this creep had followed her, called her names."

"We don't know for sure Macauley's the one that made the calls."

"He's the one that followed her out of the library last Saturday. Not the first time, she says. Besides, Vicki phoned me an hour ago, at my office. They got another threatening call this afternoon. And someone in a red car has been cruising up and down Garber Street. The landlady noticed it, and so did one of the neighbors. So I ran a check on this clown Ted Macauley. You'll never guess what he drives."

"Something tells me it's red."

"Good guess, Jeri. A red Oldsmobile. When I got that DMV report . . . I lost it. I wanted to bounce the son of a bitch off a wall. I wanted to warn him off, tell him to stay away from Vicki."

We both looked up as a car drove by on Regent Street. It slowed and pulled into a parking spot farther down.

"Why did Vicki call you?" Sid asked. "And not me? I'm her father."

"She was afraid you'd overreact."

Sid sighed. "I did, didn't I?" I nodded. "It's just that . . . she's my little girl, Jeri. I don't care if she is almost nineteen and in college. The thought of anyone doing anything to hurt Vicki . . ."

I put my hand on his shoulder and gave him an affectionate squeeze. "I understand."

A familiar figure had climbed out of the driver's seat of the car that had just parked. Now Wayne Hobart, Sid's partner, walked toward us, giving us both the eye. "Does this mean I'm a day late and a dollar short, Jeri? Has he hurt anybody yet?"

"Some words were exchanged."

"How did you know I was here?" Sid asked. "You were over in CID when I got the report on Macauley's car registration."

"Yeah, but I was in Homicide when Vicki called. So I had a sense of your frame of mind. Then one of the guys came and got me, said you were on the phone with DMV before you went steaming out of the office in what they used to call high dudgeon. So I put two and two together. Figured I'd come over here and stop you from doing something foolish."

I shivered as the rain fell in a steady curtain. "Wayne, would you take him home and keep an eye on him?"

"I'll do better than that. I think you need to come home and have dinner with me and Laurie. It's about that time and I'm hungry." Sid shook his head, but before he could say anything, Wayne jumped in. "No, Sid. We've been partners for three years now. I usually let you lead because I'm comfortable with that. But tonight I'm calling the shots. You're coming home with me."

I watched them drive away, Sid following Wayne in his car. I walked back to where I'd parked my Toyota. Another car pulled up to the curb in front of the house where Ted Macauley lived. A young woman, blond and willowy, got out, wearing a tan raincoat. She walked briskly up the sidewalk. Was this Lisa, the long overdue date? I sat in my car and waited. A few minutes later Macauley and the woman came out. I watched them get into her car and head down Regent Street, toward Ashby.

Then I started my engine. I had a date myself, to cook dinner for Kaz, who was leaving tomorrow for his trip to the AIDS conference in London. I stopped at Piedmont Grocery, fighting the usual after-work crowds, and headed for my Adams Point apartment. I was running late, but Kaz usually was too. Sometimes it was difficult to drag the man away from his work.

"Not everything that comes in a can is cat food," I told the assembled multitude lured into my kitchen by the sound of the can opener blade piercing metal. Abigail and Black Bart sat side by side in the doorway. Two pairs of eyes gazed at me expectantly.

"Sorry, guys." The can held black beans. I drained off the liquid and spooned the beans into the salad I was concocting. Abigail gruffed at Black Bart as though it was all his fault and ambled off toward the living room. I added some chopped bell peppers and corn kernels to the mixture, gave everything a stir, and set the bowl inside the refrigerator. I called Kaz at Children's Hospital. He assured me he was on his way out the door. Still, I waited until he'd actually arrived, carrying dessert, before I put the water on to boil the pasta.

It was past ten and we were curled up together on the sofa when he started making noises about leaving. "I have a meeting tomorrow morning before I leave," he murmured in my ear. "And I haven't packed yet."

"And I have all those dishes." I stretched like a cat but made no move to get up. Dishes could always wait.

"I'll leave the chocolate cheesecake here. I'm sure you'll find a use for it."

"It'll go straight to my hips."

He ran an assessing hand over my body, creating a little tingle that went straight up my back. "Well, maybe I'd better take the cheesecake with me."

I removed his hand from its exploration. "For that remark I might make you do the dishes."

He shook his head and kissed me regretfully. "I really have to pack."

I dragged myself to a sitting position and kissed him

back. "All right. I'll let you have a reprieve this time. Just so you call me when you get back from your travels."

After another kiss on my front porch, perfumed by the small lemon tree in front of the window, I watched him walk across the courtyard toward the street. Then I went back inside to do the dishes.

Seventeen

On wednesday morning Ted Macauley went to the Oakland Police Department administration building at Seventh and Broadway. There he filed a citizen's complaint, claiming he'd been assaulted by Sergeant Sid Vernon.

"Sid didn't touch Macauley," I told Wayne Hobart later that morning. I'd been doing some paperwork on a personal injury case I'd just wrapped up, when the phone rang. Wayne told me what had happened. Now Sid was facing an investigation by the Professional Standards Section of the Oakland Police Department, what used to be called Internal Affairs.

"I was there at Macauley's apartment when Sid showed up," I continued. "I'll grant you he was angry. Sid took a step toward Macauley, after Macauley called Vicki a bitch, but Sid didn't touch him. I got between them. Sid told Macauley to stop hassling Vicki. I wouldn't even go so far as to call it a tongue-lashing. Besides, how did Macauley know Sid was a cop?"

"Good question. Did Sid pull rank or anything like that last night?"

I played back the confrontation and shook my head, even though I was in my office and Wayne was several blocks away, at his desk in OPD's Homicide Section. "No, Wayne, he didn't. Maybe Vicki said something early on, when she and Emily first encountered Macauley. Vicki's housemates know what her father does."

Wayne sighed deeply. "Well, the lieutenant is not happy about this. He figures whatever is happening on Garber Street is Berkeley's show, and Sid's got no business mixing in. Even if it is about his daughter."

"Agreed. But we both know Sid. What happens now that this complaint, however bogus, has been filed?"

"One of the officers in Professional Standards will conduct an investigation, then make a report to the deputy chief," Wayne said. "The report goes back down the chain of command to Sid's supervisor, in this case the lieutenant. He agrees or disagrees with the results, sends it back up the chain, where the deputy chief decides what kind of disciplinary action will be taken."

"Such as?"

"Could be anything from an oral reprimand to termination. But they'll take Sid's record into consideration. And he's had a good record."

"He told me once he'd had an oral reprimand," I said. "But that was years ago, when he was in Traffic."

"I know. It's a wait-and-see situation, Jeri. There's not much he can do about it right now, except keep his nose extremely clean." Wayne paused, and I heard phones ringing and voices talking in the background. "You know, there's something about this that doesn't feel right."

"I was just thinking the same thing." I took a sip from the coffee mug on my desk. "I keep coming back to my original question. How did Macauley know Sid's a cop? Unless someone told him. But who? And why? You think this could be a setup?"

"Could be," Wayne said. "Sid's usually as level-headed as they come. He's got one button that can always be pushed, though, and that's his daughter. Anyone who wanted to get a reaction out of him couldn't have done

119

better than to go after Vicki. Look, Jeri, I've got to go. As Sid's partner, I can't do anything that might look like I was interfering. However, if you were to nose around a bit, unofficially, of course . . ."

"I was planning to talk with Macauley's roommate anyway. When I was at the apartment last night, before Sid showed up, I got the impression the roommate had something he wanted to tell me about Macauley. Something in connection with the whole business of harassing Vicki and Emily. I'll let you know if I uncover anything. In the meantime, keep an eye on Sid, Wayne."

"Will do."

I hung up the phone as Cassie opened my office door, wearing a gray raincoat over today's pea-green lawyer suit. "Oh, good, I was hoping to catch you." She stopped and took off the coat. Then she peered at my face and frowned. "Why so glum?"

"It's a long story." I waved her in. "Come inside and I'll tell you."

We settled into chairs, me behind my desk and Cassie in front, with her slender legs and running shoes stretched out in front of her. I gave Cassie a rundown of what had happened over the past few days, culminating with the complaint filed against Sid.

"Good Lord," she said when I finished.

"That's all you have to offer?"

"If you're looking for a crystal ball, believe me, I don't have one. Nasty phone calls and stalkers. And Sid . . . Puts my search for the perfect wedding dress into perspective, doesn't it?"

I smiled. "Is that why you wanted to talk with me?"

"Yes. A friend recommended a bridal shop in Marin County, over in San Rafael. I wanted to see if you could free up your schedule for another shopping expedition, sometime in the next couple of days."

"I'll try." My smile turned into a wicked grin. "Why don't you and Eric just elope? No fuss, no fancy dress."

"Are you kidding? My mother would disown me. She's enjoying this production. Just like she did when my sister got married." Cassie stood up. "I'll leave you to it, Jeri. I have a bunch of interrogatories to prepare."

When Cassie had gone I picked up the phone and called Ted Macauley's apartment. I was expecting an answering machine. Instead I got a human being. It didn't sound like Macauley, but I couldn't be sure. I kept my voice low and flat as I asked for David Walker. "This is Dave. Who's this?"

"Dave, this is Jeri Howard. I'm the private investigator who came over to your place last night. I'd really like to talk with you. Is there any chance we can get together? Not there, somewhere else."

"You want to talk about Ted, right?"

"Last night it seemed to me you had something you wanted to tell me."

"Yeah, I do." He was silent for a few seconds. "Listen, I was just heading out to do some shopping. I'll meet you in an hour, at Noah's Bagels, over at Alcatraz and College."

The bagel shop was near the Oakland-Berkeley border, and parking anywhere near this shopping district was difficult. Finally, I found a spot on Alcatraz and doubled back to College. Dave was at the counter, the handles of a canvas shopping bag over one arm. As I joined him, the counter clerk handed him a huge onion bagel loaded with cream cheese and salmon and a large container of coffee.

"Make that two coffees," I said, slipping several bills from my wallet.

"Thanks." He stroked his scraggly mustache. Then he sighed. "I'm gonna have to find a new place to live."

I motioned toward a bench in one corner of the bagel shop. "Why is that?"

"Ted's a real jerk," he said. "And he gets jerkier by the minute."

Dave settled his rear end onto the bench, took a large bite of his bagel, and wiped cream cheese from the ends of his mustache. "He's not what you'd call easy to live with. Last night was a prime example. When I moved in last August, I thought it was a good deal. Reasonable rent, close to campus. But I'm getting tired of the way he acts. He's always blowing off at people. And if he's gonna get into a shouting match with everyone who comes to the door—"

"So last night was not an isolated incident?" Who else had Macauley been arguing with lately? Probably everyone. He was an argumentative sort.

"There was this other old guy," Dave said. "Last week. In fact, when Mr. Vernon showed up last night, I thought it was the other guy."

"What did this other man look like?"

"I didn't really get a good look at him. He came to the door, Ted answered, like he was expecting the guy, then they went outside. I only caught a glimpse of him when I went out a few minutes later. He and Ted were on the porch, arguing. Not as tall as Mr. Vernon, but sandy hair, going gray. Looked a bit like Ted, come to think of it. I asked Ted later if that was his father, but he said no."

I filed this curious incident away for further consideration, then turned to my more immediate question. "What did you want to tell me?"

"It was when you said he'd followed those two women and called them dykes," Dave said. "What a jerk. After living with the guy, I know he thinks he's Mr. Super Stud. But what you said about him hassling those two . . . Anyway, he said he didn't know where those two women lived. But he's lying, I'm sure of it."

Now that was interesting. "What makes you think so?"

122

"Vicki and Emily. Garber Street, right?" When I confirmed this, he went on. "I saw that, and a phone number, written on a pad by the phone in Ted's room, on his desk. I was in there a couple of days ago, looking for a book. That's when I saw it. In Ted's handwriting."

"Do you think you can find that sheet of paper?" Not likely, I thought. Unless they weren't all that regular about tossing their trash.

Dave shook his head. "I was looking for it last night, right after Ted left for his date. But he came back, almost caught me digging through the wastebasket in his room."

"He came back? I saw him leave, with a woman."

"Yeah. That was Lisa. She was late. They left, and Ted came back, about fifteen minutes later. He went into his room, made a couple of phone calls, then he went out. I checked through the wastebasket again, but I didn't find the note. Then I went to bed around eleven. I didn't hear him come in after that, so I must have been asleep. He's got an eight o'clock class, so he left early this morning."

But Macauley hadn't gone to class. He'd gone to the Oakland Police Department instead. "I'd like to talk with Lisa. Does she have a last name?"

Dave grinned and pulled a slip of paper from his blue jeans. "I thought you might want to talk with her. So I took the liberty of looking her up in Ted's little black book. Her name is Lisa Spaulding and she lives over on Ellsworth."

The Ellsworth Street address was a stucco box, as I called these common architectural excrescences that dated from the fifties. Painted a dingy beige too long ago, and way overdue for some maintenance, this one was two stories of apartments arrayed over ground-level carports. It looked as though it would fall down if the Hayward fault, a mile or so east in the Berkeley hills, ever let loose in that Big One the earthquake experts kept warning us was coming. I thought about that as I mounted the exterior metal stairs to the top floor, where Lisa Spaulding lived in the end unit.

I wasn't sure I'd find anyone home in the middle of the afternoon on a weekday, but Ellsworth, between Shattuck and Telegraph, was close enough to the U.C. campus that the students who lived in this neighborhood could come home between classes. The tall willowy blonde I'd seen last night at Macauley's apartment opened her front door when I knocked. Now she peered at me through the resulting three-inch gap.

"Lisa Spaulding?" I asked.

"Yes?"

"My name's Jeri Howard. I'm a private investigator. I'd like to talk with you, about Ted Macauley."

She didn't bat an eye at the news that I was an investigator, seemingly not at all surprised that a detective would be inquiring about Macauley. Instead she repeated his name as though it left a bad taste in her mouth. "That creep. After last night, I never want to talk to him again."

"What did he do?"

She opened the door a bit wider and I saw that she was about my height and very thin, bordering on skinny, with straight blond hair that fell over her shoulders. She was wearing blue jeans and a thick blue and lavender sweater. No shoes, just a pair of fuzzy gray socks.

"What didn't he do? Got lots of time? Come on in and I'll tell you."

I accepted her invitation and stepped into a cluttered living room. A colorful yellow and orange afghan had been shoved to one end of the toast-brown sofa, and an array of books and papers were strewn across the coffee table. Lisa had been studying, and judging from the book titles I could see, she was an art major. "I've had it with this guy," she said, resuming her seat on the sofa. "I only met him a couple of months ago. We'd been out a few times. It's not like we were really close, but—"

"So what happened last night?"

She pulled her feet up into a cross-legged position. "We were supposed to go to an art exhibit in Oakland, at 'Cackac', you know, the College of Arts and Crafts. I told Ted I'd pick him up, since his place was on the way. He didn't really want to go, but the artist is a friend of mine. It was kind of a five-to-eight cocktail thing, and I told Ted we'd put in an appearance and have dinner after. But I was late picking him up, because I had a last-minute phone call. When I finally did get to his apartment, he was really steamed and he yelled at me." She looked indignant at being on the receiving end of Macauley's spleen.

"Did you make it to the exhibit?" Not according to Dave, but I wanted to hear her version.

She shook her head. "We were in my car. I had just turned left, heading toward College. Ted was still fuming. He was really abrupt. I'm not sure if it was me or if there was something on his mind. All of a sudden he said he was sorry but he just couldn't go. Some kind of an emergency. He got out of the car at the next corner and started walking back toward the apartment."

That must have been not long after I'd left. I'd just missed seeing Macauley return to the apartment. Then, according to his roommate, he'd made some phone calls and gone out again. Where? I recalled what Dave had said about the older man who'd argued with Macauley. There seemed to be more going on with Ted than a young man who wouldn't take no for an answer. But what?

Maybe someone else who knew Macauley could give me some answers.

Eighteen

"YOU AND TED MACAULEY KNOW EACH other," I told Nelson Lathrop. "You left out that fact when you were giving me your résumé."

For once, Nelson didn't look goofy. He looked chastened, and very young. His mobile mouth turned down in a frown and he avoided my eyes. It was after four. We were in the living room of the quarters he shared with Ben, who had gone off to his job waiting tables at Marquessa.

This one-car garage had been transformed by the addition of a second story that, from the outside, made the structure look top heavy. The apartment's entrance faced the backyard, and its windows faced the driveway leading to Garber Street, taking the place of the garage door. Beneath these windows were deep built-in bookcases, their tops forming a window seat. Opposite this, more shelves held a TV, as well as a tape and CD player connected to small speakers. The concrete pad on which the garage stood had been covered with a thick brownish-gold carpet, which needed the attention of a good vacuum cleaner.

I stood near the shelves. A constricted hallway behind me led to the bathroom, the kitchenette, and narrow stairs that corkscrewed upward to a single large bedroom occupied by both young men. Nelson huddled on the sofa, one of those fold-out futons on a wooden frame, leaning forward with his forearms resting on his knees.

The room didn't get much light, since the driveway was overhung by oak trees. Nelson sighed and leaned to his right, fumbling for the switch on the high-tech white metal floor lamp. All three of the lamp's bulbs came into play, throwing bright light and stark shadows against the beige walls.

"I didn't know him all that well," he said finally.

"Come on, Nelson. I saw the yearbook at Ted's apartment. You were both on the track team."

"Okay, okay. But he was a senior. I was a sophomore. I knew him, but we weren't like bosom buddies. I've barely talked to him since we graduated."

"Why didn't you say anything?"

Nelson ran the long fingers of one hand through his untidy brown hair. His eyes segued to mine, then flicked away again. "Oh, hell." He took a deep breath. "I didn't want to fan the flames, that's all."

I waited. Nelson was no exception to my rule that, sooner or later, the person who experiences my practiced private investigator silence will say something, just to fill that void. Now he wanted to explain himself.

"I've already got Marisol the queen of the man-haters biting my butt half the time just because I'm male. Can't you see how she'll react when she finds out I know this guy? It'll be all my fault, somehow."

He looked momentarily anguished, then his face reddened. I wondered if he viewed Marisol as something more than just one of the housemates.

"I like living here. I don't want to cross anyone." He sighed deeply. "When Vicki and Emily said something about this guy Macauley bothering them, how was I to know it was the same guy?" He raised shoulders and arms in an exaggerated shrug of supplication. "There's

127

more than one Macauley in the phone book. Cal's a big school, large student body, y'know."

"Enough with the excuses, Nelson." I folded my arms across the front of my cotton sweater and looked implacable. "Surely when they said the guy who was hassling them was Ted Macauley, you knew who they were talking about."

"Well, yeah. Sorta. I kinda connected the dots. Not right away, though. I mean, the guy they were talking about sounded like such a rank pig." Nelson grimaced. "I don't remember Ted being like that in high school. Of course, he was always the good-looking jock with more girlfriends than you could count. Unlike me." He shook his head.

"What do you remember about Ted in high school?"

"He was real competitive in sports," Nelson said, playing with a strand of hair. "Competitive in academics too, come to think of it. I mean, the guy's smart. He was right up there in the class standings. Always had good luck with the ladies, as I recall. That's why I just can't picture him making all those phone calls. Or doing the plants. I just can't see Macauley chopping up a lemon tree because a couple of girls—pardon me, women— wouldn't go out with him."

Personally, I liked Macauley in the role of harasser. The guy had a nasty edge that wasn't far under his handsome surface. When I'd been over at his apartment, his hostility toward Vicki and Emily had boiled over, splashing me as well. I didn't buy his excuse—and that's what it was—that the ugly words he'd hurled at them over the past few months could be dismissed as a joke.

There had to be more to it than I thought. Some ulterior motive on Macauley's part. But if there was, I hadn't figured it out yet.

Nelson shook his head again. "I know he called here a

couple of times. But how would he know where we live?"

"He knew," I said, thinking about what Dave had told me.

It was possible Nelson was lying about how well he knew Macauley or about his motivation for not telling his housemates. He said he didn't want to be accused of having anything to do with Macauley's harassment of Vicki and Emily, so he'd kept silent, figuring that saying nothing would keep him off the griddle. Did I buy his explanation? I wasn't sure.

"Anything else you remember about Ted's high school days? Anything more unusual than competitive and ladykiller?"

"Well . . ." Nelson shrugged. "He's a chem major, you know. Has a real talent for it. He used to build fireworks for the Fourth of July. Mixed the stuff right up at home. Bet that made his folks nervous." He stopped, then grinned, waggling his eyebrows. "Right at the start of his senior year, he got called on the carpet for building a bomb in the chem lab. He got suspended for a couple of days."

Maybe that's why Macauley had a copy of *The Anarchist Cookbook* next to his yearbook. I moved toward the door. "Thanks, Nelson. If you think of anything else . . ."

Nelson jerked his pointy chin in the direction of the main house. "You're gonna tell them, aren't you?"

"Yes, I am." I reached for the doorknob. "I have to. It puts a different light on the whole situation."

I left Nelson still huddled on the sofa and crossed the yard on a flagstone path that had been obscured by overgrown grass. I mounted the plank stairs to the deck and opened the back door. I felt as though I'd stepped back in time, to my first visit, watching the residents of the house sidestep each other as though their dinner preparations were an elaborately choreographed ballet. Sasha stood at the stove, stirring something in the cast-iron skillet. Emily had made yet another pot of Peet's coffee, and she poured two mugs, handing one to Vicki, who stayed out of the way at one end of the table as she leafed through the pages of a book. In front of her I saw a plate filled with a variety of raw vegetables. Vicki reached for a carrot stick and stuck it into her mouth. Rachel and Marisol both stood in front of the wide-open refrigerator door.

"Keep your dead animals away from my tofu." Rachel's voice was tart as she loomed over her shorter housemate.

"These are the best damn *carnitas* in East Oakland," Marisol retorted, a protective hand over a foil-covered pan. "Made especially for me by my friend Lupe. I won't have you referring to them as dead animals."

"Shut the refrigerator door," Sasha told them both, sounding exasperated as she waved her wooden spoon. "You're letting all the cold air out."

"Yes, Mother." Rachel laughed as she shut the door.

I smiled. The scene reminded me of dinnertime in the kitchen of the house where I grew up, a Victorian over in Alameda, where my brother and I bickered constantly, and my mother the gourmet cook told us both to cut it out. In fact, I'm sure she'd told us not to let the cold air out of the refrigerator more times than I could count.

"Want some coffee?" Emily asked me. She'd just pulled out the chair next to Vicki but hovered rather than taking a seat, ready to play hostess.

"Yes, thanks. I'll get it myself. Mugs?"

Marisol pointed to a cupboard above her dark head. I opened it and took out a mug, filling it with rich black coffee. Then I took the seat Nelson had occupied a week ago, the one at the end of the table, near the back door. I didn't see Martin, but I heard him. The little boy was in his back porch bedroom, talking to himself and singing.

A pleasant dinnertime scene, I thought, sipping my coffee. They were a family. But like a lot of families, this one had secrets.

"Why did you want to talk with Nelson?" Vicki asked after she'd crunched her way through the carrot stick. She surveyed the plate of veggies as though trying to decide which one to consume next, and finally settled on a strip of sweet red bell pepper.

I took another sip of coffee and watched the assembled housemates over the rim of the mug. "Nelson knows Ted Macauley. They went to the same high school."

"You're kidding." Surprise was written on Vicki's face.

Marisol scowled indignantly. "And he didn't tell us? What a lousy thing to do."

Rachel looked thoughtful, playing with the end of her braid, but she didn't say anything. Neither did Emily, sitting self-contained and solitary with her hands wrapped around her coffee mug.

Sasha switched off the burner on the gas stove and set the skillet on a trivet. She turned so that she stood with her back to the counter, leaning on the cabinets. "Why didn't he tell us?"

"He claims that at first he wasn't sure it was the same Macauley he knew in school. And that he had difficulty believing that Macauley would harass Vicki and Emily."

"Why would Nelson think we'd lie about such a thing?" Vicki asked. "The guy is harassing us. It's scary."

"It's not that he thinks you're lying," I said. "It's that Nelson has trouble connecting Macauley's behavior as you describe it with the Macauley he knew in high school."

"In other words, it's a guy kind of thing." Marisol's

131

sarcastic snarl told me exactly what she thought of Nelson's excuse.

Rachel waved aside Marisol's anger and focused on something else. "You think this Macauley could have gotten our new unlisted number from Nelson?"

"It's so easy to get phone numbers, though." Vicki gazed at the vegetable plate, then pushed it away. "Every time I write a check, it seems like the salesclerk asks for my phone number. And my address is printed on the check. People can read over your shoulder or overhear things. Nelson may have inadvertently let that information slip."

"He says he didn't know Macauley that well," I said. "Nelson was two classes behind. And according to him, he's barely talked with Macauley since they graduated."

"You believe him?" Sasha folded her arms across her chest.

I sipped my coffee. "It sounds as though they were acquaintances rather than friends. At least on Nelson's side. Macauley may have been aware of Nelson's living arrangements without Nelson reciprocating. We'll have to wait and see what happens next. I leaned on Macauley pretty heavily yesterday."

So had Sid. And Macauley had leaned back, filing that complaint against Sid. I looked over at Vicki, wondering if she'd talked with her father today.

Sasha opened her mouth to speak, then stopped, with a quick shake of her head that put a temporary lid on the discussion. Martin had entered the kitchen from his bedroom, making a beeline for his mother with only a cursory glance at the rest of us assembled grown-ups.

"Are you hungry, baby?" Sasha ran a hand over his dark curls. He nodded. "I'll have your dinner on the table in just a minute. Go wash your hands."

"Looking for my book," he said. "I can't find it."

"Which one?" Emily asked, leaning forward.

"Green Eggs and Ham."

Rachel laughed. "Oh, that's my favorite."

"I always liked *The Cat in the Hat* myself," I said.

"Did you look in my room and our living room?" Sasha asked him. He nodded solemnly.

"I think I saw some of your books in our living room," Vicki said, waving in the direction of the front room all the housemates shared. "On that table over by the window."

"Go look there," Sasha said, propelling him toward the door with an affectionate pat on his rear end. "Then wash up. We'll read after dinner." When he'd gone, she looked at us, grouped around the table. "We can continue this conversation later. I don't want Martin to know what's going on."

"Agreed." I got up and crossed the kitchen to top off my coffee.

I heard a crash mingling with Martin's frightened cry. The shatter of broken glass on hardwood floors told me something heavy had come through the window. I raced through the open doorway that led from the kitchen to the living room.

Something heavy, all right. Like a pipe. Only this one had a fuse protruding from one end.

The fuse was burning.

Nineteen

"STAY BACK," I YELLED, KNOWING SASHA AND the others were behind me. I flew across the room to Martin, who was backing away from the device, hugging his book to his chest. I grabbed him by the arm and ran, half-carrying him, for the kitchen. "Down on the floor, down on the floor!"

Sasha seized Martin from me as I crossed the threshold into the kitchen. I waved them toward the other end of the room, where a door led to Martin's room. We surged through into the little boy's domain and bellyflopped onto the carpet.

"Cover your ears," I shouted.

Then the bomb went off, a deafening explosion that rattled the windows and made my ears ring, despite the hands I'd cupped over them. We stayed huddled in our collective heap for a moment longer, then Martin began to sob.

Sasha raised herself to a sitting position and gathered her son tightly to her bosom, his face pressed into the hollow of her throat. She rocked back and forth, her voice unraveling in a litany, part soothing and part hysterical, murmuring a steady stream of reassurances into the boy's ear. She sounded as though she were trying to convince herself.

We scrambled to our feet. I moved to the kitchen,

followed by Vicki, Rachel, and Marisol. "Fire extinguisher?" I asked.

"Under the sink," Vicki said. "There's another one in the earthquake stash in the hall closet."

"On my way." Rachel headed for the closet. Marisol followed, detouring into Sasha's bathroom. She returned to Martin's room, carrying a blue plastic case with a red cross on the cover. She opened it and knelt near Sasha, who still cradled her son.

Vicki pulled the phone off the cradle and dialed 911 as I opened the cabinet and pulled out the extinguisher. Then Nelson came up the back steps at a dead run. He barreled through the door into the kitchen and stopped, staring at us. "What was that?"

"A bomb." Our recent conversation about Macauley was fresh in my mind.

Nelson swallowed convulsively, his face paling below his untidy brown hair. He ran both hands through his hair. "Everybody okay?" he asked.

"No, everybody's not okay," Marisol snapped, sounding rattled. "We're all scared shitless. Look at Martin. He's hysterical."

Nelson winced as though he'd been slapped. He looked around. His eyes found Emily, pressed against the kitchen wall, so pale I thought she might faint. There was panic in her usually calm blue eyes. She seemed paralyzed by fright, like some animal in the middle of a highway, oncoming headlights blinding its gaze. Nelson moved to her side and put his arms around her. She hugged him fiercely, glad of the comfort.

I moved toward the open doorway, my nostrils filled with the stink of the bomb's aftermath. But there was no fire, just a lot of smoke and debris. The persimmon sofa was scorched, its upholstery shredded. The pipe had turned into shrapnel, bits and pieces burying themselves

135

into the wall and what was left of the furniture. I shook my head slowly, thanking providence and old-fashioned construction techniques. If any of those fragments had hit flesh, we'd have been seriously injured. Or dead. But this old Berkeley brown shingle had confined the explosion to the living room. The wall between it and the kitchen probably had three or four inches of dead air sandwiched between two layers of thick plaster on top of two layers of lathe.

"We were lucky," Rachel said in a subdued voice, standing in the doorway that led to the hall, holding the other fire extinguisher.

I heard sirens in the distance, getting closer. Someone was pounding on the front door. Rachel set down the extinguisher and pulled it open, admitting one of the neighbors, who wanted to know what the hell happened and whether everyone was all right.

I moved to the gaping hole that used to be the front window, my feet crunching on the glass. Out in the street a crowd of people with stunned faces was already gathering. Dinnertime in this pleasant middle-class Berkeley neighborhood had been interrupted by the deafening roar of the bomb. Then the people disappeared from my line of vision as a Berkeley police cruiser and a fire truck arrived, lights flashing and sirens wailing like banshees. The wail stopped, leaving a pool of unnatural quiet, punctuated only by my thoughts.

This moved the hostilities several rungs up the ladder from obscene phone calls. Was Ted Macauley still amusing himself by building bombs?

"It was galvanized pipe," I told Sergeant Nguyen.

Nguyen was Berkeley's bomb guy. At least that's how he'd introduced himself. He had spent the first couple of

136

hours processing the scene, along with several technicians who were methodically sifting through what was left of the living room, bagging evidence and taking photographs. Now Nguyen was interviewing witnesses, starting with me.

I took a sip of coffee and continued describing what I'd seen lying on the Turkish rug in the living room that split second before I grabbed Martin. "About four inches long, maybe half an inch in diameter. Green fuse, maybe two feet long. Black powder, from the smell."

"You're lucky it wasn't bigger," Nguyen said, scribbling notes in a small spiral pad. "As it is, someone could have been killed."

I nodded. "But I think it was meant to scare us rather than kill someone." At least that was my take on it.

Nguyen tilted his head slightly to one side and raised his eyebrows. "Scare you? Suppose you tell me why an Oakland private investigator just happens to be on the scene when a pipe bomb gets lobbed through a window in Berkeley."

Nguyen and I were alone in the kitchen. I'd made the coffee this time, instead of Emily. The other housemates were gathered in Martin's room, with the exception of Martin and Sasha, who'd taken her frightened son to her room.

I needed the caffeine. Maybe it would dissolve my weariness. The adrenaline rush that had propelled me into the living room was gone, swept away like a wave leaving the beach, and all that was left was exhaustion.

I stared at the coffee in the mug before me. Then I looked back up at Sergeant Nguyen, who looked back, patiently waiting for me to answer.

"I'm a friend of Ms. Vernon's," I said. "Actually, I used to be married to her father, so I guess you could call me her stepmother. Vicki called me last Friday because of some things that have been happening. This has all the earmarks of a stalker case."

I gave Nguyen a quick rundown of the past two months, punctuated by the nuisance phone calls, the instances of Vicki and Emily being followed, and finally the past week's vandalism. "Inspector Culver in Property Crimes took the vandalism report. He also had the phone company put a tap on the line. But it looks like the caller is using pay phones in Berkeley and Oakland."

"You think this bomb is related?" Nguyen tapped his notebook with his pen.

"It very well could be. I've been making some inquiries, looking for reasons the people who live here might be targets."

"Got any suspects?"

I told him what I'd learned so far, outlining Sasha's work on the affirmative action front, Rachel's escort duty at the abortion clinic, and the anti-abortion protester who seemed to have made her his target for invective. For good measure I threw in Marisol's old boyfriend Peter Dace, the guy who actually had a track record of stalking.

"Then there's Ted Macauley," I said, saving my prime suspect till last. "He's been harassing both Vicki and another of the housemates, Emily Austen. Neither of them would go out with him, despite his persistent phone calls, so he took affront. Decided they must be lesbians. He of course has a different take on the situation. Says the women are overreacting. But I certainly don't think so." I told Nguyen about the first time Macauley had followed Vicki and Emily, on Telegraph Avenue, and about the most recent incident, last Saturday when he'd accosted Vicki in the library on campus.

"He's a Cal student?" Nguyen asked.

"A senior. Majoring in chemistry. He used to build

138

fireworks and bombs for the hell of it, back when he was in high school in Menlo Park."

"And how would you know that?"

"I paid him a visit yesterday. He lives on Regent Street, just over the line in Oakland. He has a copy of *The Anarchist Cookbook* on his bookshelf, right next to his high school annual. Turns out one of the housemates, Nelson Lathrop, went to the same school as Macauley. He was two years behind Ted, but he remembers Macauley's predilection for things that go boom. It seems Macauley got suspended his senior year in high school for building a bomb at school."

"I take it he's got your vote for the bomber," Nguyen said.

"He's got the know-how, he's got a grudge against Vicki and Emily, and I pissed him off. Though at the time his response seemed limited to calling me names and trying to intimidate me."

"You think he was pissed off enough to come over here a day later with a pipe bomb? That seems extreme. Or is there something else you want to tell me?"

I sighed. There was no way to get around it. "While I was at Macauley's apartment, Vicki's father—my ex-husband—showed up. He had found out about Macauley following his daughter and he was angry about it. I had to get him out of there."

"Who is Ms. Vernon's father?"

"Sergeant Sid Vernon, Oakland Homicide."

Nguyen nodded slowly. "Did Sergeant Vernon threaten Macauley?"

I answered reluctantly. "It was more along the lines of, stay away from my daughter. Vicki's his only child. He was pretty upset. Macauley filed a harassment complaint against Sid this morning. I'm not certain how he knew

Sid was a police officer, but he certainly knew where to hit back."

"Given what you've just told me, a bomb still seems like an extreme reaction," Nguyen said.

"Unless Macauley's not playing with all his cards."

"Anything's possible." Nguyen shut his notebook. "In fact, you've given me quite an array of possibilities. Now, if you'll excuse me, I have other witnesses to interview."

Twenty

"LEAVE THE REST OF IT," RACHEL SAID TIREDLY, as we finished nailing several lengths of plywood over the broken window in the living room. "We'll clean it up tomorrow."

"I'd rather clean it up now." Marisol's mouth thinned into a determined line. "That way we won't have to look at it in the morning."

She glanced at Emily for support, but her fellow housemate clutched a broom and didn't say anything. Emily hadn't said much the whole evening. Her silence concerned me, as did the frightened look that still glowed in her deep blue eyes.

It was late, past ten o'clock. Sergeant Nguyen and the technicians had departed, after staying on the scene for more than four hours. After he'd finished interviewing the housemates, Nguyen had gone outside to talk with the neighbors, to see if anyone had seen anything. Now the house was enveloped in an uneasy silence. Those who were hungry had consumed a hasty meal thrown together with what was already cooked, augmented by whatever could be found in the refrigerator.

"Marisol's right," Nelson said. "Let's do it."

"I agree." Vicki stepped away from the window, hammer in hand. She stowed that and a handful of nails in the toolbox that sat on the hardwood floor.

Nelson hoisted his broom and dustpan, then looked at me. "There's no need for you to stay, Jeri. You've done enough. Besides, I'd appreciate it if on your way home you would stop in at Marquessa and tell Ben what happened. He gets off about ten-thirty. I don't want him to walk into this totally clueless."

"No problem."

I left the living room and went through the kitchen to Martin's room. Sasha sat in a chair next to her son's bed, exhaustion etching lines and shadows on her face. The little boy was in bed, curled into a fetal position as he slept, his thumb in his mouth.

"He hasn't sucked his thumb in ages," Sasha said, her hand gently stroking Martin's face. "Took me months to break him of it."

I took her other hand. "He'll be okay."

"Will he? My poor sweet baby. He'll have nightmares."

"I'll find out who's responsible."

"Good." Her face hardened. "I won't forgive whoever did this. My child could have been killed."

I left her sitting with Martin and went back out to the kitchen. Vicki was there, standing in front of the open door of the pantry, scanning the shelves. She spotted what she was looking for and reached for a box of oversize trash bags.

"Keep an eye on Emily," I said.

"You noticed, huh?" Vicki hugged the box to her chest as she closed the pantry door. "She's acting kind of spooky."

"Yes. This rattled her. She seemed to be really frightened. As though she knows something we don't. Vicki, how well do you know Emily?"

"Not as well as I know you." Vicki's fingers toyed with the protruding edge of one of the dark green trash bags. "I met her last fall when we both moved into the house. We hit it off. We've been friends ever since. I really like her. But I don't know much about her. She doesn't talk about herself. I never pushed it. I figured it was none of my business. After all, some people are just private."

"Or maybe there's something Emily doesn't want to talk about. If this harassment has something to do with Emily . . ."

I was thinking out loud, remembering Emily's reactions to the phone calls and particularly to Martin's brief disappearance, last Saturday morning. I couldn't put my finger on it.

"She should have told us," Vicki finished. "Maybe she didn't think it would get to this point."

"But it has. I'm going to have to talk with her again."

I gave Vicki a hug and left the house, heading for downtown Berkeley. Marquessa, the restaurant where Ben waited tables four nights a week, was on Oxford Street, near University Avenue. Oxford ran north and south, one block to the east of Berkeley's main drag, Shattuck Avenue. Downtown the street briefly touched the western perimeter of the U.C. campus. I found a parking spot on the campus side of the street and stepped into the crosswalk.

I'd seen several eating establishments live out their brief lives in this particular location, most recently an Indian restaurant. Now it had a new name and a new cuisine, Italian. The place closed at ten, and it was about five minutes after. The door was locked, but I saw a young man wielding a broom in between the tables, and a woman closing out the cash register.

I knocked and she shook her head and pointed at the CLOSED sign. I knocked again, rattling the door. Looking annoyed, she stepped away from the register and walked toward me. "We're closed," she said loudly, her words muffled by the door.

"Ben Winslow," I told her, raising my voice so she could hear me. "I have to see Ben Winslow."

The woman looked exasperated, but she reached into her pocket and pulled out some keys. She unlocked the door and opened it just a crack. "I said we're closed."

"Ben Winslow. I know he works here. It's important that I talk with him."

"Well, you're out of luck," the woman said. "Ben's not here tonight. He called in sick. You might try reaching him at home."

Funny, I thought. I was just there.

"I'll kill the son of a bitch," Sid snarled.

"Calm down," I said, my voice both groggy and resigned.

Sid's phone call had roused me from a deep sleep. It must have been a deep sleep, since the cats hadn't awakened me.

Make that *cat*. Black Bart was usually content to snooze next to my feet until I moved them from the bed to the floor. But Abigail had firm ideas about when she liked to eat. The fat tabby cat had been known to use claws and teeth to persuade me to get up and feed her.

When the phone rang I'd struggled to a sitting position, hand scrabbling for the receiver as both cats jumped off the bed and trotted toward the kitchen. Sid's voice clamored in my ear as I squinted at the digital readout on my clock radio. It was after seven o'clock, past my usual getting-up time.

"Calm down? Calm down? Some lowlife scumbag hassles my daughter, then he throws a bomb through her window. And he has the nerve to file a complaint against me? I'll rip the bastard a new asshole."

144

He would too. To say that Vicki was the apple of his eye was understating the case. To say that he was angrier than he had been the other night at Macauley's apartment was also an understatement.

"Calm down," I told him again, trying hard to be the voice of reason. Not that it was doing me any good. "We don't know for sure that it was Macauley." Of course, Ted had my vote, especially after what Nelson had told me about Ted building bombs in high school. But I didn't need to go into that right now.

"Bullshit." Sid's anger burned through the phone line, palpable, white-hot. Ted had his vote for sure. I just didn't want him to do anything stupid.

I ran a hand through my untidy hair. I needed a strong dose of caffeine before I could deal with this.

"Are you at work?" I asked. He growled an affirmative. "I'll call you back." He started to argue. "Sid, I'm still in bed. I need coffee. I need to pee. I'll call you back."

I hung up the phone and swung my legs over the edge of the bed. After my bathroom pit stop I walked to the kitchen, where Abigail and Black Bart waited patiently for me to fill up their matching cat bowls. That done, I started a pot of coffee and took a shower. Only when I was dressed, breakfasted, and on my second cup of coffee did I call the Oakland Police Department's Homicide Section. Sid was on another call. I sighed, with more than a little relief, and asked for his partner, Wayne Hobart. The phlegmatic Wayne could usually be counted on to stay cool.

"Has Sid calmed down?"

"Not much," Wayne said. "He's on the horn now with Brad Nguyen over in Berkeley."

"I just don't want him to do anything rash. Such as a repeat of his visit to Macauley's apartment. It's Berkeley's case."

"He knows that. Logically." Wayne paused. "I'm not sure about emotionally. You know how he is where Vicki's concerned."

"Yeah, I know. Tell him I called. I'll be here for a while longer, but I'm going over to Berkeley myself, to see if I can get some answers to a few questions."

I hung up the phone and sipped my coffee, leaning back in the dining room chair as I watched Abigail and Black Bart wash themselves before settling into sleep on my sofa. Questions, questions, I had a lot of them. Such as what Emily Austen wasn't saying, and why Ben Winslow wasn't at work last night.

I headed for the Elmwood district. On Garber Street, I spotted a truck from an Oakland glass company. Sasha was on the lawn in front of the house, supervising the replacement of the front windows.

"How's Martin?" I asked.

"Still sucking his thumb." She gave me a lopsided smile. "We both played hooky from school today."

"Who else is home?"

"Everyone's in class, except Ben."

Since Ben worked at the restaurant four nights a week, he had arranged his schedule so that many of his classes were in the late morning or early afternoon. I left Sasha in conversation with the man who was installing the new windows and walked around the corner of the house to the garage apartment. The blinds were open and I saw Ben cross-legged on the sofa in the tiny living room. He had a book balanced on one jean-clad knee as he scribbled in a spiral notebook that rested on the other.

I knocked. A moment later he answered the door, a smile on his round face. "Hey, Jeri."

"Good morning, Ben. You missed the excitement last night."

146

"Yeah. I got the tail end of it when I got home from work."

I gazed at his brown eyes. "Nelson asked me to go by the restaurant last night, about ten, to let you know what happened. You weren't there. They said you'd called in sick."

He stared back. Then he dropped his eyes and his hand slipped off the doorknob. "Damn."

"You want to tell me about it?"

Twenty-one

"YOU DON'T THINK I HAD ANYTHING TO DO with this?"

Ben's voice was anguished as he shut the door behind us.

I looked at his stocky torso in its white T-shirt, at his earnest young face. No, I didn't really. But I wanted an explanation.

"Just tell me where you were last night."

"It's not what you think."

"I don't know what to think, Ben. You lied to your employer about being sick. You weren't at work, where you were supposed to be, when a bomb went off in the living room. Everyone is under the microscope now. You'd better talk to me. Because Sergeant Nguyen is going to talk with you soon. And he'll want answers too."

"I wasn't anywhere near here last night," he said, tripping over the words in his haste to assure me that he was innocent of involvement. "I have witnesses. I was . . . I was at this study thing, at somebody's apartment over on Fulton. It's a tutoring session."

He looked ashamed. I didn't understand why. "So you need a little help with your classes? Is that all? Ben, it's okay to be a little behind in your classes."

"It's not a little behind." He slumped onto the sofa, his head in his hands, then looked up to where I stood near the door. "I'm way behind. I'm not doing well at all. I'm struggling to keep my head above water. I'm afraid I'm going to lose my scholarship." He looked frightened at the prospect.

"Does anyone else here in the house know?"

He shook his head. "I haven't wanted to mention it. Nelson . . . I mean, Nelson, he acts like a goofball, but the guy is brilliant. And the others, all the women, every one of them, they're all like these great overachievers." His voice took on a note of longing. "I feel like I can't keep up, like I'm the stepchild. I don't know what's wrong, Jeri. I was top of my class in high school. Everybody was so proud of me when I got this scholarship to U.C. I worked for it, and I don't want anybody saying the only reason I got into this school is because I'm black. But I know people say that all the time, especially right now with all this anti-affirmative action talk that's going around."

I sighed and studied him, feeling so much older than he was, remembering my college days, fifteen or more years ago. My role had suddenly shifted away from investigator and into counselor.

"Maybe the job's getting in the way, Ben," I told him. "Four nights a week, five hours a night. That's twenty hours away from your studies."

"I need this job." His face looked bleak. "The scholarship covers tuition, and the loan is supposed to take care of everything else, but it doesn't. My belt's getting real tight, what with me trying to give my mom some extra."

"What's she going to do if you get booted out of school because your grades are in the toilet? What are you going to do if that happens?" He didn't answer.

"What's the priority here? That extra money, or you getting your education? You're the only one who can decide."

I walked across the small living room and dropped a hand onto his shoulder. "I don't for a minute think the only reason you got into Cal is because of your race. That's a bunch of bullshit. Someone saw something in you that showed promise, Ben. Don't let yourself down. Talk to Sasha about the rent. Talk to all of them about helping you out with your studies. I think you'll find they'll be happy to help you any way they can. Maybe it will take their minds off what's going on."

He sighed. "Well, I'm relieved you don't think I had anything to do with it."

My voice took on a bantering tone. "Hey, you're a history major. You don't know how to make a bomb, do you?"

"No, I don't," he said soberly. "But history majors know how to do research. I'll bet any one of us could figure out how to make one. I just wish we knew who was doing this. And why."

"Let me and the Berkeley cops worry about that."

The door of the garage apartment opened and Nelson came in carrying his usual sack of take-out food. He looked surprised to see me. "Hey, Jeri. How's it hanging?"

"It's not," I told him.

He looked confused and turned to Ben. "Yo, Ben," he said. "Got lunch here." He set the sack on the end table and started removing its contents. It looked like two fat burritos wrapped in aluminum foil and a couple of cans of soda. "Beef for you, chicken for me." He grinned at me. "If I'd known you were here, Jeri, I'd have gotten another one. You want a bite?"

I shook my head. "I've got places to go. Besides, I think you and Ben need to have a talk."

I left them in the living room of the garage apartment, for a little man-to-man over their burritos. As I went back outside, the March sky, which had started out blue that morning, had turned gray and it began to rain. I headed downtown, where the Berkeley Police Department occupied a two-story building on McKinley Avenue, near the corner of Allston Way.

Sergeant Nguyen didn't have to talk with me, a nosy P.I. from Oakland. On the other hand, my presence at the Garber Street house made me a witness, as well as a potential victim of the bomb. Nguyen didn't say anything about having talked with Sid that morning. He took me back to his first-floor office and waited until I'd taken a chair next to his desk before he spoke.

"Our analysis of the bomb debris jibes with what you told me last night," he said, consulting the file before him. "Galvanized pipe, black powder. It was fairly simple, easy to build."

"Did the neighbors have anything to offer?" I asked.

Nguyen shrugged. "It was suppertime. Everyone was in the kitchen, fixing dinner, or in the dining room, eating it. Perhaps our bomber was counting on that being the case at the Garber Street residence. We do have a report of a red car in the vicinity before the explosion. That doesn't necessarily mean that particular car had anything to do with the bomb. I'm aware that Ms. Nichols and another neighbor reported a red car cruising the neighborhood earlier in the week. But in neither case do we have a make, license plate number, or description of the driver."

"Ted Macauley drives a red Oldsmobile," I pointed out.

"I know," Nguyen said. "I already checked. And that red Camaro you saw Peter Dace's girlfriend driving is registered to Dace. But Dace was out with his girlfriend last night, according to the San Jose police. He and the girl had dinner at a Mexican restaurant, plenty of witnesses."

"He's off my A list anyway," I said. "I just don't think he'd go to the trouble. Harassment, maybe. A bomb? I doubt it. What about the protester at the clinic? The plate numbers on the van and car?"

"The van is registered to a William Wellette. He lives in Concord." Nguyen pulled a photocopy of a photograph from the file. "Is this the man you described to me, the one who seemed to know Ms. Steiner?"

I took the copy and studied it. "I don't think he knew her personally. It's just that he knows her name. He kept saying it over and over. That made me feel uncomfortable about him. Yes, this looks like him. I assume you have his photograph for a reason."

"Mr. Wellette is quite familiar to the police in several Bay Area cities, as well as some out-of-state locations." Nguyen consulted several sheets in his folder. "He's active in a number of anti-abortion organizations, some of them quite radical. His rap sheet includes arrests for obstructing clinics, making threats, the usual."

"Has he ever thrown a bomb through any windows?" I asked.

"If he has, he's never been caught. He did, however, pull a jail term last year in Portland, Oregon. For harassing a doctor at a women's clinic."

"Did he, indeed," I said slowly. "And where was Mr. Wellette last night?"

"At home, he says. Alone. At least that's what he told the Concord police when they inquired."

"Making signs about baby-killers, no doubt. Did he tell the Concord police how he knows Rachel Steiner's name?"

"He denied knowing anything about any of the staff at that clinic. Doctors, nurses, administrative personnel, or escorts."

"He's lying. I heard him."

"I plan to have a little talk with him myself," Nguyen said. "To see if he can clarify that point."

"What about Ted Macauley?"

Nguyen took his time answering. "Ted Macauley seems to be missing," he said finally.

"Missing? Since when?"

Nguyen tented his hands together in front of him. "I went over to Macauley's apartment this morning. The roommate, Dave Walker, hasn't seen Macauley since yesterday morning. Nor have any of his friends, classmates, or professors. As far as we can determine, no one has seen Ted Macauley since he walked out of the Oakland Police Department after filing that complaint against Sergeant Vernon."

Twenty-two

BY THE TIME I WENT TO SEE SID ON THURSDAY evening, the media had picked up the story. Some enterprising reporter over at Oakland's Channel 2 News had connected the dots that led from the complaint filed against a veteran OPD homicide cop to the explosion at the Garber Street house to the missing U.C. Berkeley senior. Neither the Oakland nor the Berkeley Police Department was saying much about the case. But Ted Macauley's parents, interviewed at their Menlo Park home, indignantly denied that their son could have had anything to do with the bomb. They stopped short of accusing Sid of complicity in their son's disappearance, but the implication was plain.

I needed to get Errol Seville's perspective on the whole situation. I'd tried to call him in Carmel that afternoon, but I got no answer. He and his wife Minna were out. It wasn't like them not to turn on their answering machine, but maybe they'd forgotten. I planned to try to reach them again that night.

Sid lived in the Temescal section, a North Oakland neighborhood between Broadway and Telegraph Avenue. After he and I had divorced, I went flying off to Paris. He bought a little house on Manila Avenue, a Craftsman bungalow that was a smaller version of his

154

parents' home. His current residence wasn't far, in distance anyway, from that house where he grew up, a few blocks from the campus of Oakland Technical High School, where he'd played football more than twenty-five years ago.

I stepped onto the front porch and rang the doorbell. I heard footsteps approaching the door. A curtain on the window to my right shifted and I saw a woman's face. A moment later the door opened.

"Hello, Jeri." Graciela Portillo's words were polite, her face composed, as her large brown eyes looked me over. She worked in Missing Persons and I'd met her last December while working on a case. She was divorced, in her thirties, and the mother of a ten-year-old son, according to Vicki, who had reported to me that her father and Detective Portillo had been dating for a couple of months.

"Hello, Grace," I said. I looked past her and saw Sid, in faded jeans and an Oakland A's sweatshirt, slumped tiredly on his Mission-style sofa. "May I speak with Sid?"

"Sure." She held the door open and I stepped into the living room, its hardwood floor covered with a Navajo rug Sid had picked up on a trip to Arizona. "I was just leaving. Gotta pick up my kid." She crossed to the sofa and kissed him on the cheek. "I'll call you later."

He touched Grace's hand, held it tightly for a second, then released it. I was surprised at the sting of jealousy I felt. After all, the man and I were divorced, two years this past October. If I didn't want him, I had no business playing dog-in-the-manger. Still . . .

I put that thought firmly on hold. I had more important things to talk about. Grace's expression was noncommittal as she walked past me and closed the front door.

"How're you doing?" I asked.

Sid made a noise that was supposed to be a laugh but

155

wasn't. "Oh, great, just great. Of course, I unplugged the phone because the damn reporters keep calling. I'm a real good candidate for getting my ass thrown off the force."

"You're not going to get thrown off the force." I said the words as if by rote. I had a feeling he'd been hearing the same thing all day, despite his interview with his lieutenant and the growing media attention. Hearing it from Wayne, from Grace, from Vicki, and now me. I looked through the door leading back to the kitchen and saw several cans, both beer and soda, on the tiled counter, next to a pizza box. "Vicki was here?" I guessed.

"Yeah. And Uncle Pat."

"Uncle Pat. Of course." I smiled. "I'll bet he told you not to let the bastards grind you down."

"Christ, you should have heard him." Sid got to his feet, moving slowly in a pair of beat-up running shoes. "He was threatening to call in a few markers. He probably has a few out there too."

"After thirty years, I'll just bet he does." Pat Haney had been on the Oakland force for more than thirty years. In fact it was Pat who'd steered his nephew into a career as a policeman.

Sid stood near the doorway, looking at the built-in shelves in the bungalow's dining room. The top shelf held a lot of family pictures, photographs that had become familiar to me during the years Sid and I had been together. One of them was an eight-by-ten color photograph taken the day Frank Vernon and Eileen Haney exchanged marriage vows at Our Lady of Lourdes on Lakeshore. That was three months after V-J Day in 1945, almost a year after they met one night at the Paramount Theatre in downtown Oakland. Eileen was there with her brother. Pat once told me the movie was *To Have and*

156

Have Not, with Bogie and Bacall. How romantic, I thought then, and still do.

Frank was in the Navy, a farmer's son from Missouri, who had no intention of going back to Joplin. He started dating Eileen, who'd been born and raised in Oakland. After mustering out, he found work as a longshoreman, unloading cargo ships down at the Port of Oakland. Eileen left the cash register at her father's bakery on Telegraph Avenue for a cash register at Capwell's Department Store, downtown at Nineteenth and Broadway.

Salt of the earth, both of them, according to Sid's older sister Doreen. Now as I looked at the elder Vernons' wedding picture, I wished again that I'd had the chance to get to know them. But Frank died of a heart attack six years before I met Sid. Eileen succumbed to cancer a year later.

"You want some coffee?" I asked Sid.

"Yeah, sure." He sounded distracted, and I knew why. He had bypassed the other family photographs arrayed on the shelf, the ones of his parents at various stages of their lives and the ones of Doreen and her husband and kids. Instead he'd picked up a frame and was staring at a picture of his brother Eddie in his Marine dress blues. Sid was into some serious brooding tonight.

I flicked on the light in the kitchen and set about making a pot of coffee. I never got the chance to meet Eddie Vernon either. He was killed in Vietnam, a week after Sid graduated from Oakland Tech. Doreen told me about it, the day Sid and I drove to Sacramento so I could meet his family, or what was left of it.

Eddie was in the last month of his tour of duty, Doreen said, and he had his whole life planned out. He was engaged to marry his high school sweetheart, and when he left the Corps he was going to use his GI Bill to go to college. He'd also talked about becoming a cop, just like his uncle Pat.

But all those plans got cut short by a Viet Cong barrage in the last days of the war. It hit the family hard. I could see it in Doreen's eyes when she told me her folks were never the same after Eddie died.

I leaned against the kitchen counter and watched Sid put Eddie's picture back on the shelf. Then he shambled into the kitchen and picked up the pizza box. "There's one piece left. You want it?"

"Sure. I haven't had any dinner." I tore off a couple of paper towels and stuck the wedge into the microwave. While it was heating, Sid folded the cardboard box with his big hands and shoved it into the kitchen garbage can. Then he swept the cans into a City of Oakland recycling bin at the end of the counter.

"Coffee will be ready in a minute," I said, just making conversation.

"Thanks." He looked at me with his yellow cat's eyes and mustered a ghost of a smile as he leaned over and kissed me on the forehead. "Be right back."

He headed down the hallway, his destination the bathroom. As he closed the door the microwave beeped and I took out my pizza slice. I went looking through the kitchen cupboards for a couple of mugs. I couldn't find any, so I checked the dishwasher. Pay dirt. Everything was clean, but it hadn't been unloaded. I took out a couple of mugs and poured coffee into them, then ate my pizza. When I was finished I washed my hands and set to work unloading the dishwasher.

I pulled out another mug, thick white crockery with a faded gold insignia on one side, a globe with the words "United States Marine Corps" beneath it. I wondered how long Sid had had this. It had been more than twenty years since he got out of the Marines.

Sid hadn't really thought about what he was going to do after high school. In fact, he'd thought about going to work at the port, just like his father. But Eddie's death sent him in a different direction, to the Marine Corps Recruit Depot in San Diego, with his mother saying the rosary and hoping like hell her second son wouldn't wind up in Vietnam.

Instead Sid went to Japan. That's where he met Linda, his first wife. He was in his early twenties when they married, three years into his four-year enlistment. Her father was a gunnery sergeant, a career Marine who encouraged his new son-in-law to stay in the Corps. But when it came time to reenlist, Sid decided he wanted to come back to Oakland. While he was thinking about college and several other options, Uncle Pat put in his pitch for the police force. Then Linda told him she was pregnant and Sid knew he needed to settle into something. He took the exam and made it into the hiring pool. Vicki was born two months after he graduated from the Academy.

"You don't have to do that," Sid said when he came back into the kitchen. I'd put the Marine Corps mug into the cupboard and poured coffee into two others. Now I sorted flatware from the dishwasher basket into a drawer.

"If you're like me, you'll let it sit for a couple of days before you get around to it." I pointed at one of the mugs. "Take your coffee and go sit down."

He stayed where he was and took a swallow of coffee. "Hand me those plates," he said. We unloaded the dishwasher in companionable silence, then he turned to me. "Thanks for coming over."

"I had some questions I wanted to ask you." I looked at his tired face. "But I think they can wait until tomorrow. How about a couple of hands of gin instead? As I recall, I used to beat you with great regularity."

His mouth curved up in a smile and I saw a glimmer of

159

the old Sid who had charmed me into his arms and his bed a few years back.

"The day hasn't come when you could beat me at gin rummy, Jeri Howard."

He went to get the cards while I sifted through the CDs in the rack next to his stereo system. I put on some Dave Brubeck and kicked off my shoes. We faced off over the coffee table for a couple of hours. It was about ten when I kissed him good night and headed home.

It had turned out to be a mild, clear evening, with stars twinkling in the dark blue sky above Oakland. As I climbed the steps onto my own front porch I saw Abigail standing on the back of my sofa, which was visible because her tabby bulk and her head had parted the vertical blinds covering the front window. I turned the key in the lock, my nose catching the sweet fragrance of the blossoms on the lemon tree in the flower bed in front of my window.

When I opened my front door the next morning to get my newspaper, the lemon tree had lost its head.

Twenty-three

THE TOP OF THE LEMON TREE RESTED NEATLY on my front porch, just beyond Friday's edition of the Oakland *Tribune*. The tree's lower half still protruded from the flower bed to my left, below my front window. I could make out a partial footprint in the soil at the base of the tree.

I took a deep breath, then another one, feeling cold. I felt as though someone had just walked over my grave. No, it was more immediate than that. I wasn't dead yet. But it felt as though someone's eyes were watching me. And the sensation wasn't benign.

It was a threat.

I took another breath. Then I backed away from the calling card on my front porch, shut the door, locked it, and walked back to the kitchen to use the phone to call 911, then Wayne Hobart and Brad Nguyen. Wayne arrived about fifteen minutes after two Oakland detectives and a couple of evidence techs. Nguyen showed up half an hour later.

By that time my neighbors were clustered on their front porches in the courtyard of the U-shaped building on Adams Street, talking among themselves, wondering how the vandal had gotten past the security fence and gate that surrounded our building. And why were the cops making such a fuss over a decapitated lemon tree?

"Same as the one on Garber Street?" Nguyen asked.

"Same position," I told him. "With the chopped end pointing toward the front door. That one was in a pot, though, and it had been pulled out, with the lower half and the roots tossed onto the sidewalk."

Nguyen rubbed his chin. "Interesting."

"Way past interesting."

Finally the police finished asking their questions and collecting evidence, packed up their gear, and left, taking the lemon tree with them. I asked Wayne to wait in the living room, explaining what I wanted to do and why. Then I went to the hall closet and hauled out the cat carriers. The sound of rattling latches normally caused a cat exodus, but in this case the cats were already hiding, spooked by the unusual activity. It took me a while to corral them, but finally I had both Abigail and Black Bart locked inside the carriers.

"What have you been feeding this cat?" Wayne asked as he hoisted Abigail's carrier, using both hands.

"She likes her chow, that's for sure." I picked up Black Bart, who was much lighter, and we went out the front door, past the forgotten newspaper. Out the front security gate and into Wayne's car. He drove us on a circuitous route all over downtown Oakland, accompanied by periodic protestations from Abigail, who hated to ride in cars. Black Bart just huddled in the back of his carrier, shivering. When we were both satisfied that we weren't being tailed, Wayne followed the directions I'd given him, to Dr. Prentice's office. One of the calls I'd made earlier was to my vet, who boarded animals and had an alarm system as well as someone on duty during the night.

"I don't know how long," I told her. "But I'd feel safer if you kept them here until this is all sorted out."

"I understand." She ruffled Abigail's fur. "I hope it's

not long. Abigail really hates to stay here. And you, you're going to miss these guys."

"I know. But it's safer to have them out of the apartment."

Wayne took me back to my home, which already seemed empty without my cats. I hadn't eaten breakfast and it was nearly time for lunch, so I poured cereal into a bowl and sloshed milk over it. After this repast, I picked up the phone and punched in the Sevilles' number. It rang and rang. Finally, just as I was about to hang up, Minna Seville answered.

"Minna, it's Jeri. I called yesterday but you were out. May I speak with Errol?"

"Jeri." Something was wrong. I knew it immediately. Her voice was subdued as it traveled over the phone line from Carmel, more than a hundred miles south. "Errol's not here. He's in the hospital."

"The hospital. Oh, no." Shock and dismay washed over me. Errol was in his seventies. A heart attack had finally forced him to retire. "Is it his heart?"

"He was mugged," Minna said, amazed that anything like that could happen in their pleasant little retirement retreat. "In Carmel. Right here on San Antonio Avenue, as he was walking home."

I clicked into detective mode, prompted by a disturbing thought. "When did this happen, Minna?"

"Yesterday afternoon. I'm not sure of the time. One of our neighbors found him lying in the street about a block from the house, around two o'clock. He'd been hit over the head. He was conscious but disoriented, and his head was bleeding. He's over at Community in Monterey, with stitches and a concussion."

No wonder I hadn't been able to get anyone on the phone yesterday. Questions boiled into my mind as I digested what Minna had told me. "Did anything happen before this? Anonymous phone calls? Vandalism?"

There was silence on the other end of the phone. Minna's next words confirmed my hunch.

"How did you know?" She sounded even more worried. "We've been getting breather calls for weeks. I told Errol we should change to an unlisted number, but he wants to be accessible. Then a couple of days ago someone chopped down—"

"A lemon tree," I interrupted. "It was a lemon tree."

"Yes. The one in the corner of the yard. Whoever did it left the top on our front porch."

"With the trunk pointing toward the door. I had the same caller, Minna." And the attack on Errol probably meant that I too should expect another visit. "Keep the cat indoors." The Sevilles had a large irascible tomcat named Stinkpot. Disagreeable as he was, I knew Minna and Errol would be upset if anything happened to him. "Better yet, board him. Get one of your children down there to stay with you or go stay somewhere else."

"Our oldest son's already here," she said, sounding alarmed. "And our other son is on his way. Jeri, what's going on?"

"All I've got so far is a theory," I told her. "I need to get into Errol's old files. I know he put them in storage when he retired. Where?"

The files of the Errol Seville Agency, representing my mentor's thirty-plus years as a private investigator in the Bay Area, were locked up in a document storage facility in Hayward. Minna told me the younger of the Seville daughters, Patricia, had a key. When I called Patricia at her home in Fremont, south of Oakland, I got a busy signal. As I discovered when I got her on the line five minutes later, she'd been on the phone with Minna, who alerted her to the situation.

164

"I'm planning to drive down to Carmel this evening," Patricia said. "But I'm playing in a tennis tournament this afternoon and I can't get out of it. I have to be there at two. It's twelve-fifteen now. How soon can you meet me in Hayward?"

"I'm on my way," I told her.

The storage company was located in a collection of boxy structures on Mission Boulevard, not far from Cal State Hayward. As I looked up the hill at the university's buildings, clustered on the ridge, I recalled the case I'd been working on a year ago, involving the death of one of Dad's history department colleagues. During the course of that investigation, my father had been attacked and shoved down some stairs. So I could guess how Errol's daughter felt.

"How's Errol?" I asked.

Patricia wore tennis whites. She was tall and lean like her father, with short salt and pepper hair and a lot of sun squint lines in her fortyish face. On the passenger seat of her shiny BMW I saw a tennis racket and a canvas bag. Her mouth quirked as she stuck her car keys into the side pocket of her purse. "He's doing fairly well. Demanding to be let out of the hospital, of course. But the doctors want to keep him for a few more days."

"He's safer there."

"Safe." She frowned as I pulled open one of the double glass doors leading to the storage facility's main office. "Are you sure about that?"

"Not entirely," I admitted.

Patricia signed us in at the front desk, then an attendant let us through the security door into the storage facility itself. "So this has something to do with one of Dad's old cases?"

I nodded. "I think so. A case I worked on. I just wish

165

I'd picked up the signals sooner. If I'm right, this is one very clever criminal."

"Evidently one with a grudge," Patricia said. She led the way down a long hallway lined on either side with doors, stopped at one on the right, and pulled a set of keys and an envelope from her handbag. She handed the envelope to me as she unlocked the door. "That's the inventory. I guess you know what you're looking for."

"Yes. I do."

We walked into the air-conditioned chamber, a square room lined with rows of floor-to-ceiling shelves, each shelf stacked with filed storage boxes, each box labeled with an identifying number. I pulled several sheets of paper from the envelope. The inventory listed the box numbers and contents, the whole of Errol's career boiled down into a chronology of years. I located the boxes for the year I sought. There was a folded aluminum step stool leaning against one of the shelves. I opened it and braced the legs, then moved it over to the shelf. I pulled out one of the boxes. Patricia helped me convey it to the floor.

"It was a custody case," I continued as I pulled the lid off the box and surveyed the neatly labeled file folders. "The Seville Agency got involved about six years ago. But it really began much earlier than that... With a murder."

Twenty-four

THE VICTIM OF THAT MURDER WAS A WOMAN named Stephanie Bradfield.

She died on a chilly April night, stabbed to death in the bedroom of a house in the Oakland hills. I'd seen the house. It's an expensive-looking structure, contemporary in design and constructed of stone and redwood, just off Colton Boulevard, which winds through the Montclair district. Isolated from its neighbors by the hilly terrain and a stand of eucalyptus trees, the house crowns the edge of a bluff. The deck at the back and the bedroom windows have a million-dollar view of Oakland, San Francisco, and the bay. On that night, which was clear and unseasonably cold, Stephanie Bradfield and her knife-wielding killer could have seen the lights glittering on the Bay Bridge and the Golden Gate.

How do I know the details? Well, I read about it in the papers, of course. But I knew more about it than the average citizen, because one of the investigators who arrived on the scene that cold clear night was a sergeant who'd just been assigned to Homicide three months before Stephanie Bradfield died. His name was Sid Vernon.

That was eight years ago. The file is still open. There is no statute of limitations on murder.

I know that every now and then Sid pulls that file from

one of the overcrowded shelves in his office. He sifts through its contents, wondering if there was something else he could have done to close that case, some little scrap of evidence he had overlooked. It still rankles him that the Bradfield homicide has never been solved.

Officially, that is. Sid and his former partner, Joe Kelso, are quite sure they know who killed Stephanie Bradfield.

The case file contains a cassette tape of the 911 call eleven-year-old Melissa Bradfield made the night she came home from a school play and discovered her mother, still alive but bleeding to death. Sid played it for me once. It's not pleasant listening. It makes me cold every time I think of it.

On the tape, Melissa's frightened voice veers between anguished sobs and steady calm. She moves back and forth, from the bedroom to the living room, trying to comfort her dying mother as she describes the scene to the emergency operator. Stephanie's voice quavers in the background, slurred and dying away, as life oozes from her body. The sirens draw closer, too late to save her.

That tape brings home the ugly reality of murder more than anything I've ever encountered, except the actual corpse.

As far as Sid Vernon and Joe Kelso were concerned, there was only one suspect in the Bradfield murder— Richard Bradfield. He was Stephanie's estranged husband, Melissa's emotionally distant father. Stephanie Bradfield had been on the verge of filing for divorce, citing her husband's emotional and physical abuse. Given the all too familiar pattern of such cases, it was logical for the police to consider Bradfield their prime suspect. But Bradfield had an alibi. He'd been in Pebble Beach with his assistant that evening. Try as he might, Sid couldn't shake that alibi.

"He killed her," Sid told me, more than once. "I know he killed her. But so far I haven't been able to prove it."

I wondered what Richard Bradfield looked like now, as I looked up from the meticulous and extensive file kept by the Errol Seville Agency. I recalled Bradfield as he was then, a well-built man a shade under six feet, with wavy brown hair he kept closely trimmed. He had a Roman nose and square face, with a little cleft in the chin. He favored gray pinstriped suits with pale blue shirts and red power ties. His eyes pierced right through people. Especially people he didn't like.

By the time the investigation into his wife's murder was under way, Bradfield certainly didn't like Sid Vernon or Joe Kelso. By the time the Errol Seville Agency was finished with Bradfield, he liked us even less.

Richard Bradfield had never been charged with the murder of his wife, but Stephanie Bradfield's sister had the same conviction Sid Vernon had. As far as Cordelia Ramsey was concerned, her brother-in-law was guilty of murder. And if she couldn't put him in prison for that crime, she'd take his child. So she sued him for custody of Melissa.

I leaned back in my chair and picked up the mug of coffee from my desk, staring at my office door, closed and locked. What I saw, however, was that day seven years ago when Cordelia Ramsey walked into Errol's Oakland office, where Errol and I sat, waiting to hear what this new client had to say.

Her attorney had set up the meeting, but it was Cordelia I remembered. She was a tall woman in her mid-forties, with a rough kind of beauty and a style all her own, an avenging angel with a hawk's profile and wings of gray streaking the dark red hair that brushed the collar of her camel-colored suit. The large eyes in her narrow face were a steely gray, full of anger and purpose.

"I want to know if the bastard jaywalks, spits on the sidewalk, or cheats on his taxes," she told us in a voice roughened by too many cigarettes. "Every speck of dirt. I don't care how much it costs. Just do it."

We did it.

We got the goods on Bradfield. None of it proved murder, which I think was Cordelia's secret hope, but we could and did hang the man for a number of lesser crimes.

Bradfield may have looked like a blueblood, but he was a slick operator, a streetwise hustler from Orange County. Most people didn't know he was a greedy predator until they'd been taken in. At great cost to their pocketbooks and life savings.

Bradfield Investments occupied a plush office on the twelfth floor of the Ordway Building in downtown Oakland, with a view of Lake Merritt. When Errol and I put Bradfield under our relentless microscope, we discovered that what appeared to be a legitimate small investment firm was really a boiler room operation, with Bradfield himself running a penny stock scam.

He'd found a small, capitalized Los Angeles manufacturing company, barely alive, its stock selling for less than a buck a share. He bought a pile of shares. The company's president, Sam Kacherian, also owned a pile of shares, and he was greedy, just like Bradfield. Together they manipulated the stock price until they tripled their investment. Then they cashed out, leaving the company sucked dry.

Bradfield was also playing games with the accounts of several trusting, elderly clients. The practice was called "churning," which meant Bradfield was constantly buying and selling securities for these accounts, in order to increase his commissions.

Once we'd uncovered all of this, Errol turned it over to

Cordelia's attorney. The lawyer used the information to his client's advantage in the custody case. He also brought Bradfield's crimes to the attention of the Alameda County District Attorney's Office and the Internal Revenue Service.

There were lawsuits still pending in various cases of Everyone versus Richard Bradfield and Sam Kacherian, but neither man had any money left. By the time the Internal Revenue Service swooped down on Bradfield for things like "substantial underpayment" and "failure to report income," he couldn't have had much more than the price of a burger in the pockets of one of his custom-tailored suits. Everything else he had, including the Colton Avenue house, had been seized by the IRS.

Public humiliation was hard for such an arrogant, egotistical man. I still remember the cold fury in those blue eyes when the jury foreman at his last trial read the guilty verdict.

That was the stalking trial.

Bradfield was under indictment for fraud and tax evasion when Cordelia was awarded custody of Melissa. He was out on bail and awaiting trial when he began stalking his sister-in-law.

After all, it was her fault. It was Cordelia who hired the Seville Agency and brought Bradfield's financial house of cards toppling around him. He blamed her for all his problems and he made threatening phone calls saying just that, threatening to kill her. He showed up at the art gallery she owned in Mill Valley, then flattened the tires of her car and another vehicle, owned by Cordelia's husband, an artist named Colin Derrill. Bradfield's relentless harassment had probably speeded the breakup of their marriage. That came later in the year, after Bradfield went to prison.

Bradfield's arrest on the stalking charge came when he

violated a restraining order prohibiting him from going near Cordelia's gallery or her residence. One day he showed up at her Mill Valley home and decapitated the lemon tree planted in her yard. Then he deposited the severed top on her porch, trunk end pointing at her front door.

Just as he had three times in the past week.

The son of a bitch had been leaving his calling card. Sid Vernon didn't have a lemon tree. But Vicki Vernon did.

Why had it taken me so long to make the connection?

I got to my feet and went back to the table where my coffee maker sat, replenishing my mug. Then I resumed my seat. Bradfield was the reason I met Sid. It was early into the Seville Agency's investigation. I went to the Oakland Police Department to talk with Sid and Joe Kelso, to get some background on Stephanie Bradfield's murder. Something clicked between Sid and me, and we started dating.

It was almost a year after Cordelia hired the Seville Agency to get the goods on her brother-in-law that he was convicted, first of fraud, then tax evasion, and finally for stalking Cordelia, the trial when his eyes burned with rage at the guilty verdict. And six years ago, two years after his wife was murdered, Richard Bradfield went away.

Now he was back.

Twenty-five

SID HAD NOT SPENT ALL OF THE LAST EIGHT years in Homicide. His first stint there lasted over three years, then he'd spent a two-year tour in Felony Assault before moving back to Homicide. As I recalled, Kelso had retired about the same time Sid changed jobs. I didn't know if he'd stayed retired, or if he was still in the Bay Area.

I picked up the phone and called Wayne Hobart. He was my best starting place.

"Joe Kelso?" Wayne said. "I hear he went to work as chief of police in some little town up north. Why do you want to find Joe?" I told him. He gave a long low whistle. "You really think Bradfield's behind all of this? I mean, Macauley looks good for the bombing."

"It has to be Bradfield, Wayne. Sid, Errol, and I helped put him away. You said yourself if anyone wanted to push Sid's buttons, the way to do it would be Vicki. Bradfield's pushing. See if you can find out when he got out of prison, and where. And I need to talk to Joe Kelso."

"I'll be able to tell you where Kelso is after I talk to one of his old running mates over in Robbery. Bradfield may take a little longer. I'll get back to you on that as soon as I can."

I also needed to find Cordelia Ramsey. It was a good

bet she no longer lived in that house hugging one of Mill Valley's wooded hillsides. At the time, her phone number had been unlisted, for obvious reasons. The number was in Errol's files, but when I dialed it I got someone who'd had the number for the past four years and had never heard of Cordelia Ramsey.

Wayne Hobart called just as I was about to leave my office. "Joe Kelso's chief of police up in Cloverdale," he said. I knew the town, at the northernmost end of Sonoma County, a couple of hours north of San Francisco on U.S. 101. "He's been there ever since he retired. Want me to call him?"

"Yes. Tell him I'll be in touch. Did you find out anything about Bradfield?"

"He spent five years at Wasco State prison, down by Bakersfield. Paroled to San Diego a year ago."

"Did Cordelia Ramsey file a protest?"

"That information I don't have. I do have the name of his parole officer, though." He repeated it and I wrote it down. "The guy I talked to is supposed to be sending some information about Bradfield. When I get it I'll let you know. Looks like he satisfied the terms of his parole, Jeri. He's out, free and clear, as of last December."

And the harassment of the residents of Sasha Nichols's house had started in January. Bradfield hadn't wasted any time.

Targeting the cop who helped put him in prison was just his style. Given Sid's age, Bradfield had probably guessed he was still on the Oakland police force. But how had he found Vicki? How did he know where Sid's daughter lived?

I looked at the phone number Wayne had given me, with its San Diego area code. That must be the connection, I thought. Bradfield had been paroled to San Diego, and that's where Vicki Vernon's mother and stepfather

174

lived. Sometime in that year, his path must have crossed Vicki's.

I retrieved my car from the downtown Oakland parking lot and headed across the Richmond–San Rafael Bridge, then cut through the little village of San Quentin, adjacent to the prison that dominates the peninsula jutting out into the San Francisco Bay. Then I picked up U.S. 101 south to Mill Valley and left the freeway at Highway 1, which ultimately made its way to Muir Woods and Stinson Beach. I followed the winding road west several miles until I found the cutoff that led to Cordelia Ramsey's house.

As I'd guessed, she wasn't there anymore.

I hadn't really expected it would be easy to find her. The current residents of the house were a young couple with two children who had no idea where to locate the former owner. They gave me the name of the real estate agent they'd used. I headed back down the hill to Mill Valley, only to discover that particular agent had long since moved to another firm. They must have had an address in a file somewhere, but no one would tell me anything.

I left the real estate agent's and drove to Throckmorton Avenue, downtown where Cordelia's art gallery had been located across from Old Mill Park. The gallery was now a children's clothing store, featuring exquisite and expensive baby outfits for chic infants and cutting-edge toddlers. The owner was busy with a customer, so I went outside and looked at the shop's neighbors. I was sure the stationery store had been there when Cordelia operated the gallery. The woman behind the counter fingered my business card. Then she looked up at me with wary eyes.

"I haven't heard from her in years," she said. "After everything that happened, she took Missy and left the Bay Area. I don't know if she's still in California. She liked to travel, so for all I know she's moving from place to place. Now and then I get a postcard from some exotic place."

I wasn't sure I believed her. Something in the way she spoke made me think she was holding back.

"I need to find her. Richard Bradfield's out of prison."

The shop owner grimaced as though she'd taken a bite of something sour. "They should have kept him locked up forever. I honestly don't know where Cordelia is. If I did, I'm not sure I'd tell you."

"I understand. But if you do hear from her, or from someone who might know, relay a message. Tell her to get in touch with me."

I went back outside and stood on the sidewalk for a moment, oblivious to the pedestrians and vehicles going by me on Throckmorton. If Cordelia Ramsey had spent the last few years traveling, that might explain why she hadn't protested Richard Bradfield's parole, as she had the right to do. On the other hand, Melissa would be in school, which seemed to indicate that Cordelia needed to stay put. Unless the girl was in boarding school. No, she would be nineteen or twenty now, probably starting college about the time her father was eligible for parole. So Cordelia could very well have been traveling and unavailable to comment at Bradfield's hearing.

No doubt Cordelia had covered her tracks very well. And the people she'd known here in Mill Valley would be reluctant to assist me, if the shop owner was any indication. I might need some help on this one. I retrieved my car from its parking space, pulled out my address book and cellular phone, then punched in a number. Busy. I hoped that meant the person I was calling was in her San Rafael office.

I met Rita Lydecker several years ago at the midwinter

conference of the National Association of Legal Investigators. I liked her immediately. Whoever coined the phrase tough old broad had to be talking about Rita. She was a brassy barrel-shaped bottle blonde in her late fifties who'd worked as a prison guard and a bail bondsman before hanging out her shingle as a skip tracer and investigator. Her grandkids thought it was a hoot that Grandma was a private eye.

Rita had a second-floor office on D Street near downtown San Rafael. I was right about that busy signal. She was still on the phone, polluting the air with a cigarette and waving her hands as she talked. When I walked in a wide grin spread over her face and she waved me to a chair. I opted instead for the open French doors that led out onto a small deck that she'd decorated with potted plants and a couple of refinished park benches set at angles.

"Hey, sweetie," she crowed when she got off the phone. "How the hell are you?" She ground out the cigarette in an ashtray and got up to join me in the doorway, resplendent in form-fitting black stretch pants, a bright red silk shirt, and a lot of chunky gold jewelry. She swept me into an embrace perfumed with smoke and jasmine cologne. "What brings you over to my side of the bay?"

"Business. I need to find someone."

"So tell me." Rita draped herself comfortably on one of the benches and beckoned me to the other.

"Cordelia Ramsey. Remember her?"

"Yeah." Rita ran one beringed hand through her platinum-blond hair and crossed one still-shapely leg over the other. "The redhead with the scum-sucking toad brother-in-law who offed her sister. You and Errol did a good piece of work on that one."

"Not good enough. He's out of prison. And I have a feeling he hasn't been rehabilitated."

"Guys like that never are," Rita said frankly. "The whole world would be better off if somebody just shot the sumbitches." She shook her head. "I got a case over in San Anselmo. Guy just like that. I'm afraid he's gonna kill his ex-wife, and the kids too."

Rita made shocked noises as I told her about the case. "What a hornet's nest. The bombing points at this Macauley kid. But the lemon tree—that's got to be Bradfield."

"I need to find Cordelia Ramsey. She could be in danger. I wondered if you could give me some help."

"Glad to," Rita said, getting to her feet. "Let's go over to the courthouse. It's nearly four. That only gives us an hour."

She locked her office and wheeled her Caddy over to the Frank Lloyd Wright edifice that was the Marin County Courthouse. There, we both combed through records, looking for some sort of paper trail that would tell us where Cordelia Ramsey had gone.

Cordelia would be fifty-three now. She was a San Francisco native who'd studied art in France and Italy. Ramsey was her birth name. She'd kept it through three marriages. The first was a brief one, lasting less than a year, to a fellow art student named Charles Wegman who, according to Cordelia, was lost to antiquity—and just as well. Her second husband lasted longer. He was an architect named Michael Paxton, who had his own firm in Mill Valley, not far from Cordelia's gallery. Paxton had died suddenly, a couple of years before his wife's sister was murdered.

Cordelia had then married the artist, Colin Derrill, someone she'd discovered when she bought one of his paintings. He was quite a bit younger than she was, a head-in-the-clouds type. At the time, I wondered if Cordelia had married him on the rebound from her grief at the loss of her second husband. Beyond the obvious connection of art, they didn't seem suited to one another. She and Derrill had lived in her Mill Valley home for most of their three-year marriage and had separated shortly after Bradfield's stalking trial had ended. I didn't know where Derrill was now, only that I saw his name now and then in the newspapers. I guessed he was still somewhere in the Bay Area. I had some contacts in the local art scene. I was sure I could locate him.

At five the courthouse closed and we were chased out. Rather than face Friday evening traffic, I had dinner with Rita at a Thai restaurant, talking out some ideas. When I got home, the lemon tree's stump chilled me, as did the emptiness of my apartment. I missed the cats.

But if Richard Bradfield knew where I lived, I wouldn't risk having them there.

Twenty-six

THERE'S A BLACK-WREATHED MEMORIAL ON A barren median strip at the corner of Thirty-second Street and Mandela Parkway. The parkway used to be Cypress Street. It slices through West Oakland, following the route of the old Cypress Freeway that collapsed in the 1989 Loma Prieta earthquake, killing more than forty people. I've never stopped to look at the black wreath, but I know it's there to commemorate the life and death of one of those victims.

I turned right on Thirty-second and drove the few blocks to Peralta. This was where, according to a friend of mine who was plugged into the Bay Area art scene, Colin Derrill had a studio. The building, near the Poplar Recreation Center, looked like a warehouse. No doubt it had been in a previous life. Today was Saturday, and all the real warehouses were closed. Except this one, now used as studios by several artists.

I parked next to the loading dock and walked inside, past a woodworking shop, hearing the earsplitting whine of a saw. Next to this door I saw a sign that told me C. Derrill was in unit 5A. I located 5A but the door was closed and padlocked. Now the saw's whine stopped and I heard music, some instrumental jazz piano. I doubled back to the woodworking shop and stepped inside.

The source of the music was a portable CD player set

precariously on a sawhorse. Next to this, a curvaceous brunette in brown leggings and a green T-shirt tinkered with the saw. The smell of freshly cut lumber pervaded the space.

She looked up and gave me the once-over with a pair of sharp brown eyes. "Help you?"

"I'm looking for Colin Derrill."

"He's running some errands. I expect him back soon."

"I'll wait."

I waited near the open doorway of the warehouse, watching a couple of kids ride their bikes up and down the nearly deserted street. Derrill showed up about twenty minutes later. He looked much the same as he had when he was still married to Cordelia Ramsey. He was in his early forties now, tall and loose-limbed, and his curly hair was an ashy brown that didn't show the gray. His hairline, however, had receded a bit farther.

When he saw me in the doorway he flashed a polite smile and his hazel eyes narrowed. He looked a bit confused. He knew he'd seen me before. But at the moment he couldn't quite place me.

"Jeri Howard," I told him. "I used to work with Errol Seville."

His smile dimmed. "Oh, that."

"Yes, that. May we talk?"

He was carrying a white sack that smelled like Mexican food. He delivered part of the contents to the woman in the woodworking shop. Then he unlocked the door to his studio and I followed him into his work space.

"Please, don't let me keep you from your lunch," I said.

"Thanks." Derrill unwrapped his burrito and demolished it while I circled the room, looking at his canvases. He was into big, abstract, and lots of red. I didn't know much about art, but I knew what I liked. And I didn't like what he was painting. When I was in Paris a couple of years ago I spent days staring at every Monet I could find. But a Derrill canvas made me want to blink. Often.

I stood next to a canvas that towered above me and hurt my eyes. Then I turned back to where Derrill was wiping his hands on a napkin. "Have you been in this neighborhood long?"

"No. And I'm not sure I'll stay. I was over in San Francisco, south of Market, but the rents were going up. The rent's cheap here, but we've had a couple of attempted break-ins since I moved in. What can I do for you, Ms. Howard?"

"Have you talked with Cordelia recently?"

Derrill frowned. "Why do you ask?"

"I need to find her. Do you know where she is?"

He didn't say anything. Instead he crumpled the wrappings that had held his burrito, balling them up and stuffing them into the white sack.

"Do you?"

"I know how it looked," Derrill said, regret tingeing his voice and spilling over into his hazel eyes. "Me bailing out on her right after the trial. But the marriage was over long before that. We only stayed together to present a united front, so to speak."

"I understand," I said, and maybe I did. "But do you still have any contact with Cordelia? It's important. If you know where she is, please have her call me as soon as possible."

That's all I told him. I didn't think he needed to hear about Bradfield at this point. I took one of my business cards from my purse and handed it to him.

A frown furrowed little wrinkles in his face. "She went away and started a new life. I do see her now and then, but we haven't talked since . . . well, I guess it was right before Christmas. We had dinner. She came down to meet her niece. They were going away for the holidays."

"Her niece is going to school at Cal." Even as I said it his face closed up, as though he'd revealed too much. The penny dropped.

On Garber Street, Sasha was playing catch on the front lawn with Martin, who waved at me and smiled as though he'd accepted me as part of the gang. It was a sunny afternoon, and all up and down the block I could see people out in their yards and driveways, digging in the dirt or washing it off their cars.

"Martin looks like he's recuperating," I said, glancing at the little boy as he ran across the lawn and scooped up the big yellow ball his mother had just tossed his way.

"Seems to be. He's had a couple of nightmares, though. What's up?"

"Who's home?" I asked.

"Well," she began, then dodged as the yellow ball whizzed past her. "No fair. You wait until I finish talking with Jeri. Ben and Nelson are having a serious study session at the library. Vicki went to visit her dad. Rachel went on a hike at Point Reyes. Emily and Marisol are in the kitchen, baking a cake. Today is Rachel's birthday. We're going to surprise her when she gets home."

"Carrot cake," Martin advised me. "I get to lick the beaters when they make the cream cheese frosting."

"That sounds great," I told him, ruffling his curly black hair. As they resumed their ball game, I went in the open front door, through the living room that still looked like ground zero. In the kitchen Marisol stood at the sink, whirling sudsy water around in a large mixing bowl.

"Where's Emily?" I asked.

"On the deck," Marisol said, pointing over her shoulder with one soapy hand.

The back door was open. Through the screen door I saw Emily, standing at the picnic table in the middle of the redwood deck that extended almost to the back fence of Sasha's property, where a pine tree shaded the back corner of the yard. I opened the screen door and went outside.

Emily gave no indication that she'd seen me. She seemed intent on her task, filling three bird feeders of varying sizes arrayed on the table in front of her. She had a plastic cup in her hand, using it to scoop seed from a large bag into the feeders. I watched her as she filled the two smaller ones, then I walked toward her, stopping on the opposite side of the table.

"Hi, Jeri," she said, smiling as she reached for the third feeder, a tall metal and plastic tube, and unscrewed the lid.

I placed my hands palm down on the rough wooden surface of the table.

"Hello, Melissa."

Twenty-seven

EMILY AUSTEN—OR PERHAPS I SHOULD SAY, Melissa Bradfield—stood motionless, staring at me with those deep blue eyes.

Then she set aside the tall bird feeder and the plastic cup she'd been using to scoop seed from the bag. With her right hand she picked up a stray sunflower seed and turned it over and over with her fingers.

"When did you figure it out?" She lowered her eyes, looking at the table as though she were a schoolgirl who had been sent to the principal's office.

"Not as soon as I should have," I said. "The first night I was here, when I made the joke about Emily Austen being a good name for an English major. The look on your face told me you didn't think it was funny. I should have realized that Emily Austen was a made-up name. When Martin disappeared, you were so frantic. It wasn't his being gone that triggered your reaction. I wondered then if it was something in your past, someone who threatened you."

I shook my head. "But I was concentrating on Vicki being the target, not you. And the possibility that someone the others knew was responsible for these incidents. I had plenty of suspects. But you knew, as soon as you saw that lemon tree out on the front porch. Why didn't you say anything?"

"I didn't know. Not right away." Emily dropped the sunflower seed into the still-open bag, then turned and walked to the end of the deck. She knelt and picked up a cone that had fallen from the Monterey pine in the corner of the yard onto the redwood planks. Then she stood, leaning on the railing.

"The phone calls . . . That could have been anyone. I honestly thought it was that awful Ted Macauley. It didn't occur to me that it could be—"

She stopped. From the look on her face it was evident she could not bring herself to call Richard Bradfield her father.

"When I saw the lemon tree I remembered the one he left on my aunt's front porch. Still, I didn't make the connection. I guess it really didn't dawn on me until Martin disappeared." She sighed, a deep soul-rattling sound, and her fingers plucked at the pinecone, pulling at its seeds. "I guess that's denial. I simply couldn't believe he was out of prison so soon. That he'd be able to do what he threatened."

I joined her at the railing. "What did he threaten?"

Emily looked past me at the house, not really seeing it. "He said he'd come back and kill my aunt and take me away. I believed him. So did my aunt. After all, he killed my mother."

"Very likely," I said. "Even though it was never proved."

"I know he killed her." Emily turned her head toward me. At that moment her eyes burned with a blue fire, disconcertingly like her father's eyes. "I asked her, was it him? She told me he did it."

"In words?" I recalled the tape of that 911 call, gauging the admissibility of hearsay evidence and deathbed statements. I hadn't heard Melissa's question or her mother's answer, but perhaps the girl hadn't spoken into the phone's mouthpiece.

"No." Emily's voice was a jagged whisper. "If she'd said his name, maybe the police could have done something. They could have used that tape against him. But her words were all slurred and jumbly. When I asked her, she nodded, right before she died. I know she nodded."

Emily's right hand came down hard on the railing, loosening the seeds that studded the pinecone. She pulled at one of them and it came out in her fingers. She tossed it away.

"It wasn't just some random movement of her head. And I wasn't just some hysterical kid." Her voice was angry now, as she recalled the events of eight years before. Her fingers moving faster as she pulled seeds away from the cone. "I lived in that house. I know how he treated her. I saw him hit her. And I know the policemen believed me, that older guy Joe, and Vicki's dad."

She stopped and shook her head. "But that wasn't enough, especially since his assistant lied and said he was in Pebble Beach. After the funeral he took me back to that house where he killed my mother. He acted as though we'd just go on, the two of us. Pretending like nothing happened."

Her eyes were wintry now. I couldn't imagine what it must have been like for her, the little girl who'd found her mother bleeding to death, to be in the custody of the man she, and many other people, believed responsible for her mother's murder.

"I ran away once," she said, her voice quiet now. "I was trying to get over to Marin, to be with my aunt. But I didn't get very far. You can't get very far when you're only eleven years old. He found me. He told me if I ever ran away, he'd put me in some private boarding school. That would have been preferable to living with him. But it would have taken me out of my aunt's reach."

"You didn't have to live with him long. Your aunt prevailed in the custody hearing."

"You helped with that," Emily said. "You and Mr. Seville. That's when you got him arrested. When the court turned me over to my aunt, I hoped that would be the end of it. But it wasn't. He came after my aunt. I was afraid he'd kill her."

Emily had pulled all the seeds from the cone. She looked at the denuded stub in her hand, then tossed it away, over the deck railing.

"He should have been charged with killing my mother. At least he went to jail for being a thief. And for stalking my aunt. The last time I saw him, I told him I hated him. You should have seen his face. I knew then he was crazy."

She turned and looked at me, fear vying with anger on her young face. "He's not human. He's evil. You don't know what it's been like to live this way. I hoped they'd keep him locked up forever."

"The parole system doesn't work that way."

"I know. But I can't believe they let him out this soon."

"You and your aunt should have been notified that he was up for parole."

"We buried ourselves," she said thoughtfully. "My aunt's marriage was over. She gave up her business, left the home where she'd lived for over twenty years, left all her friends. We lived in a new place, with made-up names and made-up histories. Always watching our backs, in constant fear that he might show up and make good on his threat. Maybe we covered our tracks so well the parole board couldn't find us."

I nodded. "It's possible. Tell me something, Emily. When you met Vicki, last fall, did you know she was Sid Vernon's daughter?"

Emily shook her head vigorously, her brown hair swinging from side to side. "I had no idea. Not until she mentioned that her father was a cop. Then I thought, well, it's just one of those strange coincidences life tosses in your path. I mentioned it to my aunt. She had the same view. But when you came over to the house last week, I recognized you."

"How? I don't think we ever met."

"My aunt pointed you out," Emily said. "You and Mr. Seville. It was at the Marin County Courthouse, during the stalking trial. Please believe me, Jeri. I had no idea that my association with Vicki would put her, or any of the other people in this house, in any kind of danger."

"I'm not so sure you did. I think he may have met Vicki sometime last year when he was paroled to San Diego. If that's the case, he made the connection between Vicki Vernon and Sid Vernon. Finding you might have been accidental."

Emily was stubbornly prepared to shoulder all the blame. "Of course I put everyone in danger. Look at what happened. The phone calls, the plants, the bomb through the window. I know Sergeant Nguyen thinks it was Ted Macauley, but it must be . . ." She still couldn't say his name, as though speaking the words might cause Richard Bradfield to appear right there on the deck.

"He's come after me. I don't know how he found me, but he was always clever. I should have known he'd track me down. But Jeri, I don't want to have to run away for the rest of my life."

"Neither do I. I'll do what I can to help. I need to talk with your aunt. Where can I find her?"

"Mendocino. That's where we went six years ago. She built a house on some land her second husband left her. And she owns an art gallery, just like before. I hadn't told her anything about this, but ever since Wednesday night, when the bomb went off in the living room, I've been trying to reach her by phone." Emily frowned.

"But she's not there, or at her friend's house in Fort Bragg. Thursday I was talking with Lee, the woman who works for her. Lee says my aunt is off on a buying trip. That's when she drives all over the place, looking for new artists."

"When's she due back?" I asked.

"Yesterday. But I called this morning. She hasn't returned. And Lee hasn't heard from her."

Emily looked at me, trouble and the beginnings of tears deepening the blue in her eyes. "I'm worried about my aunt, Jeri. Please go to Mendocino. Find her, warn her."

Twenty-eight

SUNDAY, BEFORE LEAVING FOR MENDOCINO, I called Wayne Hobart at home. He hadn't yet received the information Richard Bradfield's parole officer was supposed to provide. I asked Wayne if he could find out whether Bradfield had worked while on parole, and if so, where.

Shortly before noon I ate a quick lunch and threw a change of clothes into my gray nylon overnight bag. After gassing up my Toyota, I headed for the freeway. The cassette tape I pushed into the maw of my dashboard player was the soundtrack to *American Graffiti*, my preferred road music. As the familiar voice of Bill Haley belted out the opening words to "Rock Around the Clock," I headed north on U.S. 101, singing along with Chuck Berry, Buddy Holly, and the Big Bopper for the next hundred miles, all the way to Cloverdale.

The little town, with less than six thousand population, lay just below the Sonoma-Mendocino county line, with Lake Sonoma to the west. Last time I was up here the U.S. 101 freeway ended at Cloverdale, but now the bypass had been constructed around town. I got off at the south end, where a sign read, WELCOME TO CLOVERDALE GATEWAY TO WARM SPRINGS DAM.

It wasn't the dam I was looking for. I stopped at the appropriately named Corner Deli for something to drink and asked to look at a phone book. The police and fire departments were located farther north, at the corner of Broad Street and North Cloverdale Boulevard. I parked out front, went inside, and gave the woman at the front desk my business card, asking if she'd call the chief of police at home and tell him I was in town. Half an hour later his big voice boomed at me as he pushed open the outer door.

"Jeri Howard, I'll be damned."

Joe Kelso looked older, grayer, and he'd put on some weight, but he didn't have the tired face and the worry lines I remembered from his days in Oakland Homicide, when he and Sid had worked together. He was more relaxed, his voice bantering.

I smiled at him. "I think retirement is agreeing with you, Joe."

He laughed. "Retirement? Is that what this is? Hell, Jeri, I'm just as busy as I ever was. Did you know some lowlife broke into Cloverdale Propane the other night? That's a crime wave around here."

"Beats Oakland, I take it."

"It does indeed." His face turned more serious. "I have maybe one murder a year. And I clear it. We get our share of domestic violence and thievery, of course. A little drug traffic here and there, mostly evil weed, but no drive-by shootings. Yeah, it beats the hell out of Oakland."

"How's Brenda?" I asked as he poured us each a cup of coffee and ushered me into his office. He shut the door and gave me a rundown on Brenda, his wife, and their children and grandchildren. We chatted for about half that cup of coffee, then I cleared my throat. "Joe, have you talked with Sid or Wayne lately?"

He cocked an eyebrow at me. "No. Should I?" I didn't answer right away. "Say, Jeri, I thought you were maybe heading up the coast for some rest and relaxation and just stopped to shoot the breeze. Is this business?"

"Sid's got an internal affairs situation," I told him.

"Sid Vernon?" Joe bellowed, slamming his fist against his desk. "No way. No way in hell. The man's straight as an arrow."

"It gets worse," I said. I sat back in the chair and told him what I knew and what I'd guessed.

"Bradfield," Joe said, the name leaving a bad taste in his mouth. "That son of a bitch. If only we'd been able to nail him for killing his wife. So Melissa Bradfield is Vicki Vernon's roommate. And Cordelia Ramsey lives in Mendocino now."

I nodded. "Melissa is now Emily Austen. Cordelia took the name Perdita Paxton. Paxton was her second husband's name. And she owns an art gallery, like before. That's the business she's been in for most of her adult life. But if Bradfield makes that connection, and remembers the second husband came from Mendocino, that means he could track her down. Emily says her aunt was due home Friday, but she hasn't been able to get Perdita on the phone. That's why I'm on my way up there."

Joe reached for the phone and a Rolodex full of cards. "The town of Mendocino's unincorporated. They don't have any police. For law enforcement they rely on the sheriff's station at Fort Bragg. I know a deputy up in Ukiah, the county seat. He can tell me who handles that part of the coast. I'll give Sid a holler too. You stay in touch, Jeri."

I used the rest room at the police station, then went back out to my car. Highway 128 led northwest, gaining elevation as I went over a series of slow-going switchbacks and left Sonoma County for Mendocino County. Now I was in steep forests of oak trees, twisting and

193

winding along the narrow two-lane asphalt with its double yellow line that indicated no passing. The road required concentration, and my slow speed frustrated the driver of a beat-up pickup, so I pulled over at one of the frequent turnouts to let him pass.

After he whizzed by me I saw a lumber truck barreling toward me from the opposite direction, hauling a load of huge redwood carcasses bleeding bark. As the truck went by, sucking wind, a bit of bark flew at my windshield, hitting the glass with a thump that left a red-brown mark. All along the road I saw distinctive bark, left here and there by the lumber trucks.

I caught up with the car ahead of me, then braked as I saw both its taillights and the familiar orange triangle that read ROAD WORK AHEAD. It was followed fifty yards or so by another that indicated we were entering a slide area. The spring rains had softened the soil under the pale green hillsides, sending a plume of dirt and gravel into the roadway. A CalTrans crew, all in orange coveralls and driving orange vehicles, was clearing away the debris. After a short wait the flagman waved us through.

The highway twisted and turned as it climbed, then descended and widened as I entered the Anderson Valley. Here they grew hops and sheep, and more recently apples and wine grapes. In the late nineteenth century the valley developed its own dialect, called Bootling, and some of it still survives, in and around the town of Boonville.

I slowed as I drove through Boonville, then picked up speed again and continued through vineyards toward Philo and Navarro. The road followed the North Fork of the Navarro River until it joined its southern counterpart and became simply the Navarro River, running wider and wider through a corridor of tall redwoods that created a tunnel of perpetual shadow, with the occasional shaft of sunlight dancing through the towering trees, dappling the road as it wound through the river canyon.

I pulled off the road at the campground, shut off the engine, and got out of my car to stretch my legs, listening to the quiet, marveling as I always did at the redwoods. They were mostly second growth, perhaps 125 years old. All the forests on this coast had been extensively logged in the last century, but some of the old-growth redwoods survived at Hendy Woods State Park, where a hundred acres of redwoods stretched over three hundred feet toward the sky.

A car went by on the highway. After it had gone I was alone in the dark woods, standing next to a cut-off stump wide enough to serve as the foundation for a small building, with only the rustling of leaves and ferns and the distant music of water over rocks as the Navarro River headed toward its destination. And I knew so must I. It was late afternoon and I wanted to get to Mendocino while it was still daylight.

I got back in my car and back onto the highway. The river widened with purpose, swollen with water from the spring rains, paralleling the highway. As I passed Hop Flat I saw the high water marks showing where the river had crested fifteen feet above this roadway in past floods. Now as the highway straightened out, the river was broad and tidal as it passed under the bridge looming on my left. Highway 128 ended here and the asphalt ribbon past that bridge became Highway 1, the Coast Highway.

The people who made the signs advising a twenty-mile speed limit weren't kidding. The steep climb offered some breathtaking views of the river as it joined the Pacific Ocean, but that was for passengers. All my attention was dedicated to making it around those curves without driving off the bluff. Finally, I rounded a curve and looked north at the spectacular Mendocino coast. It was eight more miles to Mendocino, over a grassy marine terrace, then inland through a tight curve, then up and down again, dropping to sea level at Little River.

Finally I saw Mendocino, across the bay, with the tower of the Presbyterian church rising to meet the coastal fog as it rolled toward the mouth of the Big River this spring evening. The headlands jut west into the Pacific Ocean, high bluffs licked on three sides by the restless waves, with the forests to the east.

This wild beautiful coast first knew Pomo Indians and Russian fur traders. Then the Gold Rush came, bringing more people to California and more demand for buildings to house them. Mendocino was founded in 1852, its enterprise the logging of the surrounding redwood forest. I'd seen old black and white photographs of loggers felling trees, with the resulting cut timber covering the flats of the Big River. These logs were hauled down to sea level by bull teams, loaded onto oceangoing vessels. But the last sawmill closed in 1938, and World War II lured residents from the coast. Isolated then as now by geography and the weather, Mendocino fell into neglect, its buildings boarded up and sagging. In the fifties and sixties the town slowly woke as artists moved in, their work filling the art center and the galleries. Now the summer and weekend visitors filled the bed and breakfast inns and ate at the town's restaurants.

Many of the logging men who came to Mendocino had been New Englanders, and they'd recreated the architecture they'd known back home. Most of the homes were built in the 1870s and 1880s, though some dated back earlier, and they were of that style of architecture we called Victorian. The other architectural feature of Mendocino was its distinctive water towers, necessitated by the town's low water table and perpetual water shortage.

These structures dotted the village, broad and square at the base and gradually narrowing at the top.

Since it was Sunday, I took a chance that the Joshua Grindle Inn on Little Lake Road might have a vacancy. The inn had one room available that night. I checked in and presented my credit card. The water tower here contained rooms instead of water. Mine was at the top of the tower, a little aerie with a tiny bathroom, toilet, sink and shower stall, windows on all four walls that slanted inward, and a skylight in the roof.

I'd stayed at this inn twice before, while I was married to Sid, on a couple of rare weekends away from our busy schedules. We'd shared one of the suites in the house itself, coming down to the breakfast room in the mornings to chat with fellow travelers over breakfast, sipping sherry in the parlor after dinner at one of the restaurants in the village.

Not this trip. I'd have this double bed with its white chenille bedspread to myself. I was here on business, not for pleasure, though just being in Mendocino was a pleasure to me. I set my overnight bag on the blue carpet at the foot of the bed and went into the tiny bathroom to use the toilet and wash my face and hands. Then I looked out the west-facing window, where the sun was heading down toward the marine layer, twilight covering the headlands, bringing with it fog and a breeze that ruffled the trees at the back of the inn.

But I didn't have time to linger and enjoy the view. I looked at my watch. Nearly five. I went outside and locked the door, then headed down the stairs that clung to the outside of the water tower.

Twenty-nine

PERDITA PAXTON HAD NAMED HER GALLERY Perdu, French for "lost." I wondered if her choice of names, for herself and her business, meant what I thought it did.

I angled the Toyota into a parking space midway on the block of Main Street between Lansing and Kasten. Perdu was near the Mendocino Hotel, located on a path that led from Mendocino's Main Street to Albion Street, not far from the entrance to the Kelley house, once a residence and now the village historical museum. Main Street had buildings on the north side only, unless one counted the old Ford house, now the interpretive center and museum for the Mendocino Headlands State Park.

I looked across the street and the grassy meadow criss-crossed with paths, toward Mendocino Bay. In the fading light I saw white foamed waves crashing on the bluffs to the south and the headlights of a car as it rounded the curve I had so recently traveled, heading onto the Big River bridge. A man and a woman passed me, holding hands, talking softly. I watched them walk toward the Mendocino Hotel, where they stopped to examine the menu posted outside the hotel restaurant.

I walked back between two shops to a small courtyard between the streets. Several businesses fronted on this plaza, with its flagstones and flowers. The gallery was on my left, up several shallow redwood steps and through double doors to a long narrow room built on three levels. I stepped inside, onto the middle level. Paintings and prints hung on the walls on either side of me. To my left, on the lower level, I saw a large abstract sculpture of a woman, constructed of terra-cotta. Grouped around this were low tables displaying pottery and ceramics, not crowded together, but several pieces distanced from the others, so that each had its own space. The same sort of motif was used on the upper level to my right, only the large piece was made of metal and looked like a bird. The smaller objects around it were polished wood, made of cherry, oak, and walnut.

Opposite the door I'd come through a long lighted case displayed jewelry that was more art than something to wear. The glittering metal and stones had prices to match. I saw no one in the gallery, but when I crossed the threshold, a low chime had sounded. Now the door behind the case opened and I faced a young woman, probably in her mid-twenties, with short dark hair and dark eyes, wearing a long black dress and high-laced boots. She looked at me and glanced discreetly at her watch.

"We're just closing," she said.

She had me there. It was now past five. But she hadn't locked the door yet.

"Are you Lee?"

"Yes," she said, managing to draw the one syllable into a long inquiry.

"I'm Jeri Howard. Emily Austen called to let you know I was coming."

"Yes, she did. But I don't understand why." Lee's eyes were curious. "Perdita sometimes takes longer for her buying trips than originally planned. But Emily seemed rather upset that Perdita wasn't here."

I looked at Perdita's employee. How much did she know about her employer's past? Very little, I suspected.

"It's probably nothing," I said. "But wouldn't Perdita call you if she was coming back late?"

"Well, usually she does," Lee admitted. "But she hasn't this time."

"Do you know where she went?"

"North. She didn't give me an itinerary."

"Has anyone else been in here looking for her recently?"

"You mean people I don't know?" In response to my nod, Lee shook her head and looked mystified. "Not that I know of. Is something wrong? I wish you'd tell me."

"I think it would be better if Perdita told you herself."

She looked disappointed, then shrugged and stepped from behind the counter, keys in hand. "I have to lock up now. If Perdita should call tonight, where are you staying?"

"The Joshua Grindle. But I have a cellular phone." I wrote that number on the back of one of my business cards and handed it to Lee. She activated the alarm system, then turned out the lights. Once outside, I waited while she locked up the gallery. Then she said good-bye and walked off in the direction of Albion Street. I went back to my car.

The house where Emily and her aunt had lived, until Emily went to college, was on the north side of the headland, off Heeser Drive, on a short street that dead-ended behind Mendocino's school. There were half a dozen or more homes on this meadow, all with spectacular views of the Pacific Ocean north from Agate Cove to Russian Gulch and beyond. Most were built of redwood, weathered silver by the elements. Two of them were larger versions of the town's ubiquitous water towers. One of these, farther west off the dirt road, was Perdita's. It was

200

three stories, and the topmost room, Emily told me, had been hers.

The light was fading as I parked my car and approached the house, which was larger than the water tower rooms at the inn. Here the stairs were inside, and there was a deck with a railing on three sides of the structure. The windows were covered with pleated horizontal shades that kept me from peering inside. I didn't see the Volvo Emily told me her aunt drove. I knocked on the door and called out, but got no response. All I could hear was the crash of waves on the bluffs behind me and the musical tinkling of a wind chime from one of the other houses nearby.

I scribbled a note on one of my business cards, stuck it into the crack of the door, and headed back to town. I had dinner at 955 Ukiah, seated alone at a table for two, sipping a glass of chardonnay and chatting with the owners' self-assured daughter, a girl of ten or twelve, who ate calamari with a side of capers and recommended several items on the menu.

When I left the restaurant I decided to check out the place next door, Sweetwater Gardens, which offered hot tubs and saunas. There was no time limit for the group tub, the young woman at the desk informed me, and clothing was optional.

It seemed like a Mendocino kind of thing to do. I bought a bottle of mineral water, rented a towel, and went into the communal dressing room to strip and shower. The tiny courtyard was surrounded by a high redwood fence, and the tub itself was up a few steps, one side open to the night. I saw two women there, talking as they relaxed in the water. I discarded my towel and joined them, luxuriating in the hot water, cooling myself down with sips from the cold mineral water.

On the ceiling above the tub I saw a stained-glass panel in deep blue, representing the night sky, with yellow stars and a yellow moon. I leaned my head back and looked at the real night sky, closer to black than blue, dusted with smaller sparkling dots of stars. Then the two women and I were joined by two men, one bearded, the other German. We politely ignored each other's nudity as we relaxed in the hot tub.

Finally all my mineral water was gone. I felt like a lazy boiled shrimp. I clambered out of the tub and showered off the bromine from the water, then walked back to the inn, where I fell into a deep sleep under the white chenille bedspread in my little tower room.

I woke early the next morning, just past seven, craving coffee, but the inn didn't serve breakfast until after eight. Once dressed, I set out for a walk. The headlands were shrouded with fog this morning, cottony billows obscuring the roofs and the water towers of the village. I walked down Little Lake Road toward Lansing Street and climbed several concrete steps into Hillcrest Cemetery.

Old cemeteries fascinate me. The gravestones reveal something about the people who built a town, where they came from, at least. In this cemetery a lot of people came from Ireland, Italy, and the Azores, and there were lots of members of the same families all buried together. I knew at one time there had been a sizable Chinese population here. In fact, farther out on Albion Street was an old Chinese temple, the oldest on the north coast. But there were no Chinese graves here that I could see.

Interspersed with the older graves I saw more recent ones and located several Paxtons, presumably the family of Perdita's second husband. Was he buried here? I couldn't recall the man's name. At the top of the hill I saw a tall redwood cross and a lovingly tended plot covered with bright spring flowers. Here lay a boy of thirteen, not long in his grave, and very much missed, from what I saw. Others in this cemetery had no one left to tend their graves, like the woman farther down the hill. The rusted remains of an iron fence that once decorated her chipped and leaning headstone were now piled on the weedy site.

A few paces away I found two stones side by side, both broken off and lying atop the graves they marked, with the stubs of marble at the head of the graves looking like broken teeth. They were the McCartie brothers, John and Jeremiah, and one of them had died in 1876. Weather and time had softened and blurred the words carved on the broken stones, but I could see enough to tell me Jeremiah McCartie had been shot to death in Mendocino. Who was he, and how did he come to that fate here on the rugged coast, such a long way from his birthplace in Ireland?

I left the cemetery and walked up Lansing, past St. Anthony's Catholic Church, to Heeser Drive, where I turned left and headed in the direction of Perdita's house, past the sign that warned me this was a private road. Several of her neighbors were home. In fact, one man looked at me curiously as he exited his house and walked toward his truck. I saw nothing at Perdita's house that would indicate anyone was there. My business card was still stuck in the door.

My stomach growled, despite the big meal I'd had last night, so I walked back to the inn, where coffee and breakfast were now being served in the dining room. I helped myself to fruit and yogurt, frittata and muffins, as the assembled guests did the usual check-in with one another. None of the inn's rooms had phones, so after breakfast I used my cellular phone to call Joe Kelso at the Cloverdale police station. He wasn't in, but the officer I spoke with told me he was fairly certain Joe had made that phone call to Ukiah.

I checked out and headed for Main Street. I was in the

courtyard between Main and Albion at ten, speculating whether the fog would burn off by noon and waiting for Lee to show up to unlock the doors. Today she wore a long gray skirt and an oversize burgundy sweater, her neck and shoulders swathed with a woolen shawl and a matching cap covering her dark hair.

"She didn't call," Lee said as she unlocked the door. She looked somewhat taken aback to find me on the gallery's steps. She also looked worried. "It's not like Perdita not to check in."

Where the hell was Perdita Paxton? I felt frustrated as I retraced my steps to Main Street. Should I drive up to the sheriff's station in Fort Bragg?

Deciding to wait a couple more hours, I walked all the way down to the end of Main Street and onto one of the paths that threaded the grassy headlands, making my way down to the edge of the bluff where several large pieces of rusted metal and wood were all that remained of the chutes used to load cargo from the bluff to the old dog-hole schooners that sailed this coastline, with shallows and rocks and shifting sandbars, tackling the bad currents and worse weather. Large wharves were impossible in Mendocino Bay, so the lumber was loaded by means of an apron chute, a wooden slide running from the bluff to the deck of the ship. At the turn of the century they were replaced by wire chutes using heavy cable, and passengers disembarking from a ship would ride a large trapeze to shore.

At the end of the headland I looked down on the beach where the winter storms had tossed up piles of driftwood. In one inlet a tire floated near an overhang, debris of a less picturesque sort. The rocky sides of the bluffs below me had been polished and smoothed by the incessant waves. They were dangerous, prey to the sneaker waves that could rise suddenly to snatch unwary humans from the rocks. There are several natural bridges at the end of the headland, graceful arches carved by a millennium of wave action, water insinuating itself into the rock, smoothing and polishing, like a fickle hand that has toyed with the land over hundreds of thousands of years, and will for thousands more, until the arch weakens and falls into the sea.

I stood at the end of the bluff and looked west, out at the gray Pacific Ocean, conscious that there was nothing between me and Japan, nothing but several thousand miles of cold, heaving water. Then I walked all the way around the headland, back to Perdita's house, stepping onto the redwood deck. I knocked at the door, then circled the house.

I heard the sound of car tires on gravel and walked back to the front of the house, hoping to see Perdita Paxton's Volvo. Instead I saw a white sedan, its driver's side door bearing the wave and redwood crest of the Mendocino County Sheriff's Department. The man who opened the door was about my age, six feet tall, with sandy hair and a clean-shaven face. He wore a short-sleeve brown shirt decorated with a seven-point star, green fatigue pants, and a gun strapped at his side. He put his hands on his hips and surveyed me from Perdita Paxton's driveway.

"Hello." His voice was friendly, noncommittal, but there was definitely an official inquiry behind it, as though he were debating whether to run me in for trespassing. "I'm Sergeant Sullivan. Mind telling me what you're doing here?" One of Perdita's neighbors who'd seen me at the house last night or earlier today must have called the sheriff's station in Fort Bragg.

"My name's Jeri Howard." I walked toward him, keeping my hands in the open where he could see them. When I got close enough I saw freckles dusting his cheeks, making him look younger than he was. "I'm a private investigator from Oakland. I'm trying to locate Perdita Paxton."

"Got some identification?"

"In my purse." I reached slowly and brought out my license, handing it to him. "Joe Kelso of the Cloverdale Police Department was supposed to call your office in Ukiah, to let them know I was coming up here."

Sullivan didn't say anything as he examined my license. Then he reached into the cruiser for his radio. I heard enough of his side of the conversation to confirm that someone had indeed called the sheriff's station to report me. Finally he ended the transmission and returned my license.

"Kelso called," he said. "Early this morning. But I didn't get the word until now. I've been out in the field. So tell me what this is about."

Before I could say anything, a Volvo turned off Heeser Drive and came up the road, raising a cloud of dust. It pulled into the driveway next to the cruiser. A woman opened the door and got out, a tall woman whose hair had once been a rich dark red. Now the shoulder-length locks were as gray as the silvered lumber used in constructing her house. An Airedale terrier, female, scrambled out of the car, stopped, took a protective stance, and barked a warning.

"Steady on, Molly," the woman said, in the deep raspy voice I remembered so well. She looked regal despite the navy-blue sweat suit she wore, its dark blue color enlivened only by the yellow and red scarf tied loosely around her neck. I saw the same hawk profile, the same sharp gray eyes. Now she addressed the sergeant. "Hello, Neil. What's going on here?"

"This woman says she's a private investigator," the sergeant began.

Now the gray eyes narrowed and scrutinized me closer. "Of course. I recognize you now. Jeri Howard. You worked for the Errol Seville Agency. How's Errol? Are you still with him?"

"Errol retired. He and his wife moved to Carmel. I'm on my own now."

Perdita Paxton smiled briefly and crossed her arms over the front of her sweatshirt. "I assume you haven't dropped by to see me just because you're in the neighborhood."

"Emily sent me. She couldn't get you on the phone, so she got worried."

"I went out of town for a few days." Now she frowned. "Why is Emily so anxious to find me?"

"Richard Bradfield is out of prison," I told her.

Her mouth tightened and her eyes hardened into two gray stones.

"Bloody hell."

Thirty

"IS THAT THE GUY?" SERGEANT SULLIVAN ASKED.

"Yes, it is," Perdita said.

"Guess I need to hear about this."

"Indeed you do. Come inside. I'll make some coffee."

Perdita opened the back door of her Volvo and reached inside for a small black overnighter. Then she walked past me and the deputy, up onto the deck. She sifted through her keys, stuck one into the dead bolt, and opened the door.

The Airedale preceded us into one large space that was both living room and dining room, the floor covered with a thick cushiony oatmeal-colored carpet. The dog made for the large front window, immediately to our right. Beneath this was a small green area rug, frayed at the edges and covered with wisps of black and copper fur. The dog circled, then sprawled on the rug. Perdita set down the bag she carried and opened the pleated ivory blinds that shaded the window, revealing a vista of grassy headlands and the Pacific Ocean, stretching into the blue sky now that the fog had burned off. To the right a series of headlands and pine-covered slopes swept north toward Fort Bragg.

"May I use the phone?" Sergeant Sullivan asked her.

"Help yourself. It's on the desk." She picked up her bag. "I'll take this upstairs and be right back."

She started up the carpeted stairs, just this side of the

far right corner of the room. In the corner itself was the desk she'd pointed out to the sergeant, tucked under the slanting ceiling below the stairs that climbed to the upper floors. The desk looked like oak, with a matching two-drawer filing cabinet, its top serving as a stand for the small laser printer. One end of the desk held a laptop computer. At the other I saw a cordless phone and a small answering machine, its red light blinking furiously from what must have been all of Emily's calls.

The sergeant sat down in the padded blue office chair and picked up the phone. While he talked I had a look around. The sofa, low and contemporary in design, angled in front of the window, with low tables on either side holding pottery and an assortment of books. Behind this a small rectangular table, made of polished wood, with two woven place mats, sat in the rear left corner, with several tall bookcases on the wall that was to the left of the front door. The kitchen was at the back, between the stairs and the dining table, a compact walk-through space with white appliances. Beyond this I saw a small utility room, the off-shoot I'd seen jutting from the back of the structure. The room contained a washer, dryer, storage cabinets, and a tiny bathroom visible through an open pocket door.

The place was a marvel of economic and utilitarian design and looked almost monastic, with little decoration, save a couple of prints on the wall and a photograph of Emily on one of the bookshelves. Perdita evidently left the objets d'art at her gallery and lived here, solitary except for the company of her dog.

She came back down the stairs now and walked into the kitchen, where she took a bag of coffee from the freezer, spooned grounds into the filter of her coffee maker and poured in the water.

"Emily says you built this place when you moved up here."

"Yes. My second husband owned the land. We had intended to build a vacation home. The house where he grew up is in the village. But he hadn't lived there since he left for college. After his mother died, we sold it. It's a bed and breakfast inn now."

"A beautiful view." I gestured toward the window.

"Yes," she agreed, looking past me at the light shifting on the constantly moving surface of the Pacific Ocean. "Emily loves it here."

"But you don't."

"It's quiet and isolated. Much too quiet and isolated, since Emily went off to college." Perdita stopped. We listened to the water and steam of the coffee maker. The strong smell of fresh-brewed coffee filled the room.

"It made sense at the time," she continued. "After everything that happened, I wanted to get away from people. The simplicity of small-town life, a good environment for Emily. Just the two of us, safe from the world outside."

"Safe," I repeated. I wasn't sure any of us were safe. "Does Bradfield know about your ties to Mendocino?"

"Maybe. My sister may have told him. Bradfield's a very clever man. That's how he's been able to get away with so much for so long. I'd say we must assume he knows my second husband was from Mendocino, though Mike and I lived in Mill Valley all the time we were married. Mike died ten years ago, two years before Bradfield killed Stephanie."

She looked past me at Sergeant Sullivan. "I'm sure you've heard that old saying. Just because you're paranoid doesn't mean they're not out to get you. That's why my neighbors and the Mendocino Sheriff's Department are particularly diligent about keeping an eye on me and my property."

210

The sergeant hung up the phone. Perdita opened a cupboard, took out three red ceramic mugs, and poured coffee into each. "I know you laid it out for the sheriff when you moved up here," Sullivan said as he stood up and moved toward the kitchen. "That was before I took over this territory, but I've seen the file. I guess Ms. Howard better bring us up to date."

"Absolutely," Perdita said. She handed both of us a mug and picked up her own, gesturing toward the sofa that faced the ocean. "Why wasn't I notified that he was up for parole? Wasn't I entitled to give a statement at his hearing?"

"Yes," I said, even as the officer nodded. "But I can guess why you weren't contacted. You've buried yourself deep up here, with the name change."

I took a seat at the end of the sofa. Sergeant Sullivan remained standing. Perdita sat down at the other end of the sofa, leaned forward, and shook her head. "The Marin County D.A. knew where to find me."

"They may have had some personnel changes," Sullivan said. "Right hand not knowing what the left hand is doing."

I nodded. "And Emily tells me you've done some traveling since she graduated from high school."

"Yes. I went to Egypt last year. I wanted to see the pyramids before I got too much older. So it's possible someone tried to contact me and I was gone. And the last few days I've been driving all over Northern California with a friend who's an antique dealer. A buying trip, an excuse to get away. We were gone longer than we planned. But why are you here, Jeri? It's not only to tell me about Bradfield being out of prison. How did you find out? What's going on?"

"I got into this matter because of something that happened at the house where Emily lives. Maybe coinci-

211

dence, maybe not. I didn't realize until a few days ago that Emily was Melissa Bradfield. Then it all started to make sense."

"You better back up," Sullivan said, taking out a notebook. "Start at the beginning."

I told them everything that had happened since the day Vicki Vernon called to tell me about the plants, and all that I'd learned about the events leading up to that incident.

"Damn it," Perdita said, scowling, when I'd finished. "Why didn't Emily tell me any of this?"

"I don't think she was sure it was her father, not until the lemon tree. As I've discovered in my investigation so far, there are several people with reasons to harass Emily's housemates. All of the people living there have experienced problems." I took a sip of coffee. "Everything that's happened has Bradfield's fingerprints all over it. My guess is that he's decided to go after every one of us who had anything to do with putting him behind bars. And we both know that you are high on that list."

Perdita laughed grimly. "Probably the number one spot. If he's out of prison, I'm sure he'll come after me."

"He certainly found Emily," I said. "I'm not sure how he found Vicki Vernon, but he was paroled to San Diego. That's where she grew up. Sid's still at the Oakland Police Department, simple to locate. As for me, I'm in the phone book. It would have been easy for Bradfield to discover that Errol retired and moved to Carmel."

"So you think this guy Bradfield will head up to Mendocino, once he figures out Ms. Paxton is here?" Sullivan grimaced as he looked up from his note taking. "I don't think we can provide you with round-the-clock protection. I'll have to check with my boss."

"I'll be fine," Perdita assured us, a determined look on her face. "I've got the dog. And a gun I know how to use.

212

I'll call my friend in Fort Bragg. He'll come and stay with me."

"I'd prefer to catch Bradfield before it gets to that point," I said.

Sullivan seconded me. "So would I."

Thirty-one

WHEN SERGEANT SULLIVAN LEFT, PERDITA called Emily in Berkeley. After a long talk with her niece, she offered me crackers, cheese, and fruit, washed down with a mellow zinfandel from an Anderson Valley winery. We sat at the small dining room table, where a narrow window looked out on the stand of pine trees at the back of her property. On the slope above I saw the back of one of the Mendocino school buildings.

"My friend's coming down from Fort Bragg later, for a late lunch. I don't cook much," she said. "I never did. Emily was the chef around here."

"Why 'lost'?" I asked, giving voice to the question I'd had since I found out she named her gallery Perdu, and herself Perdita. "Emily Austen I can understand. She's an English major, so she chose two of her favorite authors. Lost . . . well, lost I can guess."

A smile softened Perdita's face. "Emily Dickinson and Jane Austen. Those two helped a very troubled, frightened little girl escape the demons. I told you she loved it here. She needed the small-town atmosphere, a place where you know all your neighbors. I worried about her going to Cal, with that big campus and the crazy Berkeley scene. I'm glad she moved into that house. Emily likes the people there. I met them last December, right before Emily and I went to Hawaii over the holidays. I like Vicki especially. I'm pleased she and Emily have gotten to be close friends. Emily needs that."

I nodded. "They seem to have meshed."

"Why lost, you ask," Perdita continued. "It's simple. I lost the life I had, the life I loved. I miss that life, terribly." She paused as she raised her wineglass to her lips. "I miss having season tickets to the American Conservatory Theatre, the ballet, the symphony, the opera. I miss the museums and the galleries."

"But Mendocino has the arts," I said. "In smaller measure, I grant you. Besides . . ." I waved my hand in the direction of the big front window and the sweeping view of the ocean. "There's the land and the ocean."

"Oh, I know, Mendocino's one of the most beautiful spots on earth. There's something about the land up here that draws one. And I know I can go over to the art center and see a play." She shook her head, her words wry. "But it's not the same. It's not for me. I knew that the first time I saw this place, back before the tourists and the inns and the restaurants. The artists had just started moving up here when I met Mike Paxton, and he brought me up here to meet his family. Most of those buildings on Main Street were boarded up or falling down."

She sipped her wine again, remembering. "Mike's dad hadn't worked in months. He'd been laid off from the lumber mill up in Fort Bragg. His mother took in washing to make ends meet. Mike didn't want to live here either, not permanently, anyway. He'd gone to school to be an architect. There aren't many jobs up here for people in that field. He found a job in San Francisco and later we bought the house in Mill Valley. But he felt the pull of this Mendocino coast. I suppose someone who is born here always does."

"Did you come up here often?"

"Oh, yes. On weekends, holidays, to be with Mike's

family. They were rather close-knit, while the parents were alive. They thought I was somewhat avant-garde because I kept my birth name, before it was fashionable." She laughed. "Mike's sisters married men who lived in other states, then his father and mother died and the house was sold. We still came up here frequently, staying in one of the inns, or with friends. I've always been interested in the art scene up here. I'd look for new artists, buy things for my gallery in Mill Valley. We'd just bought the property and Mike was designing this house when he had his heart attack. I put those plans away until I left the Bay Area. Then I built the house, just the way he designed it. For two people. Only it was me and Emily instead of me and Mike."

She pushed away her chair and carried her plate to the kitchen, returning with the bottle of wine. She offered it to me, but I declined. Then she poured herself another glass.

"I'm still angry," she said. "About losing my life. It was something I had to do for Emily and I understood that. But I owned that gallery for a long time. It filled a space when Mike died. My gallery was well known, respected. I had the contacts, the connections. That life was important to me. It represented a time when control, autonomy, held a place in my world. I pulled my own strings."

She raised the glass to her lips and drank, a bitter expression on her face, as though the wine had gone bad. "But all that was lost when Richard Bradfield murdered my sister."

"You have a gallery here," I reminded her.

"Yes." She put down the wineglass. "And I need to go there, before I consume the rest of this wine and get even more maudlin. Did you drive over here?"

I shook my head. "I left my car parked over on Ukiah

Street. After I went to the gallery this morning, I walked. I've prowled every path on the headlands, waiting for you to show up. I spent last night at the Joshua Grindle Inn and planned to drive back this afternoon."

She glanced at her watch. "Wait a bit and have lunch with me and my friend. I'd like you to meet him." She stood up and headed for the kitchen.

"Sounds good to me," I agreed. "Let me make a few phone calls first."

I checked in with Wayne Hobart, Rita Lydecker, and Joe Kelso, letting them know I'd located Perdita and warned her that Bradfield was probably looking for her. Then Perdita, the dog, and I piled into the Volvo and headed for the village. Lee looked relieved when Perdita and I entered the gallery, carrying cardboard cartons that had been in the trunk of her Volvo. Molly was at our heels and she trotted through the gallery, straight for Perdita's office.

"I'm so glad you're back," Lee said. "Emily is looking for you, this woman is looking for you."

"It's all right, Lee. I've talked with Emily. You've met Jeri Howard." Perdita set her carton on the floor and I did the same.

"There are some messages on your desk. What have you got there?" Lee indicated the box.

"I found the most marvelous pottery," Perdita said, tossing words over her shoulder as she opened the door behind the counter that led to her office. "Up in Dos Rios, of all places. It is out in the middle of absolutely nowhere, but this woman's work is terrific. I've got a couple of small pieces with me, and I took some photographs of the rest. I asked her to put together a portfolio." Perdita sat down at her desk and picked up several small yellow sheets torn from a message pad.

Lee opened the box and took out an elongated vase

fired in dark blues and grays, with touches of red and rust on its length. She made appropriate noises that indicated she agreed with Perdita's assessment of the potter's work and set the vase on the glass counter. The second piece was squat, in the same general colors.

After Perdita had made her phone calls, she and Lee hauled out the gallery's record book and entered information concerning the potter and the two pieces Perdita had bought. "I'll price them later this afternoon," Perdita said, consulting her watch. "Tom should be here in about twenty minutes. Come on, Jeri, let's take Molly for a walk before he gets here."

Molly keyed on the word "walk" and headed for the door of the gallery, waiting expectantly for Perdita to open it. Perdita snapped a well-worn leather lead onto the dog's collar and we set out along Main Street, heading toward the ocean. The afternoon sun blurred as it slipped behind the layer of fog hugging the Pacific. Once we'd left the pavement for the path leading onto the headlands, Perdita released the dog. Molly woofed and raced through the grass, pursuing something only she could see.

"Tom's your friend from Fort Bragg," I said. "Does he know?"

"That I'm Cordelia Ramsey, a woman with a past?" Perdita laughed, then shook her head. "No. I didn't burden him with my baggage. I saw no need to give him the details. To him, I'm Perdita, a widow, raising a niece, running an art gallery. That's all he needs for now."

As we caught up with the Airedale, Perdita told me more about Tom Jeffries. He was a widower, a retired businessman from the Los Angeles basin who'd moved to the north coast last year to open an antique store in Fort Bragg. In addition to old furniture, Jeffries was interested in art. He and Perdita met last fall at a Mendocino Arts Center reception.

Molly romped toward us, then sprawled in the dust path, panting. "Had enough, old girl?" Perdita asked. The dog barked and got to her feet. Perdita snapped the lead onto Molly's collar. We turned back and headed toward Main Street.

"I was thinking of Bradfield's assistant," Perdita said.

"So was I." When I'd reviewed the Seville Agency file a few days ago it occurred to me that the employee who'd provided Bradfield's alibi for the night of the murder might be in danger. And not because the alibi was ever shaken.

A bird broke cover in the bushes ahead and Molly barked furiously, straining at her lead. ". . . lying, of course," Perdita said, partly drowned out by the clamor. "Bradfield killed Stephanie, there's no doubt in my mind. But that testimony about the penny stock scam . . ."

"Could earn a spot on Bradfield's enemies list," I finished. The D.A. in the fraud trial had elicited some damaging information from Bradfield's loyal assistant.

As we walked along the sidewalk toward the Mendocino Hotel, a boxy vehicle that turned out to be a Land Rover angled into a parking spot next to Perdita's Volvo. A man got out, tall, lean, and silver-haired, wearing a red flannel shirt under a corduroy jacket, blue jeans, and boots. He looked comfortable, sure of himself, equally at home in a business suit or this more informal attire.

Molly barked once and Perdita unclasped the lead. The dog ran to greet the man, her stubby Airedale tail wagging with affection. He leaned down and ruffled the dog's ears, then straightened as Perdita and I approached. When Perdita stopped beside him, he leaned over and kissed her on the cheek. Then he looked at me with brown eyes in a tanned, lined face and stuck out his hand. "Tom Jeffries," he said. "Call me Tom."

"Jeri Howard." I shook his hand. He was in his late

fifties, I guessed, a little early for retirement. But maybe he'd wanted to retire while he was still vigorous enough to enjoy it.

"You two hungry?" Jeffries asked.

"Ravenous." Perdita put her arm around his waist. "Let's stash Molly at the gallery and head up to the Bay View Café."

"Good thing you live in a town with restaurants," he told her affectionately. "Otherwise you might have to learn to cook."

"Perish the thought." Perdita gave a mock shudder as she led the way toward the courtyard. I followed, feeling like the third wheel on a two-wheel bicycle, my mind already racing ahead as I thought of what I needed to do when I got back to the Bay Area.

Thirty-two

"HAVE YOU FOUND OUT ANY DETAILS ABOUT Bradfield's parole?" I asked Wayne.

It was early Tuesday morning. I'd returned from Mendocino the night before, checking in with Emily and the other Garber Street residents before going home to my empty apartment in Oakland. They'd had no phone calls for several days, which alarmed Emily. She was quite sure her father had gone up to Mendocino after her aunt. I thought it more likely that the caller—who was probably Bradfield—was letting all of us stew before he made his next move.

When he'd answered the phone, Wayne reported that Sid was in good spirits, despite the internal affairs investigation. The media interest had cooled because the reporters' attention had been drawn to a nasty political battle between the Port of Oakland and the City Council. Macauley's parents had backed off their accusations once the news about their son's bomb escapade in high school had come to light. And yes, Ted Macauley was still missing.

Now Wayne gave me the details he'd gleaned from a long talk with a friend in the San Diego Police Department. "Bradfield cleaned offices during his parole. He worked for a company down there, name of San Diego County Cleaners. They contract janitorial services with various businesses. When I talked with Bradfield's parole officer last Friday, he told me the guy stayed out of trouble, reported in regular. But as soon as he finished his year, he quit the job. Didn't even give notice, according to his supervisor. Drew his last paycheck, closed his bank account, left town. He'd been living in a studio apartment in North Park. Landlord says Bradfield just cleared out with no warning. Left the keys in his mailbox and didn't collect his deposit."

"Sounds like he had someplace he needed to be," I said. Was that location the Bay Area? So Bradfield could start harassing the inhabitants of the Garber Street house?

"Guess so," Wayne said. "He's a private citizen now, so he doesn't have to check in with anyone. The bottom line, nobody knows where Richard Bradfield is."

"What about transportation? Surely he must have had a car."

"He did in December but he doesn't anymore, at least not the same one. My pal in San Diego ran a check on the vehicle. It turned up in a used car lot down in Garden Grove. Been there since January. Say, Jeri, my friend faxed me a picture of Bradfield. It's not the greatest, but it's fairly recent. Want me to fax it to you?"

"Thanks, Wayne. I'd like to know what he looks like now, in case I come face-to-face with the guy." I was ready to hang up the phone, then something else that had been at the back of my mind reasserted itself. "What about Sam Kacherian, Bradfield's partner in the stock scam? I know he went to prison, just like Bradfield. He must be out too. Maybe he could give us a line on Bradfield."

"Good thought," Wayne said. "I'll see what I can find out."

I rang off. A moment later the fax machine began

humming. I leaned over to watch the telecopied photograph of Richard Bradfield take shape. The black and white fax couldn't tell me if his brown hair was showing some gray, but it was a fair likeness of the man I remembered. The square face showed some lines that hadn't been there before, and there were bags under the eyes and a hint of a jowl at the jawline.

I used my fax machine to make several copies of Bradfield's image, then I logged onto my computer. I dialed up a database on California corporations. San Diego County Cleaners was located in downtown San Diego, but I discovered that it in turn was owned by a company called Belston Enterprises. In fact, Belston, which was headquartered in Santa Ana, down in Orange County, owned a number of similar companies all over Southern California.

Garden Grove was in Orange County, I recalled, glancing at the notes I'd made during my conversation with Wayne. And it wasn't far from Santa Ana. In fact, if memory served, Garden Grove was where he'd grown up.

I printed out the information on Belston Enterprises. Then I picked up the phone and called Errol Seville's number in Carmel, guessing he was out of the hospital by now. He had in fact been released the day before. He sounded chipper for a seventyish man who'd been mugged a few days before. I gave him an update of the situation.

"It seems to me," Errol said slowly when I'd finished, "that Sam Kacherian is dead."

"How in the world would you know that?"

Errol thought for a moment. "You know, I think I read something in the newspaper. Not here, though. Let's see . . . It must have been the San Fernando Valley newspaper. Minna and I were down in Woodland Hills a couple of months ago, visiting friends. Kacherian lived in Encino before he got caught with both hands in the till. I think his wife divorced him. She may still live there. Tell you what. I'll make a few phone calls."

"I'd appreciate whatever you can dig up. One other thing, Errol. What happened to Bradfield's assistant?"

He thought for a moment. "Haskell? I don't know. Nothing in the files?"

"Not that I could see. Nothing after the stalking trial. I'll have to dig deeper."

I pulled the Bradfield file from the box, hoping to review it again later in the day. But I had several other cases demanding my attention, particularly since I'd been gone for nearly two days. I turned my attention to paperwork, a trip to the courthouse, and an appointment with an attorney on Harrison Street. Shortly after three I detoured to Berkeley and found Sasha at home on Garber Street. The bombed-out living room looked bare and clean, the sofa having been removed and the debris swept out.

"I'm waiting for my insurance company to come through so I can plaster and paint," Sasha told me as she conducted me to the kitchen. "They're not quite sure how to categorize a pipe bomb."

Vicki and Emily had just come home from class and were raiding the refrigerator for provisions to tide them over during a planned study session. "I have something I want to show you," I told Vicki, opening the flap of the manila envelope I carried. "It's a copy of a photograph."

Emily looked at me and the envelope, her mouth tightening as she guessed the subject of the picture. "Don't show me. I don't want to see."

My hand stopped and I looked into her troubled blue eyes. "You don't have to."

"Come on, Emily." Sasha put her arm around her tenant. "Let's go for a walk. Martin should be coming

224

home from school any minute, and I told him I'd meet him at the corner."

"She's pretty freaked out by all of this," Vicki said after they'd gone. "Guilt tripping, says it's all her fault. If I were gonna be some big deal psychologist, I'd say she thinks she should have been able to save her mother."

"We could speculate about that sort of thing all night." I pulled the photocopied picture of Richard Bradfield from the envelope and handed it to Vicki. "Take a good look. Have you ever seen this man before?"

Vicki held the picture between thumb and forefinger, shifting slightly for a better light. She narrowed her eyes and studied the likeness. "He looks familiar," she said finally. After another pause, she shook her head. "But I couldn't say where I saw him."

"Do me a favor," I said as I slipped the picture back into the envelope. "Call your stepfather in San Diego. Ask him to find out who does the janitorial work in the building where he has his dental office."

"One of the janitors? That could be it. I worked there all summer, sometimes late. I'll make the call right now."

Vicki went upstairs in search of her address book, returning just as Rachel came home from class. "We had another demonstration at the clinic today," she told me. "But that guy—Wellette—he wasn't there. Maybe that Berkeley cop scared him off."

"Could be. The guy's got a record."

Rachel opened the refrigerator, looking for sustenance, while Vicki punched in a number. Her stepfather was busy with a client, but the dental office manager looked up the information for her. Then Vicki hung up the phone and turned to me.

"Is San Diego County Cleaners the right answer?"

I thought it was the right answer, I told myself as I

drove back to Oakland. At least to a portion of the mystery.

Vicki's stepfather had his dental practice in a building in San Diego's Hillcrest district, not far from the janitorial firm's downtown address, or from the location of the apartment where Bradfield lived during his parole. If Bradfield was part of the crew cleaning that building, that could explain how he might have encountered Vicki. As for how he keyed in on the fact that she was Sid Vernon's daughter, perhaps he'd overheard someone say her name.

The phone was ringing as I unlocked my office door. I snatched up the receiver before the answering machine picked up the call. On the other end of the line was Brad Nguyen at the Berkeley Police Department.

"Ted Macauley's car turned up," he said, "with bomb paraphernalia in the trunk."

Nguyen told me Macauley's red Oldsmobile Cutlass had been abandoned in a cul-de-sac off Centennial Drive, up by the University Botanical Gardens. No one knew how long the car had been there, but since Macauley's disappearance, a description and plate number had been out on the computer. Finally someone noticed the car and reported it earlier that day. The site, in the hills above U.C. Berkeley, was close enough to campus that whoever had abandoned the car could have hiked down.

"When we popped the trunk we found a length of pipe, some fuse, and some caps. Some black powder residue as well."

"Fingerprints?" I asked.

"I'll let you know as soon as I get the report. I hope when the press gets hold of this we can turn up a witness who saw the car being ditched."

Nguyen's news added another variable to the debate.

Having discovered the possible hand of Richard Bradfield in what was going on, I was reluctant to return to
Ted Macauley as instigator. He'd receded from his
former position of best suspect, in my personal lineup
anyway.

It was true the college student had the knowledge necessary to build the bomb. He drove a red car, like the one
that had been seen on Garber Street right before the
explosion. And he'd been acting oddly before the explosion and his disappearance. Witness his bailing out on his
date with Lisa Spaulding the night Sid and I had shown
up at his apartment.

Suddenly I recalled what Macauley's roommate Dave
told me, about the older man who'd shown up at the
apartment a week earlier, looking for Ted. Sandy hair
going gray, Dave had said. And he'd thought the man
looked like Ted.

I dug out the Oakland *Tribune* story I'd clipped for my
file, about Ted Macauley's disappearance and the complaint against Sid. A photograph of Macauley had accompanied the article, small and a couple of years old. I
compared it with the photocopied picture of Bradfield that
Wayne had faxed to me. The only similarity I could see
was the shape of the face, but neither likeness was good.

Was I reading too much into this, seeing the black
hand of Richard Bradfield everywhere I looked?

The phone rang again. This time it was Errol.

"Sam Kacherian is indeed dead," he said. "He committed suicide. At least that's the way it looks. I called an
old friend of mine, down in L.A. I was right about seeing
Kacherian's name in the newspaper when Minna and I
were in Woodland Hills. It was just after the New Year,
the first week in January."

Errol gave me what information he had obtained from
his friend. Kacherian had been paroled to Orange County

last year, about the same time Bradfield was paroled to San Diego County. Kacherian had worked at a number of jobs during that time and had been laid off from the last one, a few days before he was found in his Tustin apartment, dead of a single gunshot to the head. The gun, an unregistered .38 caliber, was in Kacherian's right hand. Tests showed residue on that hand, indicating the dead man had fired the weapon.

An apparent suicide, despite the lack of a note. At least, that's how the local police were treating it.

Kacherian had reason enough to kill himself, I supposed. He was out of work, alone, since, as Errol had said when we'd talked earlier in the day, Kacherian's wife had divorced him after his arrest. He'd come a long way down the ladder from the days when he was the president of Kacherian Manufacturing, with a factory and offices near the Los Angeles airport and a big house in Encino.

"What sort of jobs was he working at?" I asked. Errol didn't know, but his L.A. contact was supposed to dig up some more information. I thought of Bradfield's car turning up in that lot in Garden Grove, which wasn't far from Tustin either. I couldn't help wondering if Richard Bradfield had been anywhere near Tustin when Sam Kacherian died.

"Any luck with Haskell, Bradfield's assistant?" Errol asked.

I looked at the Errol Seville Agency file, which I'd hauled out of the box a few hours earlier. "That's next on my to-do list."

Thirty-three

IT HAD BEEN SIX YEARS SINCE HASKELL'S DAYS in court, forced on the point of a subpoena.

Tuesday evening, after talking with Errol, I refreshed my memory of Richard Bradfield's assistant by going back through the old files. Of course, I remembered Haskell quite well. One of my jobs on the investigative team had been to take a look at Bradfield's alibi for the night of his wife's murder.

The alibi had blond hair, brown eyes, and a little birthmark just to the left of her full lips. Her tall slender figure and long legs looked terrific in the successful career woman suits she always wore. I'd always thought her looks were what got her hired. Her employment record certainly wasn't that remarkable.

Andi Haskell was about twenty-five when, after a succession of office jobs, she went to work for Bradfield Investments as the boss's administrative assistant. Sometime after that their relationship expanded to include the bedroom as well as the office. She was twenty-eight the night her lover's wife bled to death in the Colton Avenue house.

The day Stephanie Bradfield was murdered, her husband and his assistant drove down to Pebble Beach, a journey of approximately two and a half hours. Ostensibly they were there to meet with a new client, a retired general who lived in a big house on Seventeen Mile Drive. As it turned out, the meeting with the client appeared to be a smoke screen to disguise Bradfield's meeting with Sam Kacherian, who just happened to be in Pebble Beach that day.

If Bradfield and his stock scam accomplice ran into each other on the putting green, who would give it a second thought? Of course, we figured Kacherian's presence provided another layer of smoke between Bradfield and his wife's murder.

Bradfield and Haskell checked into the lodge just after noon and had a late lunch with their new client. Then Bradfield played golf with Kacherian, had a few drinks in the bar, and retired to Haskell's room for an intimate room service dinner for two, followed by a romantic night together. The next morning they had breakfast in the hotel dining room, where they conducted some business at the table, enough so that the server remembered the file folders and the calculator. Then they checked out of the lodge and drove back up to Bradfield's Oakland office, where Sid Vernon and Joe Kelso were waiting for them with the news of Stephanie Bradfield's death.

It certainly appeared that Bradfield did not have enough time to get from Pebble Beach to Oakland, stab his wife, and return to Pebble Beach to spend the night with Andi Haskell. Particularly since Haskell and the room service waiter backed up Bradfield's story about the intimate dinner in her room. Of course, the waiter only remembered delivering the meals to a beautiful blonde in a blue silk robe that showed a tantalizing glimpse of her bosom, a woman who smiled and gave him a hefty tip.

So where was Andi Haskell now? She was thirty years old when her boss went to jail. But she helped put him there. She was a hostile witness, unsmiling, subdued, and monosyllabic, unwilling to say anything damaging about the man who was both her employer and her lover. Despite all that, it was Andi Haskell who, when asked about a particular set of files in Bradfield's office, inadvertently revealed too much about Bradfield's relationship with Kacherian. I remembered the look on Bradfield's face that day in court, when he realized the damage her testimony had caused. And it had. Confronted with Haskell's words, Kacherian rolled over on his former accomplice.

Haskell had been facing the prospect of jail time, but our investigation, and that of the D.A., didn't provide any evidence that she'd been involved in the stock scam. So she was free to disappear. I agreed with Errol that I needed to find her, if only to warn her that she might be in danger from Bradfield. How difficult would that be, six years after the fact?

Haskell's address at the time of the Bradfield affair was a condominium on Moraga Avenue in Oakland, in Montclair just this side of the Warren Freeway, and not far from her lover's Colton Avenue address. She had purchased it about a year after she went to work for Bradfield.

After leaving my apartment Wednesday morning, I drove to the Alameda County Courthouse to find out whether Andi Haskell was still paying taxes on the condo. Not this year. Not for five years, in fact. She must have put the place on the market about the same time Bradfield was being tried in Marin County on charges of harassing Cordelia Ramsey. The real estate records didn't provide me with a forwarding address, but they did give me the name of the real estate company that handled the transaction.

It was a large firm with branches all over the Bay Area. I headed for my office to make some phone calls. When I finally connected with the real estate agent who handled the sale of Andi Haskell's condo, she told me that all she knew was that her client had gone back to Colorado.

"Back to Colorado," I repeated. It made sense. Our investigation had unearthed the information that Haskell had attended the University of Colorado, but we hadn't pursued that part of her life before she came to the Bay Area. We had focused on Bradfield's background rather than hers. "You're sure that's what she said?"

"I think so." The woman paused. "It's been a while, you know. But I seem to remember her using that phrase. Back to Colorado. Anyway, the only address I have for her is a post office box in Denver."

Denver's a big city, I told myself as I replaced the phone in its cradle. Good place to lose oneself. Should I contact an investigator there? Or could I narrow the parameters of the search?

There had been another employee in Bradfield's office, a woman who worked there as a secretary and receptionist. I sifted through the files until I found the woman's name, an address, and phone number. Stella Contreras. I'd interviewed her a couple of times when the Bradfield case had come to a full boil.

Five years ago she'd lived on Damuth Street, not far from Dimond Park, right here in Oakland. When I punched in that phone number, however, I got an answering machine that told me the number now belonged to someone named Truong. So she'd moved, or she'd gotten another phone number. I considered driving down to Damuth Street to scout around. Instead I reached for the phone directory that covered Oakland, Alameda, Berkeley, and San Leandro. There was more than one Contreras listed, of course. No Stellas, but several with Oakland exchanges and the initial S. She could have moved farther away during the intervening five years, but this was a place to start.

I tried to picture Stella Contreras, coming up with a

vague image of a middle-aged Hispanic woman with a round face and streaks of gray in her short, upswept black hair. According to the file, she'd been registered with a temporary agency in Oakland before Bradfield hired her. Maybe she'd gone back to that agency when her employer had been arrested.

I picked up the phone again and struck out with my first try. "No, she's not registered with us anymore. Hasn't been for several years."

I thanked the woman who'd answered the phone and disconnected the call. Back to the phone directory, this time the Oakland yellow pages. I flipped through the thick book until I found the listings under "Employment-Temporary." There were a lot of them, including a firm on the third floor of my building.

I walked down the hall to ask Ruby, head of that firm, if she'd ever had Stella Contreras on her rolls. No luck there. It looked as though I had a date with my phone. I went back to my office and made myself another pot of coffee. When I had a mugful of fresh dark brew, I settled back into my office chair and started dialing.

It took me the better part of an hour to work my way through the listings. Finally, toward the end of the alphabet, I hit a fresh trail. "Yes, we did have a Stella Contreras registered with us last year," said the crisp voice on the other end of the wire. "She found a permanent situation. A law firm here in Oakland."

"Could you tell me which law firm?" I asked.

It was on the sixth floor of the Ordway Building. Ironic, considering that Bradfield's office had been on the twelfth floor of that same downtown high-rise overlooking Lake Merritt. I got off the elevator, looked around, and spotted a sign indicating that the law office was on the city side of the building. Bradfield's suite had been on the lake side, with a view past the body of water to the hills beyond.

I recognized Stella Contreras immediately. She looked a bit older, with more wrinkles in the round face and a lot more gray mixed into the black. But her hair was still done in that upswept helmet, decorated with the thin wire headset that ran from her left ear to her mouth.

"Mrs. Contreras?"

She looked up from her station at the reception desk and frowned, as though she thought she knew me but couldn't quite place me. The phone rang, although in this case it was more like a low insistent trill. Her focus shifted from me to the headset as she said good afternoon and repeated the name of the law firm. When she'd directed that call she fielded another, then in a lull turned her attention to me again. By that time I had my identification in my hand.

"I don't know if you remember me," I said. "Jeri Howard, investigator with the Seville Agency. I talked with you about the Bradfield case."

The look on her face told me she remembered very well indeed.

"Oh, God. That mess." The phone rang again and she answered it, with the same professional pleasant voice as before. Then she frowned at me again. "I hoped I'd never hear his name again. What do you want now?"

"I need to find Andi Haskell."

Now her face turned incredulous. "What makes you think I'd know where she is?"

A man in a business suit came through the law firm's doors and advised Stella Contreras that he had an appointment. She took his name and called the attorney he was there to see. Once he'd been ushered into the inner sanctum, Stella Contreras flashed me an exasperated look over her console. "Look, I've got a lunch break coming up in about half an hour. If you want to talk with me, wait until then."

I took a seat in the reception area and leafed through a couple of magazines. When the relief receptionist showed up, Stella Contreras took her handbag from a drawer in the reception desk and joined me at the door. "Forty-five minutes," she said, glancing at her watch. "That's all I've got. Let's go downstairs."

There was a cafeteria on the second floor of the Ordway Building. I offered to buy her lunch, and she accepted, opting for a bowl of vegetable soup and a cup of herbal tea. I took coffee and led the way to a small table near the entrance.

She dunked a lemon-scented tea bag into the hot water and wrinkled her nose. "I don't know what I can tell you. I haven't seen Andi Haskell since I quit that job. Right after Bradfield was arrested. Why do you want to know, anyway?"

"Bradfield's out of prison," I told her.

I saw a little frisson of worry in her eyes. But Stella Contreras had less to fear from Bradfield than did the rest of us, who'd helped bring him down. Contreras had only worked for him a short time, and she'd been a functionary, not involved in the day-to-day workings of his business. Not like Andi Haskell.

"They should have kept him locked up," she said. She picked up her spoon and dipped it into her soup. "After what he did to that poor woman, his sister-in-law. Defrauding all those people. And I know the police think he killed his wife. I'm glad to be out of that, I'll tell you. But what makes you think I know where Andi Haskell is?"

"I've got a line on her." I sipped my coffee. "She sold her condo and moved to Denver. At least, her forwarding address is a post office box in Denver. I know you worked in that office less than a year. But during that time, did Andi Haskell ever say anything about where she was from? Did she ever mention any family? Any roots? Any connections?"

Stella frowned and wrinkled her nose again, keeping an eye on the clock. She blew on her tea and took a swallow while she thought about it.

"Andi liked to ski," she said finally. "She was up in the Sierras every chance she got. There was a snapshot on her desk. Her, on a ski trip. She was wearing a gold knit cap and a gray sweatshirt with a gold buffalo on it. Isn't that the symbol of the University of Colorado?"

"Colorado Buffaloes," I repeated, nodding. "Big Eight Conference. She went to school there, in Boulder."

"I thought so." Stella shrugged. "Don't ask me where that came from. She must have mentioned it at some point. But that was a long time ago. She'd be in her mid-thirties now."

"Was she alone in the photograph?"

Stella concentrated on her soup for a moment before answering. "There was a woman with her. Tina something. A friend from college or high school maybe. I think this Tina lived here in the Bay Area and they kept in touch." She consulted the clock again and took another mouthful of soup. "You know, talking about college, I think she commuted to class. Once, right before everything happened, I was talking about my daughter, going to school up at Chico, living in the dorm. Andi said something about not being involved in that living-on-campus experience, because she'd lived at home and commuted. Family finances, that sort of thing."

"So she might be from a town near Boulder, Colorado." If that was the case, it would narrow my search somewhat.

"Her mother was a widow. Worked as a salesclerk, I

think." Stella said the words quite suddenly, then looked at me, perplexed. "I can't believe I remembered this much. It's not like I knew Andi that well."

"But things come up in conversation," I said. There was something about getting a witness talking that helped those little bits of information float to the surface. "Do you remember anything else about her friends, other than the one named Tina?"

"No, no. Just Tina. I wish I could remember her last name. But I didn't even know Andi that well. I picked up on the fact that she was having an affair with Bradfield. Maybe that's why I kept her at a distance." She sighed and looked at the clock, then turned her attention back to her lunch. "Sorry. That's all I remember."

I stood up. "Here's my card. If you recall anything else, please call me. It's important that I locate her as soon as possible."

"Is she in some kind of trouble?" Stella Contreras asked.

"I hope not," I said. "But I'd feel a whole lot better if I could talk with her."

Thirty-four

TINA SOMETHING RANG A BELL.

In fact, I'd seen the name earlier that day in Errol's files. It was on the loan application Andi Haskell had filled out when she bought her condominium.

The Seville Agency had dug out the financial information on that earlier real estate transaction to see if Bradfield had purchased the place for Haskell. He hadn't, but he'd given her a liberal salary and a big Christmas bonus that went right into the down payment.

At the time Haskell was buying the condo, she'd written down the name of a personal reference, one Tina Kellner, who worked at a bank in San Francisco. There was a business address and phone number. I picked up the phone, hoping she was the woman in the ski picture Stella Contreras had mentioned.

Unfortunately, as I discovered when I tried the number, the bank had been gobbled up by another bank, about four years ago. That was something that happened a lot these days. I tried the surviving bank and eventually learned that Tina Kellner was one of those superfluous, redundant employees who get laid off when companies gobble other companies. The woman on the other end of the phone, in the bank's Human Resources Department, told me she had no idea where Kellner had gone after that.

I hung up the phone and reached for the telephone

directories stacked on the bookshelf behind my desk. The San Francisco listings contained several Kellners, but none of them was answering the phone this afternoon. The ones who had machines weren't forthcoming with any information that would help me pinpoint anyone named Tina.

I heaved a sigh, stared at the clock, and debated what to do next. For all I knew, Tina Kellner had an unlisted number. Or she could have married and moved to L.A.

I locked my office and went down to the lot where I kept my Toyota. Then I headed across the Bay Bridge to San Francisco, where I combed through the property tax records until I found Tina Kellner. She owned a condominium on Leavenworth Street on Russian Hill, in one of the newer buildings. It took me longer to find a parking space than it did to determine that she wasn't home. At least no one answered when I buzzed her unit. I tried buzzing her neighbors instead. On my third try I got the answer I needed.

"I remember when she got that job," Tina Kellner told me later that afternoon.

We were suspended midway up a San Francisco financial district high-rise, the headquarters of Pacific Gas & Electric, on Beale Street. It was late, the light fading. When I looked out the window I could see heavy traffic on the lower deck of the Bay Bridge, as commuters headed out of the city, toward home.

"She was so excited," Kellner continued. "Personal assistant to Mr. Moneybags. If only we'd known then what was going to happen. She'd have run the other way."

"She ran away afterward."

I turned away from the window and took a seat in one of the chairs in front of Kellner's desk. It was beige, like the rest of the furniture in her office. The neutral color was enlivened here and there with touches of green and blue, from the pottery on the small table next to me to the framed poster from a Napa Valley winery on the wall between the door and the window.

"Who could blame her for running?" Kellner said, thrumming her fingers on the smooth polished wood of her desk. "Dragged through the papers like that. After she got involved with Bradfield, I saw less and less of her. It had been well over a year since I'd seen her. Then one morning I picked up my *Chronicle* and there she was, in the middle of this scandal over in Oakland. Poor kid. So I called her. She was glad to hear from me."

She stopped, reflecting on events that had taken place years ago. Then the intercom on Kellner's phone buzzed. She picked up the receiver. "Yes?" She listened for a moment, then said, "Tell him I'm in a meeting and hold my calls. Thanks."

She looked at me and shook her head. "I haven't talked with Andi Haskell since she left the Bay Area. Her choice, I guess, not a surprising one either. I don't know if I can help you find her. Or if I should."

"Would it make any difference if I told you Richard Bradfield is out of prison?"

Now Kellner grimaced. "Yes, it would. Do you think she's in some kind of danger?"

"Possibly," I said. "Just tell me what you know about her. If she went back to Colorado, I need to know where to start looking for her. Where was her hometown?"

"I'm not sure I remember," Kellner said, after thinking about it for a moment. "Andi was an acquaintance rather than a friend. Besides, she was the kind of person who didn't reveal much of herself."

"How did you meet?"

"During our last year at the university, on a ski trip.

Then we both moved out here and ran into each other at some alumni thing. We stayed in touch because of the C.U. connection. She never talked about home much. Her father was a farmer. But he died when Andi was in college. I don't know if her mother's still there."

"So it was a rural community," I commented. "Would she go back there?"

Kellner shrugged. "I'm not sure. She liked the Denver-Boulder area. And she'd want to be close enough to the mountains to ski. She's probably in Denver."

"That jibes with what the real estate agent told me. A post office box in Denver."

"Her sister lived in Denver," Kellner said suddenly. "Older sister. Her name's Leanne. She's married to a man whose name ends in 'ski.' Russian or Polish. Andi used to joke and say she should have married him, just for the 'ski.'" She furrowed her brow, then shook her head. "Can't think of the name. Maybe it'll come to me. I've got your numbers. I'll call you if it does."

"I talked with someone else who worked in Bradfield's office. She says Andi lived at home while going to college."

"That's true. She didn't live on campus. My recollection is that she lived with an aunt and drove back and forth every day. But I'll be damned if I can remember where."

I probed further but was unable to elicit any more information from Tina Kellner. I thanked her and made my way down to the lobby. Driving back to Oakland, I pulled together the threads I had so far. The town where Haskell had lived during her college days must be close enough to Boulder to commute. Whether that was the farming community where she grew up or the home of an aunt was open to speculation.

I unlocked the door to my office, checked my answering

machine, and discovered that the red light held steady. No messages.

I pulled out my map stash and dug around in the box until I found a map of the state of Colorado. I unfolded it, spread it out on the surface of my desk, and stared at the pale yellow shape that denoted Denver and the smaller dot that was Boulder, hugging the edge of the Rockies. With my finger I drew an invisible half circle around Boulder, then looked at the names of the towns within a likely commuting radius. Most of them were in Boulder County. That's where I'd start.

I picked up the phone and called United, making a reservation on an early morning flight to Denver. Then I went home to pack a few things. Ordinarily I'd have had to make arrangements for someone to take care of the cats, but they were still at Dr. Prentice's office. I was just sitting down to a solitary dinner when Tina Kellner called.

"Sikowski," she said without preamble. "Andi Haskell's sister is married to a guy named Sikowski. Don't ask me what wrinkle of my brain that was hiding in. And I think you may be looking for a town that starts with an L."

"How do you know?"

"When I got home from work I went through some old photo albums. I found some pictures of Andi. In one of them she's wearing an old letter jacket, blue and white, with a big L."

Thirty-five

IT WAS STILL DARK THURSDAY WHEN I PARKED my car in the long-term lot at Oakland International Airport. I carried my gray nylon bag into the terminal and walked up to the United counter to pick up my ticket. Then I headed for the gate, where I consumed a cup of coffee and read a paperback mystery while I waited to board.

I located my seat, on the right side just ahead of the wing, then stashed my bag in the overhead compartment. Once all the passengers had boarded and were properly cinched in place, the big jet backed away from the concourse and taxied into position. After a brief pause, as though gathering strength for the two-and-a-half-hour flight, the jet blistered down the runway and took off, asphalt pavement giving way to dark blue water as we angled over San Francisco Bay, turned sharply, and headed east over the Central Valley, toward the rising sun.

I settled back on the cushions, opened my paperback, and tried to ignore the small child behind me who was rhythmically kicking my seat. Finally the kid stopped, admonished by his mother. I read, periodically distracted by the scenery far below my little window. The peaks of the Sierra Nevada were still white with snow. I saw a lake below, its blue water free of ice, a bare shore showing below the waterline, and a dam visible at the far end. The surrounding slopes, blue-green with trees, were brushed by wispy trails of cloud. I saw remote canyons hidden between folds of rock, then another lake, covered with ice reflecting the sun.

By the time the flight attendants had made their way up and down the aisle, proffering beverages and a euphemistically named snack, we were east of the Sierras and over the Great Basin that encompasses much of Nevada and Utah. The ground below looked like thin, worn brownish-gray velvet, humped and rolling, dotted here and there with trees. Utah's Great Salt Lake Desert looked tan and sandy, with large uneven salt flats.

I remembered the old saw about the Mormons: if they had approached Salt Lake City from the west instead of the east, they would have turned back. Still, it was beautiful, even if it was a bit desolate.

More mountains appeared to the east, faint shadows that grew larger as the jet ate up distance. From the air the western slope of Colorado's Rockies was an arid broken landscape. The word "badlands" leaped into my mind as I gazed down on rugged bluffs and ridges, dusty red-brown earth in the broad sweep of valleys between networks of peaks and canyons, like a moonscape, a rocky rift zone, changed by geologic shifts over thousands of years. Uneven ribbons of reddish earth alternated with gray-brown layers of sediment and rock in what looked like an ancient riverbed. Was that dusty winding ribbon a road? A stream? I couldn't tell. Then I saw a straight narrow ribbon, with tiny cars moving along it, and in the distance an equally miniature town, laid out in a neat grid, surrounded by larger squares of cultivated land, roofs of buildings glittering in the sun.

The mountains loomed closer, dark blue-gray where there was vegetation, brown rock where they were bare. Finally I saw high snowcapped peaks and white clouds.

Below there was a large pear-shaped lake, its narrow end butting up against a steep slope, the layer of ice over the water pale blue and dusted with snow.

This was the Continental Divide, where the mountains look as though they never lost their white cover. Then we flew into clouds and I could see nothing outside the tiny window except atmosphere that resembled cotton candy. Above me the light flashed, indicating that passengers should fasten seat belts. The pilot came on the intercom, with a deliberately cheery voice announcing that we would be experiencing some turbulence as we neared Denver. Suddenly I saw snow softening jagged peaks and the dark blue-gray folds of mountains as the jet came down from the cloud cover, bucking and bouncing over frozen lakes with silvery ice.

Then we were out of the clouds and into a bright blue bowl of a sky, flying over brown and gold hills dotted with towns and bisected by thin ribbons of highways. Through the window and off to my right I saw the sky-scraper towers of Denver, the Queen City of the Plains.

It had been several years since I'd flown to Colorado, so this was my first glimpse of the new airport. Its white peak roof resembled a vast circus tent on the high plains northeast of town. Once we'd touched down and taxied to the terminal, I waited until a majority of the passengers had grabbed their bags and herded themselves toward the door. Then I stood up, stretched, and pulled my bag from the overhead.

Inside the B concourse I found a phone and checked the Denver metropolitan area listings for Haskells and Sikowskis. It was past ten in the morning and I didn't have any luck finding any of them at home. I took the lower-level train that ran between the various concourses and found the car rental counters, where I picked up the compact sedan I'd reserved.

A short time later I'd made my way to U.S. 36, and sped northwest through the Denver suburbs and the outlying towns. Finally, the sedan crested a hill and headed down into Boulder, which sprawled along the edge of the front range of the Rockies. It had been a while since I was there but I remembered some of the landmarks. The Flatirons, smooth brown rock surfaces, towered above the redundantly named Table Mesa in the southern part of town. Directly ahead of me I saw a large cluster of red sandstone buildings, the University of Colorado.

The hills that rolled down off the ridge toward town looked dry and brown, while the mountains that rose at Boulder's western perimeter were blue-gray, touched here and there with white, as a reluctant winter gave way to an early spring. I contrasted this with the green rainy landscape resulting from a Northern California spring. Where I came from, dry and brown was the norm in summer. So was living at sea level, with higher humidity. I recalled that the last time I'd been in Colorado, both the dryness and the altitude had bothered me.

I found the county courthouse, its red-gold marble facade echoing the red-gold sandstone of the university buildings. It was downtown on the Pearl Street Mall, and I located the building with more ease than I did a parking place. Once inside I found my way to the recorder's office, where I asked the clerk to search the name Haskell in the county's computerized records. Anything recorded by a court should have been there. I was having a lucky streak today. Tina Kellner had told me Andi Haskell's father died while Andi was in college, about fifteen years earlier. There was a death certificate on file for one John A. Haskell, Longmont, Colorado. After the death certificate had been recorded, it was mailed back to a lawyer's office in Longmont.

"Probably a joint tenancy," the clerk told me. "If both

spouses had owned the property as joint tenants, the surviving spouse would have had to file the death certificate
in order to sell."

Further digging into the county records provided more
information on that particular real estate transaction. The
assessor's office told me who was paying taxes on the old
Haskell farm. It looked like the present owner was a firm
called Front Range Development, but that wasn't who'd
purchased the farm from Estelle M. Haskell fifteen years
ago. I went to the voters division and consulted registration records, which gave me the current address of the
person I was looking for.

Finally, I tucked my notebook into my purse and
walked back out to my rental car. I pointed it northeast on
Highway 119, the straight diagonal route to Longmont.

Thirty-six

"JOHN WAS SOME YEARS YOUNGER THAN ME," Dean Lester said. "Healthy as a horse, I thought. Then one day he just dropped dead of a heart attack, right in the middle of harvest. To up and die sudden like that . . ."

Lester shook his head. He was a round-faced balding man, probably in his mid-sixties. His round torso matched his face, which was lined from years spent in the sun. We were seated in the cluttered living room of a small one-story brick house on the west side of Longmont. It was a good-sized town, with a view of the foothills and the Rockies looming to the west. Lester lived in a neighborhood of well-tended older homes lining the tree-shaded streets, on Bross Street near the corner of Longs Peak Avenue. I'd called him from a phone booth at a strip mall on the south side of town. When I explained who I was and why I was in town, he invited me over.

In fact, he seemed eager for the company. He was a widower, he said, on his own for three years now. His sole companion was a middle-sized floppy-eared dog, his fur a mix of black, tan, and white, looking like he had some shepherd and hound in his ancestry. This man-and-dog bachelorhood might have accounted for the lived-in condition of the house. Lester made a good pot of coffee, though, and we were using it to wash down some pastries I'd picked up at a bakery next to the phone booth.

Once the social niceties were out of the way and the dog had left off sniffing my feet and stretched out on the carpet near the coffee table, Lester told me about Andi Haskell's father. "He had a half-section, just like me," Lester said, explaining that a half-section was 320 acres. "We grew corn, soybeans, some sugar beets."

"When did you purchase the farm?"

"Several months after John died, around Thanksgiving. Estelle wasn't interested in farming it herself or hiring anyone to do it. And I figured she needed the money, what with Andrea in college. She took my offer and moved in with her sister." He took a sip of coffee, then continued his narrative. "I sold both places after my wife died. My kids were after me to retire, none of them wanted to run the farm, and that development company made me a good offer. So I sold the place and bought this house. My daughter wanted me to move in with her, up on the north side of town. But I said no thanks to that. Me and old George are comfortable here."

The dog raised his black and tan head and thumped his tail against the carpet before settling back into slumber.

I guessed that Andi would have been in transition from her sophomore to her junior year at the University of Colorado. Lester confirmed this.

"Yes, Andrea had been going to college a couple of years when her dad died," Lester said, wiping his fingers on a paper napkin. "In fact, I think she was in summer school that year."

"Was she living here at home while she went to college?" I asked. "It's certainly close enough to commute."

"Oh, yes, lots of people drive to the university every day. But I thought Andrea lived there in Boulder." He stopped. "Well, I'm not sure. My wife would have known." He said this last with a tinge of sadness that made it clear he missed his wife. I wondered how long they'd been married.

"Weren't there two Haskell daughters? One is married, I believe."

"Leanne," Lester said. "She was four years older. She married that Sikowski boy from here in Longmont. I believe they live somewhere down in Jefferson County. Seems to me Estelle said he worked at the Federal Center in Lakewood."

I leaned toward him, pleased to learn that the Sikowski I was looking for came from Longmont. Now if I could just get a first name to narrow that list I'd copied from the Denver phone book. When I asked, Lester thought for a moment. "The name Steve comes to mind, but I'm not sure. Now, his dad owns a car dealership here. Sikowski Ford. On North Main. You can't miss it. All you need to do is go over there and talk to his dad. I'm sure he can tell you where to find the boy."

"That would help considerably. Now, you said Estelle Haskell moved in with her sister after she sold the farm. But I gather that wasn't here in Longmont."

"No, somewhere closer to Denver."

"Any idea where they're living?"

"My wife would have known," he said, for the second time. "I think they stayed in touch for a while. Let me see if I can find it in her address book." He got up and went back into the kitchen, where I heard him rummaging around in drawers. A moment later he came back, carrying an address book, the kind with three rings and a vinyl cover that was supposed to look like leather. He opened it to the section marked H and peered at the words written on the lined pages. "Here's the book, but the only address I see is the farm, and that's not good anymore, of course. There's a phone number here, with Estelle's name next to it."

"May I look?" I asked, holding out my hand. He nodded and handed over the book. The Longmont address for the Haskells, the farm, had long since been crossed out. Beneath this the name Estelle Haskell and a phone number had been written in blue ink.

"This isn't a Longmont exchange?" I asked.

"No. I'm sure it's somewhere in the Denver area. My wife would have known. Sorry, I'm just not good at keeping up with people."

"Mind if I use your phone? I have a credit card."

He waved his hand. "Oh, don't worry about how much it costs. Just go ahead and make the call. Anything I can do to help. Phone's in the kitchen."

I crossed the worn blue and white linoleum to a wall phone hanging next to the kitchen counter. At my feet were a couple of large blue plastic dog bowls, one full of water, the other licked clean. The phone number I'd punched in rang three times, then was picked up by an answering machine that told me Margaret and Estelle weren't available to answer my call, but if I wanted to leave a message, I could wait for the beep. I hung up instead.

Back in Lester's living room I told the old farmer that there had been no answer. "That's a shame. But you can try again later. Want some more coffee?"

"No thanks. I'd better be going. Maybe I can get some information at Sikowski Ford that will help me track down Andrea's sister."

He seemed a bit regretful at seeing me go. He and George walked me out to my car, George primarily to raise a leg against a tree in the middle of the yard. Lester waved an arm at a neighbor as we went down the sidewalk. "There's Mrs. MacDonald," he said. "She might know about Estelle Haskell. Let me ask her."

We crossed the lawn to where the older woman, wearing a housedress and carrying a canvas shopping bag, had just opened the driver's side door of her dark brown sedan. "Mrs. MacDonald, this is Jeri Howard," Lester began. "She's looking for Estelle Haskell."

"Actually, I'm looking for her daughter, Andrea," I said, wanting to forestall any information that I was a private investigator, in case this sharp-eyed woman who was looking me up and down with great curiosity would be disinclined to talk. "Mr. Lester tells me Estelle Haskell now lives with her sister. Would you happen to know what the sister's name is, or where they live?"

She considered this for a moment, then spoke in a tart voice. "Well, I can't help you with the daughter. But Estelle's sister is Margaret Todd. And they live down in Broomfield."

Thirty-seven

I FOUND SIKOWSKI FORD WHERE DEAN LESTER said I would, on North Main just past Seventeenth Avenue. Finding the elder Sikowski was more difficult. He wasn't at the car dealership. I finally persuaded one of his employees, who was evidently disappointed that I didn't want to buy a brand-new car, to tell me where I could locate his boss. Turned out Sikowski was taking a break at a restaurant about a block farther north.

It was a typical coffee shop, with padded orange vinyl booths lining the wall to my right, tables in the middle, and a counter with stools on my left. The waitress behind the counter was working the cash register, and she barely glanced at me as I looked around for likely prospects. By now it was mid-afternoon. The lunchtime crowd had long since departed and it was too early for the dinner trade, so there were only a few customers in the place.

The car salesman had given me a sketchy description. Sikowski was tall, had gray hair, and was wearing a blue suit. All the men I saw in the coffee shop were seated, so tall wouldn't help me as a description. There were a couple of gray-haired men in blue suits. One was with a woman, the two of them sharing a table near the entrance. My eyes roved over them, dismissed him, then looked toward a booth midway toward the back. The man sitting there was alone, facing forward, and he was wearing a blue suit.

"Gordon Sikowski?" I asked, walking over to the booth.

He looked up from his coffee and the remains of a piece of pie. "You found him." He had a high forehead and a thinning head of hair. Behind his friendly smile were a pair of narrowed hazel eyes and the unspoken question asking who I was.

"Sit down, have some apple pie. It's the best in town." I slid into the seat opposite him. "What can I do for you?" he asked.

"My name's Jeri Howard," I said. I decided to be straight with him. I took a business card from my purse and handed it across the table. "I'm looking for a woman named Andrea Haskell. I understand your son is married to her sister."

"That's true," he said as he examined the card. Then he pushed away the plate that had held his pie, the pale brown crockery sliding across the yellow Formica surface of the table. "Why are you looking for her?"

"That's something I'd prefer to discuss with her." I leaned back against the padded orange seat.

"But you don't know where she is," he said, looking cagey.

At that moment the waitress appeared at the table, holding a coffeepot and a brown mug. "No, thanks," I told her. She shrugged, freshened Sikowski's cup, and padded away.

"I hope you might be able to tell me where she is," I said, "if you know. If you don't, I'd like to know where to locate your son and his wife."

"Well," he said, drawing out the word. "I don't know if I can do that."

"Why?"

"I'm a great respecter of privacy."

"So am I, Mr. Sikowski. But this is important."

"I suppose it must be, if you came all the way back here from Oakland, California." He mulled this over for a moment. Then he cocked one gray eyebrow at me. "She was in some kind of trouble, wasn't she? Back there. I thought that was all over with."

He waited for me to respond. I wondered how much he knew about what had happened back in California. "Perhaps it is," I said. "Let's just say I'm trying to forestall a recurrence."

"I don't know whether to believe you or not."

"Look, Mr. Sikowski, I know she lives somewhere in the Denver metropolitan area. I know at some time your son and his wife lived in Jefferson County and your son worked for the Federal Center in Lakewood. Sooner or later I'll track them down. A name like Steve Sikowski will be easier to find than Smith or Jones. But it would save time and make my job a whole lot easier if you'd just tell me."

I was going by what Dean Lester had told me. I didn't know for sure that the younger Sikowski's name was Steve or that he and his wife still lived where they had fifteen years ago when Andi Haskell was in college. My words must have hit some mark, though. I saw a flicker in Sikowski's eyes.

"I don't know where she lives," he said, his voice a little less friendly than it had been. "And if you're such a hotshot private eye, I guess you can just go looking for my son. Maybe he won't be as easy to find as you think."

Well, that backfired, I told myself as Sikowski stood up and walked over to the coffee shop counter. "How much do I owe you, Aggie?" I heard him ask the waitress. She named a figure and he said, "There you are, and keep the change."

I waited until he'd left the shop, then I picked up the menu that was stuck between the salt and pepper shakers, thinking I'd better eat something while I was there. I scanned the offerings and waved at the waitress.

"Mr. Sikowski recommended the apple pie," I told her.

She smiled. "That's his favorite. Has a piece every day about this time. Want to try a slice?"

"I think I'll have some lunch first." Outside, the sky was darkening, and my stomach reminded me that I needed something other than those pastries I'd consumed at Dean Lester's house. "Is this turkey sandwich made with the real thing? Carved off the bird, I mean, not that pressed stuff." She assured me it was, so I ordered turkey on whole wheat, a large iced tea, and the pie.

"I didn't get a chance to ask Mr. Sikowski about Steve and Leanne," I said, as she wrote down my order. "Haven't seen them in a while. I wonder, does Steve still work for the federal government? Are they still in Lakewood?"

"Oh, no, hon," the waitress said as she moved toward the kitchen. "Steve works for the state now, but Leanne's still teaching school. They built a nice big house, out in the country, west of Arvada."

Sikowski was right about the apple pie. After I finished the sandwich, I polished off a big wedge. Then I visited the coffee shop's bathroom before leaving. In my car I consulted my map.

I'd passed through the edge of Broomfield earlier in the day when I drove from Denver to Boulder. The town was at the southeastern corner of Boulder County, part of the town straddling into Adams County to the east and Jefferson County to the south.

I started the car and drove south on U.S. 287. As the afternoon wound toward evening the sun edged toward the peaks of the Rockies. Once it slipped behind the mountains it created an early twilight. When I reached

Broomfield, I pulled the rental car off the highway into the parking lot of a convenience store, cut the engine, and got out, looking for a phone. There was one, just to the right of the convenience store's entrance, and it looked like the phone directory was intact. I leafed through the pages and found what I was looking for, a listing for Margaret Todd and an address on Emerald Street.

It was a one-story house, constructed of brick, like so many of the homes I'd seen in Colorado. In the fading daylight it looked yellow, with brown trim and a well-groomed lawn and flower beds. There was no car in the driveway leading to a closed single garage. The house itself had a shut-up look, beige drapes drawn across a picture window that faced west. I parked at the curb and walked up several shallow cement steps to the porch. I couldn't tell by looking at the mail slot next to the front door whether the mail had been collected.

I rang the bell. No answer. I listened for a moment and didn't hear anything. Then I walked next door and rang that bell. This time my summons got me a young woman about my own age, who looked as though I'd interrupted her dinner preparations.

"Mrs. Haskell and Mrs. Todd," she repeated, after I'd asked my question about the whereabouts of her neighbors. "They've been gone a couple of days. Couldn't say where they went, or when they'll be back. I do know they like to go up to Central City or Cripple Creek to gamble."

I thanked her and walked slowly back to my rental car. The towns the neighbor had mentioned were old mining communities up in the mountains. They dated back to Colorado's gold rush, which had come about ten years after California's. In recent years the residents had voted in casino gambling.

I was tired, not relishing the prospect of driving any farther when it seemed that I'd spent the whole afternoon on the road. But I had to give Arvada a try. On my map Arvada looked much larger than Broomfield. I stopped at a generic chain motel near the intersection of Wadsworth and Eighty-eighth, produced my credit card, and acquired a room with a double bed and a phone. I started playing telephone roulette with the Sikowskis who had Arvada interchanges, pushing back that little voice that told me it was quite possible the Sikowskis I was looking for had an unlisted number.

Forty minutes later, after a series of dead ends, no answers, and answering machines, I got a helpful teenage male who cheerfully told me his parents were indeed Steve and Leanne Sikowski. He even gave me the address, in a collection of sizable brick homes on big lots west of Indiana Street, out by the Arvada Reservoir. By the time I located the house, in the dark western reaches of the city, it was past seven. But there was a big American sedan and a four-wheel-drive vehicle parked in the double driveway. That meant someone was home.

Thirty-eight

Not that it did me any good.

Leanne Haskell Sikowski, a schoolteacher according to the waitress in Longmont, wouldn't let me through the front door. Instead she preferred to glare at me through the screen mesh, as though she'd like to send me to the principal. She was an older version of the Andi Haskell I remembered, not as tall or slender, but with the same hostility that had radiated from her younger sister when she'd been on the witness stand six years ago.

"I have nothing to say to you," she said, her voice icy. Frown lines showed between her eyebrows, accentuated in the harsh overhead glow of the porch light. I guessed that her father-in-law had called to warn her that I might show up on her doorstep. She didn't seem surprised to see me, only determined not to give me any information.

"I need to talk with your sister. It's important. If it weren't important, I wouldn't have flown out here from California."

"If it's about that business in California, that's all in the past."

"Sometimes the past can show up." As I spoke the words I was aware that, to Leanne Sikowski, that's what I represented. Something in the past, something she was trying to protect her sister from. In some ways I couldn't blame her. But if I could connect the dots to find Andi

Haskell, so could Richard Bradfield. And he knew her better than I ever would.

"At least contact your sister and ask if she would meet with me," I said, my voice placating, not showing the frustration I felt. "I understand your wish to protect her, but perhaps it's a decision she should make herself." I took one of my business cards from my purse and wrote down the name of the motel and my room number. "This is where I'm staying tonight."

Leanne Sikowski reluctantly unlatched the screen door and reached for my card. Her expression didn't change, though. I wondered if she was taking the card just to get rid of me.

Whether she talked to her sister or not, Andi Haskell didn't call me that night. The phone didn't ring at all, even as I sat on the bed and flipped through channels, finally settling on a movie.

After breakfast Friday morning I checked out of the motel and headed back up Wadsworth to Broomfield, planning to try Andi Haskell's mother and aunt again. Maybe they'd returned from their sojourn in the gambling towns of the Colorado Rockies, with more money than they'd had when they left. With luck, I could get to them before Leanne Sikowski called to warn them I was looking for Andi. Luck, I thought with a sigh. I'd had a run of it yesterday in Boulder and Longmont, but it had played out by the time I got to Arvada.

When I parked outside the house on Emerald Street, I saw a late model Pontiac parked in the driveway. The drapes that had covered the front window the day before were open to admit the morning light. I rang the bell. A moment later the door was opened by a sixtyish woman with short iron-gray hair and glasses with round tortoise-shell frames, wearing a bright blue sweat suit and running shoes. I wasn't sure if this was Estelle Haskell or

Margaret Todd, but she set me straight as soon as I'd asked the question.

"I'm Mrs. Todd. Everybody calls me Maggie," she said. "Come on in."

The living room was carpeted in beige plush and furnished with an overstuffed gold sofa with a matching chair. There were green plants on a glass-topped coffee table that had been moved under the wide front window in order to take the best advantage of the sun. African violets in ceramic pots crowded the end tables on either side of the sofa. An upright piano rested against the wall opposite the window, its top covered with family pictures. Here was Leanne Sikowski, a man who looked like a younger version of his car salesman father, and two teenage boys.

And here was a five-by-seven of Andi Haskell, certainly more current than my memory of her. The blond hair was styled differently, much shorter, and she wasn't alone in the photograph. She was with a dark-haired man who had a round friendly face, and there was a baby on her lap, a little girl about a year old, with her mother's blond hair and her father's brown eyes. So Andi had married and had a child.

"Estelle's down in the basement, doing laundry. We've been away for a couple of days. Got back late last night. Come on, it's this way."

I followed Maggie Todd through the dining room, with its plain square table covered with a frilly white tablecloth, and as she made a right turn into the kitchen, which had a smaller harvest-type table that looked as though it got more use than the one in the dining room. Houses in Colorado usually had basements, and just past the door that led out to the garage were some carpeted stairs leading down to this subterranean level.

"Estelle," Maggie hollered. "You got company." Then

her voice returned to its normal tone. "What did you say your name was? Jeri? Is that short for Geraldine?"

"Jerusha, actually. It was my grandmother's name."

"Jerusha. Say, that's pretty. You want some coffee? I got a fresh pot here, and some coffee cake that Estelle made this morning." She didn't wait for an affirmative. Instead she opened the cupboard next to the stove and took out a cup and a plate. I helped myself to the coffee as she cut me a wedge of the streusel-topped coffee cake.

"I can have a cup with you and Estelle," she said, glancing at the digital clock on the microwave oven, "then I have to go over to the Senior Center for my tai chi class."

We pulled out chairs and sat companionably at the kitchen table. "It's delicious," I said after the first bite.

"Oh, Estelle's a wonderful cook. Not me. I'm handy around the house, though. Repairs and painting and keeping up the garden. After our husbands died, the only sensible thing for these two widow women to do was to move in with each other."

I heard footsteps coming up the carpeted stairs, then Estelle Haskell rounded the corner. She was older than her sister, more white-headed, slower in her movements. She wore brown slacks and a white blouse, both of which seemed loose on her slender frame.

"Who is it, Maggie?" she asked her sister, then she stopped and peered at me through a pair of bifocals. "Do I know you? No, I don't know you."

I got to my feet. "Mrs. Haskell, I'm Jeri Howard. A private investigator from Oakland, California. I'd like to talk with you about your daughter Andrea."

"A private eye." Maggie Todd straightened in her chair. "You didn't say that at the front door. That's fascinating. How did you get into that line of work?"

Mrs. Haskell wasn't the least bit interested in how I

got into the detective business. All that had registered from my introduction were her daughter's name and the city of Oakland. Her blue eyes took on the same suspicious look I'd seen in her elder daughter's face last night. "What do you want with my daughter?"

"If I could just talk with her—"

The old woman cut me off with a sharp gesture and an even sharper voice. "She's left that part of her life behind. She got tired of that mess out there in California, all that traffic and the ridiculous cost of living and the wrong kind of people."

I wondered who Estelle Haskell deemed the wrong kind of people. Were they black, brown, poor, or simply not from Colorado? Was Richard Bradfield the wrong kind of people? I picked up the coffee and took a swallow before speaking carefully. "What did your daughter tell you about California, about her job and the man she worked for?"

"Why, she got laid off," she declared. "After she'd worked for that fellow for years, and been such a good assistant. And she couldn't find another job. So she sold her condo at a loss, because of those ridiculous real estate prices. Then she came back here where she belongs. With her family."

It sounded as though Andi Haskell hadn't exactly been truthful when she told her mother why she'd moved back to Colorado and the bosom of her family. After another sip of coffee I set the cup on the kitchen table, conscious that Maggie Todd was looking at me speculatively through her round glasses.

"Something has come up that I need to discuss with Andrea," I told them.

Mrs. Haskell dismissed me imperiously. "She doesn't want to talk with you, or anyone from those days. And don't you keep trying to find her. She's married now, and

I'm not going to tell you what her name is. You just go back to California and leave my daughter alone."

She waved her hand in the direction of the front door, and I took that as my cue to exit. "I'll walk you out," Maggie Todd said, standing and bouncing a little on the soles of her running shoes. "Got to get over to the Senior Center."

Neither of us said anything until we were outside, she with her car keys in her hand. "Do you know what happened in California?" I asked her. "I'd like to know, to see if your version jibes with mine."

"Yes, I do know." Maggie Todd's face turned thoughtful. "So does Estelle, though I think she's come to believe that fairy tale she told you. That's what she told all her bridge-playing cronies, and every time she tells it, she believes it's the truth." She paused and jingled the keys in her hand, her tai chi class momentarily forgotten.

"I know my niece was involved with that man she worked for, Richard something-or-other. He was a crooked businessman and got charged with something related to his financial shenanigans. Andrea said that he went to jail for that. And for harassing some poor woman, his sister-in-law. I'm not clear on why he was harassing this woman."

"She sued him for custody of his daughter, and won. Did Andrea tell you he was a suspect in his wife's murder?"

"No." The older woman looked horrified. "Why wasn't he charged with that?"

"He had an alibi for the night the murder was committed. Your niece."

"You think she lied?" The question came in a subdued whisper.

"Yes, I do."

"Oh, my God," she said. "Why have you come here? Why are you trying to find Andrea?"

"Because this man—Richard Bradfield—is out of prison now. Andi alibied him for the night his wife was murdered. When she testified in court about his business, her testimony was instrumental in his conviction for fraud. I'm convinced that Bradfield is harassing people who helped put him in prison. I'm convinced because I'm one of those people. And so is your niece. I think Andi is in danger, Mrs. Todd. Won't you at least let me warn her?"

She opened the door of her car but made no move to slide into the driver's seat. After a sidelong glance at the house, she turned to me. "Her name's Andrea Wood now. She works in the administrative office at Boulder Community Hospital."

Thirty-nine

I DROVE BACK TO BOULDER, COMPLETING THE triangle my rental car had drawn since yesterday. Boulder Community Hospital was a tan brick building on the west side of North Broadway, backing onto a park. I left the rental in the lot, next to a sign that warned me the structure had been built in the Goose Creek flood plain and the lot was subject to flooding.

Inside the hospital, I approached a volunteer who directed me to the hospital's business office. I didn't find Andrea Wood there, but a cheery-voiced coworker with a name tag that identified her as Marilyn said, "You just missed her. She went to lunch."

Belatedly I glanced at my watch. It was nearly noon. "Any idea where? Maybe I can catch up."

"Well, I'm not sure." Marilyn looked at the calendar on Andi's desk. "This says Pour la France, noon. You know where that is?" I shook my head. "Downtown on Pearl Street Mall, around Tenth, I think. It's not far, about seven blocks. Andrea walked, I'm sure. Parking's so bad down there you'd be crazy to take your car."

I took Marilyn's word and set off in the direction of Boulder's main business district. As I walked I noticed patches of dirty snow at the curbs and the edge of a nearby parking lot. All the vehicles seemed to be stout-hearted, mountain-climbing, four-wheel drives, with ski racks and bike racks, dusty and dirty with the residue of the filthy winter slush. The reason that the owners of these stalwart vehicles hadn't washed them was that this pleasant sunny day was an anomaly. Those tiny buds taking a risk on the ends of bare branches were fair game for a late spring snowstorm.

I reached the Pearl Street Mall and stopped to get my bearings. I was a couple of blocks west of the courthouse, where I'd begun this search the day before. I asked a passerby where Pour la France was and set off in the direction indicated. I crossed Eleventh Street, saw the restaurant's sign, and slowed my pace. It wasn't quite warm enough, at least not in Colorado, for tables to be set up on sidewalks. As I walked past the restaurant I spotted two women seated at a table for two near the front window. One of them looked very much as she had in the photograph I'd seen at her mother's house earlier today. Andi Haskell, short blond hair combed back off her face, wore a long gray skirt, boots, and an oversized blue sweater. I saw a gray coat with a hood draped over the back of her chair.

It looked as though they'd just been seated, chatting over the tops of the menus as the server showed up with glasses of water. I had some time to kill. On the other side of Tenth Street, a few doors down, I saw Peaberry's Coffee. I bought myself a latte and a lemon bar and sat at one of the coffeehouse's outdoor tables, keeping one eye on the entrance of Pour la France.

I had heard Boulder referred to as Little Berkeley, but since I was familiar with the real Berkeley, I was more aware of differences rather than similarities. University towns were alike in that they were full of students and the students all seemed to be carrying books in backpacks. But these kids were tan and fresh-faced, looking as though they belonged on the ski slopes instead of in class. They certainly appeared less world-weary, and less diverse, than their Telegraph Avenue counterparts.

Finishing the lemon bar, tart enough to bring tears to my eyes, I walked back toward the restaurant and saw Andi and her companion still in conversation over sandwiches. I crossed Pearl Street and skulked on the other side, consuming the rest of my latte as I examined the display in the window of a mystery bookstore called The Rue Morgue. Finally, as I was disposing of my cup in a nearby trash can, I saw Andi, now wearing her coat, and her lunch companion come out of Pour la France and walk up Pearl Street in the direction of Broadway. They parted at the corner, where Andi hugged her friend, then turned and walked briskly back toward the hospital.

I caught up with her as she crossed Mapleton Avenue. When she heard my voice saying her name, that old name, she froze. Then she turned slowly and stared at me, startled blue eyes widening over the thick gray wool.

"I know who you are," she said, as though confronted by a ghost. "I saw you at the trial. You worked for that private investigator. How . . . how did you find me?"

"Your aunt told me."

"Damnation." The word exploded from her. "She knows she's not supposed to say anything."

"Like your mother or your sister," I said. "And they didn't. Fortunately, I was able to convince your aunt that this is important."

She huddled deep into her coat, whirled, and started walking again, up Broadway, the heels of her boots making rapid clicks on the sidewalk. I followed, keeping pace with her. We were still a couple of blocks from the hospital, but we were covering ground.

"Look, I know your name is Andrea Wood now. You're married, you have a child. I don't like upsetting your life, but I think you should know. Richard Bradfield is out of prison."

She stopped at the next corner, waiting as a car made a right turn off the side street onto Broadway. "What has that got to do with me?" she asked as she stepped off the curb.

"He's harassing people again. Little things like hacking the tops off lemon trees, just the way he did before." From her indrawn breath I knew that caught her attention. We approached another corner, this one with a traffic light that showed an amber Don't Walk signal. "It occurred to me that Bradfield might be after anyone who helped put him in prison."

"I didn't help put him in prison." Her silhouette was repeated in the window of the florist's shop on the corner. "You did."

"What about all that information about the penny stock deal?"

"I had no idea that he was involved in that scheme, or any of the others." Impatient, she punched the button decorated with a walk signal and gazed up at the light, willing it to turn green. "I didn't realize the significance of what was in those file folders until later, when I had to testify in court."

"I don't think people like Bradfield make such fine distinctions. You don't want him, or anyone from those days, to know where you are. That tells me something. You're afraid of him, aren't you?"

"Wouldn't you be?" she asked as the walk signal flashed. We crossed the street.

"I certainly am. You see, my lemon tree was one of those that got decapitated. I think we should talk, Andi."

"I have to get back to work. I'm late." She stopped and glanced at her watch, and I did the same. It was after one. But Andi's feet didn't seem to be moving just yet. She stood there, looking at me with narrowed eyes, as though she were trying to make a decision. "I get off at five. Maybe . . . maybe I could leave early."

I looked at her, trying to guess if she'd take the opportunity provided by the next four hours to disappear. If she did, I'd have to start hunting all over again. But hassling her on her job didn't seem like the best way to get her to talk.

Should I trust her? Did I have a choice?

"I'll be in the hospital lobby at four-thirty."

Forty

I HAD ENOUGH OF SITTING AROUND HOSPITALS when my grandmother died. Spending the next few hours hanging around Boulder Community Hospital, inside or out, until Andrea Haskell Wood got off work didn't seem like an acceptable option. Besides, I was hungry. I crossed Broadway in search of food, finding a deli inside a small supermarket. Then, with a paper-wrapped pastrami on rye and a bottle of mineral water in hand, I walked back to the hospital parking lot.

I drove west into the mountains. As Canyon Boulevard narrowed from four lanes to two, it became Colorado Highway 119, snaking up the canyon at the side of Boulder Creek. I pulled off the highway just past Four Mile Canyon Drive and found a spot by the creek to eat my lunch. Spring brought snowmelt, and the creek ran high, water rushing past me on the rocky creek bed, which still had spots of ice visible at the opposite edge of the stream, where the sun had not yet reached to warm them. I leaned down, stuck a hand in the water, and felt its icy chill.

When I'd finished my sandwich, I balled up the debris and stuck it in the litter bag the rental company had provided along with the car. I wheeled back onto the road and kept going up into the mountains, stopping once again when I saw the sign for Boulder Falls. I hiked back up into a notch on the north side of the roadway, careful where I stepped on a path still slick here and there with ice. When I reached the falls I was rewarded by the sight of tons of water rushing and roaring over the rocky cliff.

I reached Nederland, some twenty miles west of Boulder, by mid-afternoon. The town itself was on the other side of the Barker Meadow Reservoir, which contained a huge amount of water behind its dam. As I had a cup of coffee at a restaurant whose windows afforded a magnificent view of the snow-covered peaks all around me, I found myself wishing I had more time to explore. As it was, I needed to head back for Boulder.

By four o'clock I'd parked once again in the lot at the hospital and found a bathroom inside. Then I hung out in the hospital gift shop until I saw Andi, fifteen minutes later, her gray coat draped over one arm as she walked toward me. We went outside. The temperature had dropped as the sun disappeared behind the mountains that loomed so close, draping Boulder in an early twilight and making me glad I'd worn my jacket. She too felt the chill, and stopped to put on the coat.

"Your spring weather isn't what I'm used to," I said. "Back home it's rainy but warmer than this."

"I remember," she said. "I lived in the Bay Area for a long time. This spring weather is deceptive. We sometimes get blizzards before May." She walked down the steps. "There's a place across the street where we can get some coffee."

I followed her to a place called Vic's Espresso and News, next to a wine shop in a shopping center on the other side of Broadway. We settled at a table near the front door, with a latte for me and a mocha for her. I sipped mine and burned my tongue. Andi made no move to reach for her cup.

"I had three phone messages waiting for me when I got back from lunch," she said slowly. "One from my sister, warning me that you were trying to find me. Ditto from my mother. And one from Aunt Maggie, saying I should hear what you have to say."

"I take it you've decided to do that."

"I'm here, aren't I?" She stared at the mound of whipped cream atop her coffee, then gave me a quick sidelong glance from her blue eyes. "But I warn you, now I have to pick up my daughter at day care. I can't stay long."

"I saw her picture at your mother's house. Pretty little girl. What's her name?"

"Alice." She smiled.

"How long have you been married?" I asked.

"Four years. His name's Keith. I met him right after I moved back here. Right here at the hospital, about three weeks after I got this job. He sells medical equipment. He's on the road a lot."

"Does he know about Richard Bradfield?"

She frowned and reached for her cup, avoiding an answer for the moment as she sipped her mocha. "I gave him an edited version."

"How edited? As edited as the one you gave your family?"

"Look," she said, setting down the cup. "I have a life here. A damned good one. It's the most important thing I have. I don't want to screw it up."

"But you're afraid of Bradfield."

"Aren't you?" she countered, piercing me with her eyes.

"Of course I am. I'd like to stop him before he damages anyone else's life. Including yours."

She considered this for a moment, using a long spoon to stir the whipped cream into her coffee. When she spoke again, the words came reluctantly. "I don't know how I can help you."

"Tell me about your relationship with Bradfield. How did it start?"

"I got sucked into something bad," she said slowly. "And I didn't realize how bad until it was over." She compressed her lips. Then she sighed. "I came to San Francisco after I graduated from college. I lived in the Marina for a while. I'd worked at a few secretarial, administrative assistant jobs in the city, mostly in the Financial district. I was getting bored with it, though. Then I saw the ad for this job in Oakland, for a lot of money. That's what attracted me. The salary. It was so much more than what I'd been making with my other jobs. I applied, I got hired. That was ten years ago."

"And your relationship with Bradfield?"

Her mouth tightened again, as though she were reluctant to speak of him. "He was like a big spider. Sitting in the middle of a web. I got tangled up in that web. I did some things I'm not proud of, things I'd just as soon forget."

The memories were painful for her, I could see it on her face. It appeared she'd done a lot of soul-searching over the past five years. Time and distance, and a new husband and baby, will do that. I wondered if the things she wanted to forget encompassed only her affair with Bradfield and the fraud he'd perpetrated on his clients. Or was there something in all that soul-searching that involved the murder of Stephanie Bradfield?

She took another sip of coffee before continuing. "A very attractive, well-paid web, of course. And he was a handsome, self-assured spider. It didn't happen right away. It was about a year after I took the job. I became more and more attracted to him, emotionally involved."

"And sexually."

She didn't respond right away. "If it means anything," she said finally, "I had deluded myself that he'd leave his wife for me. Oldest story in the book, of course. I knew they had problems. That they'd separated before, then gotten back together. For his daughter's sake, Richard said. When I got involved with him, he told me how unhappy he was in his marriage, that the only reason he stayed with her was Melissa. I didn't know he'd abused his wife, not until later."

"After Stephanie Bradfield was murdered, and Cordelia Ramsey hired the Seville Agency," I finished. "Everything fell like a row of dominoes. When the dominoes stopped falling, and Bradfield went to prison, you sold your condo and headed back to Colorado."

"There certainly wasn't anything left for me in California. The Alameda County D.A. thought I was involved with Richard in defrauding those old people and that penny stock business. But I wasn't. In fact, I was appalled when I realized what was going on. I was naive, yes. I thought Richard and Mr. Kacherian were legitimate businessmen. But I had nothing to do with any fraud. Or with harassing Cordelia Ramsey."

She paused to sip some coffee. "That didn't stop all of them from going after me. The full-court press from the district attorneys in Alameda and Marin, and the IRS thrown in for good measure. When Richard was arrested, Bradfield Investments folded and I didn't have a job. I did some temp work, but I also had to borrow money from Aunt Maggie. I didn't ask Mother for help, because I didn't want to explain it to her. I went through two years of pure hell, in debt up to my ears. And I couldn't leave until it was over. Every penny I got out of selling my condo went to pay my bills. I had nothing left by the time I moved back here."

"What did you tell your family?"

"My mother? The bare minimum. Can't you just picture her reaction if I told her I was that man's mistress?

275

My sister knows more, but not everything. Aunt Maggie knows all the gory details." Andi shook her head. "I don't like to talk about it. For obvious reasons."

"When did you break off the relationship?"

"I didn't." The words came out in a whisper. "The police did it for me."

"You are afraid of him."

"Of course I am." Her mouth quivered slightly. "When you told me he was out of jail, my heart dropped into the pit of my stomach."

I spread my hands wide. "But according to you, he doesn't have anything to fear from you. Unless it was your testimony at one of his trials."

She shook her head. "It's not that. I only told the truth. I was subpoenaed. I had to testify. I thought Sam Kacherian was just another client, one of Richard's occasional golf partners. After that day I testified in court, I thought Richard would realize I didn't mean to hurt him. But that was just more of Andi being naive, wasn't it? I saw it in his eyes when I left the witness stand that day and walked past the table where he and his lawyer were sitting."

I nodded. People like Bradfield didn't care much about the truth or what other people were compelled to do. They only care about themselves and how the world affects them.

Andi took another sip of her mocha, then held the tall glass between her hands. She shivered, and I didn't think it was because of the blast of air that came through the door when a customer entered the coffee shop.

"You can't imagine what it's like to learn that someone you once cared for is a monster," she said. "Someone who defrauded people who'd entrusted their money to him. Someone who could stalk Cordelia Ramsey. Someone who could . . ."

"Murder his wife?" The words dropped onto the table with a thud. Andi stared at her coffee as though she expected some demon to rise from the cup.

"He swore he didn't kill her," she said, her voice barely rising above a whisper. "I believed him. Probably because I wanted to believe him."

I stirred my latte with a spoon. "But you've had eight years to think about it, haven't you, Andi? Have you come to any conclusions?"

"Oh, yes, I have." Her eyes came up to meet mine. "Would you like to hear them?"

Forty-one

"HE DID KILL HIS WIFE," I SAID.

"He wasn't with me. I lied to the police."

Andi Haskell took a deep breath. She probably needed it. Her words came slowly, carefully, as though she were having trouble getting them past the tight lines around her mouth.

"That day at Pebble Beach . . . After we met with the client at his house on Seventeen Mile Drive, we went back to the lodge. That was about three. I thought Richard and I were going to spend the rest of the afternoon and evening together, maybe stroll around Carmel and have a romantic dinner at some secluded restaurant. But . . ." She shook her head. "Not to be. As we were walking from the parking lot toward the lodge, who should we run into but Sam Kacherian and a friend of his."

"Yes, we knew Kacherian was there in Pebble Beach," I said. "We figured it was a planned encounter, not chance."

"They played it that way," Andi said. "Chance meeting, I mean. Kacherian and Richard were all hail-fellow-well-met, gee-I-didn't-expect-to-run-into-you. That sort of thing. At the time, I believed it. I don't believe it now. I was the beard, so Richard could meet Kacherian." She smiled, but she wasn't amused.

278

"Anyway, Kacherian had someone with him, another businessman. They invited Richard to play golf and he accepted. I was disappointed. But I didn't say anything. That was about three-thirty. I asked Richard about dinner. Order room service, he said, and he'd be there about seven-thirty. Richard went to his room to change. I spent the afternoon at the spa, getting a massage and a facial. I went back to my room sometime after six and ordered dinner."

I recalled the statement of the room service waiter who'd brought the meals to Andi Haskell's room. According to his watch, he'd delivered them at 7:35. Melissa Bradfield had discovered her dying mother about eight-fifteen that night. The coroner estimated Stephanie Bradfield had been stabbed sometime during the previous hour, perhaps about the same time Andi answered the door in Pebble Beach wearing her blue silk robe. Richard Bradfield was supposedly behind that door, which would have made it impossible for him to be in Oakland, a two-and-a-half-hour drive from Pebble Beach.

But Andi had just admitted lying about that.

"What time did Bradfield show up?" I asked.

"After nine. It may even have been nine-thirty. When he was late, I was upset, though not surprised. I figured he was talking business with someone and had lost track of the time. That happened a lot. Now that I've had a few years to look back on it, I realize I was always playing second fiddle." Bitterness colored her voice.

"I'd been looking forward to that trip to Pebble Beach since Richard mentioned it a month before. I'd learned the drill, you see. Being involved with a married man meant I wasn't able to spend a lot of time with him. I learned to appreciate those times when I could be with him. Certainly never on holidays or weekends. I was

279

afraid to be demanding or greedy for his time, for fear I'd lose him."

Now she shook her head. "I look back on it now and wonder how I could have deluded myself so thoroughly. I doubt that he ever really cared." She stopped and took a deep breath. "But you don't want to hear about that. You want to know about Pebble Beach. I'm not sure exactly what time Richard finally arrived. Except that it was a long time after seven-thirty."

"What did he say when he got there?"

Her eyes got a distant look, as though she were trying to recall Bradfield's exact words. "He was contrite, of course. He always was. When I asked where he'd been, he told me he, Kacherian, and Kacherian's friend had been in the bar, talking business. But he asked me not to say anything to anyone, because the three of them were putting together a real estate deal and they wanted to keep it under wraps until it was certain. Later I thought he didn't want me to say anything about their meeting because of that stock scheme."

"Now you don't think so?"

She shook her head. "It was his wife's death Richard was worried about. I didn't see him from about three-thirty until after nine. He would have had plenty of time to drive from Pebble Beach to Oakland and back again. He could have killed her."

"But you were his alibi."

"Yes." She smiled faintly. "He used me. I let him use me."

I let that subject pass on to another. "The man who was with Kacherian. This is the first I've heard of him. Do you have any idea who he was? Can you describe him?"

Andi tilted her head to one side. "Kacherian introduced him, said he was from Orange County. He was a good-looking older man. Tall, gray hair, brown eyes, I think. Distinguished, in his mid-fifties, I would guess. Very dapper and self-assured, as though he'd be comfortable in blue jeans or a business suit."

I sat up straighter. The man she was describing sounded a lot like someone I'd met recently.

"He said something about wanting to look at antiques later," Andi continued. "Maybe he was a collector. His name was . . . let's see . . . a president's name, or close to it. Tom. That's it. Tom Jeffries."

When Andi left the coffee shop to pick up her daughter at day care, I took up residence at the nearest phone booth. Wayne Hobart wasn't at his desk in the Oakland Police Department Homicide Section. But I found Rita Lydecker in San Rafael.

"Drop whatever you're doing," I told her, "and find out everything you can about a man named Tom Jeffries. He's in his late fifties or early sixties. Eight years ago he was in business down in Orange County. He retired sometime last year. Right now he owns an antique store in Fort Bragg."

"And you'll tell me what this is about when you get back," Rita said. "I'm on it."

I argued with myself all the way to the Denver airport. Was it possible that Tom Jeffries had simply retired and moved to Fort Bragg, where he then met Perdita Paxton? That could very well be all there was to it, plain truth and coincidence. Coincidences happen all the time. And plain truth? Less often, to my cynical investigator's mind. Tom Jeffries's retirement and move to the north coast had coincided with Richard Bradfield's parole.

Still, I thought, I could be overreacting to Andi Haskell's revelation. So, the man had once played golf with Sam Kacherian and Richard Bradfield. And presumably had discussed some sort of deal with them. So what? That didn't

281

mean he was a bosom friend. Just business. That's all it could be, just business.

I didn't recall Jeffries's name coming up when the Seville Agency uncovered the penny stock scam involving Kacherian's company, but that didn't mean he wasn't involved or that he didn't know about it. Once Errol had passed the information to our client's attorney, the agency's involvement in the investigation had passed to the district attorney's office. Jeffries might have been a peripheral player whose participation had come up later. Or maybe there wasn't enough evidence to charge him. Even if Jeffries had been implicated, I told myself, that didn't necessarily mean he was now entangled in some sort of conspiracy to get Perdita Paxton.

From what Andi Haskell said, it was Kacherian whom Jeffries knew, not Bradfield. Besides, Perdita said she hadn't told Tom Jeffries anything about her life before she moved to Mendocino. But did he know she was really Cordelia Ramsey? Did he know that Richard Bradfield was suspected of killing his wife that day he and Kacherian saw Bradfield in Pebble Beach? In a way, Jeffries and Kacherian were Bradfield's backup alibi, one he could have brought into play if Andi Haskell hadn't told the police her lover had been with her when his wife was stabbed to death in Oakland. But Andi had come through.

I didn't have answers, only a feeling of disquiet when I thought of Perdita and Jeffries and their budding relationship. Richard Bradfield was an ingenious killer with a long list of names and grievances. He'd decided it was his turn for payback. I didn't want Perdita's name ticked off that list.

When I got to the Denver airport I turned in my rental car and headed for the terminal. By then it was seven, cold and dark, and the woman at the United ticket counter said the weather reports were predicting snow. I'd purchased an open-ended ticket when I left Oakland for Denver. There were two more flights out of Denver to Oakland that night. One left in forty minutes, but the flight was full. I tried for a standby on that one. It didn't work out. I was stuck with the flight that left at nine-fifteen.

I found a bank of phones and called Wayne Hobart at home. "Where are you?" he asked. "I've been trying to reach you."

"Colorado. I just talked with Andi Haskell."

"Richard Bradfield's alibi for his wife's murder," Wayne said.

"Not anymore."

"She'll talk? Sid will be glad to hear that. Of course, we have to catch the son of a bitch first."

"Why were you trying to reach me?"

"Macauley's still missing," he said. "And Colin Derrill's in the hospital."

"Since when? And how bad?"

"Since last night. He was leaving his studio sometime after seven. We know it was after seven because he was on the phone with a friend before that. He got waylaid, beat up pretty bad. He's in a coma."

"Damn," I said, loud enough that the person at the next pay phone glanced my way. "So you can't ask him if his assailant was Bradfield?"

"Bradfield? It's possible. But that studio of his is in a lousy neighborhood. His wallet was gone and so was his watch. We've got some punks in this town who kill people for less than that."

"When I saw Derrill a few days ago, he told me he'd had some break-ins at his last place. What if Bradfield was looking for information on Cordelia Ramsey's whereabouts? She was married to Derrill when Bradfield began stalking her. He might have guessed they had stayed in touch."

283

"It's possible," Wayne conceded. "I'll alert that sergeant up in Mendocino County, just to be safe."

"Thanks, Wayne. Listen, I know Sam Kacherian supposedly killed himself in January. Errol found out that much from a friend of his down in L.A. But I've got some questions. Where did Kacherian work before he got laid off? He must have had a car, to get his job. Was the vehicle found there where he killed himself? If not, where is it?"

"You think Bradfield killed him?" Wayne asked.

"Kacherian lived in Tustin. The car Bradfield had while he lived in San Diego turned up in Garden Grove. Not far as the crow flies. Bradfield could settle a score and gain some transportation at the same time."

"I'm on it," Wayne said. "I'll talk to you when you get back."

I hung up the phone. Then I discovered that Andi Haskell had also told the truth about how suddenly springtime blizzards could cover the Denver area with a blanket of white.

While I was waiting at the gate, hoping to catch the standby, I'd noticed the first few snowflakes floating down outside the plate-glass windows that lined the concourse. The snow fell more steadily as the flight took off without me. I paced the length of the concourse and had dinner at one of the terminal restaurants. When I checked one of the overhead screens to verify my departure time, I discovered my late evening flight had been delayed, first by twenty minutes, then forty, then an hour.

The sky kept falling, whitening the runways and frosting the windows. Back at the phones I called Perdita Paxton's number in Mendocino, but got the answering machine instead. I left a message, asking that Perdita call me at home in Oakland. But by the look of the snow outside the window in Denver, I wasn't sure I'd be there. I disconnected and called the Garber Street house. Rachel answered.

"I'm stuck in Denver," I told her. "There's a blizzard outside."

"Well, it's raining here. Sheets and sheets of water, pouring from the sky. The weather report last night said chance of showers. Hah! Right now it's a certainty."

Wonderful, I thought. That could cause delays on the Oakland end of the flight. Assuming I ever got off the ground in Denver. "Any more calls? Is Emily there?"

"No, to both questions," Rachel said. "Emily and Vicki drove up to Mendocino earlier this afternoon. Hope they got there before the rain did."

"Mendocino. What time did they leave?"

"About three. They were hoping to beat the traffic." Rachel picked up my concern. "Is there a problem, Jeri?"

"I'm not sure. If the weather cooperates, I should be home late tonight. I'll know more tomorrow."

At least I would if Rita was fast. Which she usually was.

I tried Perdita Paxton's Mendocino number again. Still the answering machine. I didn't leave a message. Directory assistance didn't have a number for Tom Jeffries in Fort Bragg. He must be unlisted, I thought. I waited twenty minutes and called Perdita's number again. This time I got a recording that told me service had been temporarily disrupted. Pacific Bell must have been having some problems with the storm front rolling in off the ocean. Telephone communication with the Mendocino coast was no longer an option.

I called Errol instead. Fortunately, the phones were still working on the Monterey peninsula. "North coast is getting the worst of it," Errol said. "We've had a lot of rain, though. Where are you?"

"Denver. I had an interesting conversation with our old friend Andi Haskell." I gave him a rundown of what

Andi had told me. Then I made the same request of him that I'd made of Wayne Hobart: more information about Sam Kacherian's death.

As I hung up the phone I checked my watch and sighed. I walked to the gate and discovered my flight had been delayed yet again. I found an uncomfortable seat with not enough light, pulled out the paperback I'd brought with me, and tried to read. The airport had filled with disgruntled passengers, noisy crying children and their restless parents, harried-looking businessmen and -women in suits who weren't going to make it to that early morning meeting in Chicago or New York City. Unable to concentrate on my book, I went to get some coffee and paced the concourse while I drank it, poking my nose in all the airport shops.

When I returned to my gate, the seat I'd vacated had been taken in my absence. So I sat down on the carpeted floor, leaning against my gray travel bag, and listened to the elderly man next to me regale his companion with tales of getting stuck at airports throughout the West.

Finally, I dozed off. But it was a fitful sleep. I woke up every time an announcement blasted through the airport's loudspeaker. Each time, I looked out the window and saw only white.

Snow. The damn stuff was pretty, if you didn't have to go anywhere. For the duration, I was stranded, and the ticking clock told me I was running out of time.

Forty-two

MY FLIGHT FINALLY LEFT DENVER FOUR HOURS late, touching down at Oakland International at three o'clock Saturday morning. I went home, exhausted, slept for a few hours, then woke to a dark gray sky and the sound of rain pattering on my roof.

My apartment certainly seemed empty without my cats, as gray and gloomy as the weather outside. I knew from my earlier conversations with Dr. Prentice that Abigail and Black Bart were both well and missing me. I missed them too. I wondered how long it would be before the danger was over and I could bring them home. But the decapitated lemon tree outside my front window was a reminder of just how potent that danger was.

I showered and dressed. By eight I was in my office, drinking coffee as I listened to the radio recital of power outages, flooding, and traffic accidents caused by the storm that had swept through the Bay Area over the past twenty-four hours. The weather was supposed to improve today, but so far I hadn't seen any evidence of it and neither had the guy who was updating me on the hour and half hour. Besides, there was another front waiting offshore, gathering strength.

The mail had piled up in my absence. The red light on my answering machine blinked at me as well. I sifted through the mail, then checked the messages, mentally sorting through what could wait and what couldn't. The last message was from Wayne Hobart. He'd talked with the police department down in Tustin. I picked up the phone.

"You were right about the car," Wayne told me when I reached him at home. "Kacherian had a little Nissan that was missing when they found the body. Turned up a day later in San Luis Obispo."

"Another car got stolen there, right about the same time," I guessed.

"Right again. This one wound up in Oakland. Two days after it was stolen."

"About the time the phone calls started at the house where Vicki Vernon lives. I'm willing to bet a car was stolen in Berkeley when Ted Macauley's vehicle was abandoned up by the botanical gardens."

"Several, in fact. I've already talked with Brad Nguyen in Berkeley. Macauley's car was probably ditched Thursday or Friday. Two cars were stolen from that neighborhood on Thursday, and two on Friday. None of them located so far."

"What about Kacherian's job?"

"Not much there. He worked for one of those packing stores. You know, where you can take in your Christmas presents and they'll box 'em and send 'em. It was a seasonal job. He started working there before Thanksgiving, and he was let go after the holidays."

"What was the place called?" I wrote down the name of the company and thanked Wayne, asking how Sid was doing.

"He took a couple of days off, went up to Sacramento to see his sister. Maybe this will have blown over by the time he gets back."

"I hope so." The rain spattered against my office window, reminding me of what else was blowing over.

288

After I disconnected, I called Rita Lydecker. "Anything on Tom Jeffries?"

"Yeah. You in your office? I'll fax the stuff to you."

I waited impatiently for the fax line to ring, then snatched the pages as they came out of the machine. Then I switched on my computer and logged onto some databases. With the information Wayne had given me coupled with Rita's fax, it didn't take long to connect the dots. I leaned back in my chair and stared at the screen in front of me.

"Bingo," I said.

It took me nearly five hours to get to Mendocino.

First I had to fight my way past my own fatigue, then through a midday Bay Area traffic jam caused by the nasty weather. It was still raining as I inched my way across the Richmond–San Rafael Bridge and onto Highway 101. The traffic thinned out as I drove north.

I bypassed Cloverdale and got on Highway 128, heading northwest toward the coast. But the previous night's storm had washed a lot of mud and debris onto the twisting two-lane road. At a couple of places only one lane was open as highway crews pushed the obstacles out of the way. When I reached the long tunnel of redwoods that ran alongside the Navarro River, I saw signs warning of flooding. Fortunately, the river had receded, leaving only a scum of mud on the asphalt ahead of me.

When I got to the coast it looked as though that promised Pacific front was taking its time to make landfall. Above me the sun tried to pierce through the cloud cover, but the clouds hovering offshore were angry and dark, hugging the boiling, surging ocean. As I drove across the Big River bridge into Mendocino the waves assaulted the headland to the west. It started to rain again.

I tried Perdita's house first. No one home. Then I

drove down Main Street and angled the Toyota into a parking spot.

Lee was behind the counter at Perdu and she looked surprised to see me. "You drove up from Oakland? I thought the road was closed. We didn't even have electricity or phones last night."

"It's open now. But just barely. Looks like another front is moving in."

"This weather," Lee said, shaking her head. "It rained like crazy last night, but it was sunny two hours ago."

"Where's Perdita?"

"She's not at home?"

"No. And she wasn't there last night."

"Probably went out to dinner. She doesn't cook. Her niece and a friend came up for the weekend, got here just before it started raining hard. I wonder if—" Lee stopped. "Maybe they went up to Tom Jeffries's place in Fort Bragg."

"Where can I find him?"

"His house is up north of Pudding Creek," Lee said, consulting her watch. "But it's past three. He should be at his store." Lee jotted an address on the back of one of Perdita's business cards. "You can't miss it."

I pointed the car north again, speeding up the asphalt ribbon. The rain stopped by the time I drove into Fort Bragg. I found Tom Jeffries's antique store easily enough, on Franklin Street, which paralleled Highway 1, which became Main Street when it entered town. But Tom Jeffries wasn't there. Instead an older woman held court behind the counter.

"You just missed him," she said. "He and Mrs. Paxton and the girls went to the botanical gardens. He said something about picking up some plants he'd ordered before the rain starts again."

I found a phone booth and looked up the Mendocino

County sheriff's substation. It was on South Franklin. I stopped there, looking for Sergeant Sullivan, but he was out in the field. I left a message, then retraced my route south, over the Noyo River, to the Mendocino Coast Botanical Gardens. I pulled off the highway onto a gravel parking lot and parked near the restaurant, which was now closed. There weren't many vehicles in the lot, but one, a Land Rover parked near the entrance, looked like the one Jeffries had been driving when I met him last week.

The sign at the entrance said the gardens were open until five. Although the sun was trying its best, it didn't seem like a day for a walk in the gardens. I went through the gate, where there was a shop that sold everything from seeds to the usual T-shirts. There was also a window where a white-haired man collected admission fees. I looked around but didn't see any of the four people I sought. A young couple in jeans paid the old attendant. Then they strolled off, arm in arm, past a middle-aged man who stared at a display of succulents as though he couldn't decide which variety he wanted to buy.

"Do you know Tom Jeffries?" I asked the man at the store. "Tall, silver-haired man, on the lean side. He's with an older woman and two young women, college-age. They may have had a dog with them, an Airedale terrier. Jeffries was supposed to pick up some plants."

"Can't say as I do," he said, shaking his head. "But we've had several people in and out today, in spite of the weather. There's Emma. Let's ask her."

He looked over my shoulder at a woman in a smock who'd just come into view, carrying a nursery catalog. I repeated my question and she nodded, pointing at a cluster of large plants in plastic containers. "Yes, they were here. In fact, that's Mr. Jeffries's order right there."

"Where did they go? It's important that I find them."

"He wanted to show them how the rhododendrons would look," Emma said. "They've started blooming but they won't peak until May." She reached for one of the folded brochures and opened it. One side was a map of the gardens. She pointed. "Here are the coast rhododendrons, where the north and south trail meet."

I pulled out my wallet and gave the old man the admission fee, then set out, map in hand, through beds of perennials and then an expanse of different types of heather. Ahead of me I saw masses of camellias and daylilies. I found the south trail easily enough, and the area where the coast rhododendrons grew, but I saw no people, save the young couple I'd seen earlier. I stopped at the junction of the north and south trails and listened, hearing only the wind and the crash of waves on the shore to the west.

Wait. Was that a dog barking? I listened again. Yes, it was a dog. I thought it must be Molly, the Airedale. The sound came from somewhere ahead of me. I looked down at the map. I had a wealth of trails to choose from, all narrower than the one I was on, winding through the woods and into the canyons formed by Digger Creek and Schoefer Creek. Were they hidden from view on one of them or had they stayed on the broader trail that led to the coastal bluff?

I started walking, sticking with the north trail as it continued west. I thought I heard voices to my left and detoured down the Pine Forest trail to Fern Canyon. But the voices I'd heard belonged to two women strolling along the banks of Digger Creek. They had a cocker spaniel with them. The dog barked at me as I approached.

"Have you seen a man and three women, with an Airedale?"

One of the women nodded. "Yes. Butchie and the

Airedale had quite a romp. That was about fifteen minutes ago. They were heading in the direction of Cliff
House."

I consulted the map again and saw the structure she
referred to, almost at the end of the bluff that jutted out
into the ocean, with a picnic area nearby. I got back on
the main path, then left it again on the Shore Pine trail.
Up ahead I saw a grassy meadow, then a glint of black
and brindle and the distinctive Airedale cut as Molly
raced across the path in front of me. I heard nothing but
the steady crash of water on rocks. But Molly must have
heard something else. She altered course, heading across
the meadow for the trees.

Cliff House at the Mendocino Coast Botanical Gardens
certainly wasn't as grand as the San Francisco landmark I
associated with the name. This was a small enclosed rectangular shelter, reached by a narrow path and a series of
steps leading down from the main trail. With redwood
planks for walls, it was little more than a viewing platform
perched on the edge of the cliff.

I went through the only door, at the southwest corner
of the structure, and saw a wide glass window that faced
north and looked down at the waves crashing on the
rocks below. Across a cove I could see the Georgia
Pacific lumber mill dominating the coastal skyline of
Fort Bragg. Closer to home I saw Perdita Paxton standing at the railing in front of the window, with Tom Jeffries next to her, his arm around her waist.

"Hello." My voice echoed as I spoke.

"Jeri. We didn't expect to see you." Perdita looked
surprised.

So did Tom Jeffries. He dropped his arm from her
waist as they both turned from the glass to face me.

"No, I'm sure you didn't. Where are Vicki and
Emily?"

"They went on ahead with Molly," Perdita said. "Around the bluff, I think. We're supposed to meet at the main entrance. Jeri, is something wrong?"

"That gives us time to talk, then." I gave Tom Jeffries a hard-eyed stare. "Tell me, Mr. Jeffries, about your relationship with Richard Bradfield."

Forty-three

PERDITA PAXTON WENT WHITE AROUND THE mouth and stepped away from Tom Jeffries. Her gray eyes chilled as they raked his face, as though she'd never seen him before.

"I didn't know you knew Richard Bradfield," she spat out.

Jeffries stared at her, confused. "I didn't know Bradfield," he protested. His eyes moved from Perdita to me as he shook his head. "Not well, anyway. And I certainly didn't have a relationship with him. Business or otherwise."

"He worked for you, in a manner of speaking," I said. "So did Sam Kacherian."

"That's nonsense. Bradfield had his own company. As for Sam . . ." Jeffries stumbled a bit as he said the next words. "I don't know what you're talking about."

"Belston Enterprises, Mr. Jeffries. You were a senior vice president of Belston, until you retired last year. Belston owns a chain of packing stores, all over Southern California."

"Belston owns a lot of businesses." He was hedging. He knew where I was headed.

"Sam Kacherian worked in several of those stores, after he was paroled."

Jeffries sighed heavily and looked at Perdita's stormy

face, hoping for some comfort. He didn't get any there. "Look, Ms. Howard, I knew Sam Kacherian a long time. He'd just spent five years in prison. I know, I know, he committed a crime. But he paid for it. I was just trying to help the man get back on his feet."

"So you talked with Belston's former general counsel, the one that got appointed to the parole board a few years ago." Now he looked startled. "Oh, yes, I checked that too. It's amazing what you can find out with computers these days. Your pal made sure Kacherian was paroled to Orange County, close enough to the San Fernando Valley so he could at least see his children regularly, even if his ex-wife didn't want to have anything to do with him. He had a job waiting for him, in Santa Ana, courtesy of Belston's Human Resources director. But he couldn't make it to work on time, so the manager let him go. You found him another job, in Tustin. But he got laid off after the holidays."

"He was having a hard time adjusting," Jeffries said.

"You know Kacherian is dead."

Now Jeffries looked pained. "Of course I do. I attended his funeral. But what the hell does all this have to do with Bradfield?"

"Bradfield was paroled about the same time Kacherian was. To San Diego. Where he worked for a janitorial firm called San Diego County Cleaners."

"Is that supposed to mean something to me?" Jeffries demanded.

"Considering that Belston also owns that firm, yes, it's supposed to mean something. Did you help Bradfield get a job too?"

"Of course not." I watched his face as he denied it, trying to decide if he was telling the truth.

"Then how do you explain it?"

"I can't explain it. Unless my friend in Human Resources somehow thought that I meant . . ." He shook his head. "No, no, it must be a coincidence. Just where is this leading, Ms. Howard? Sam may have been involved in that stock thing, but he had nothing to do with whatever else Bradfield did."

He turned to Perdita. Her eyes were as cold and gray as the sky on the other side of the plate-glass window. "What's going on, Perdita? Why are you looking at me that way? How in the hell does this involve you?"

"You have no idea who I am?" Her voice was icy. "I'm supposed to believe this is all coincidence."

He moved toward her but she moved away, toward the other end of the window. He stopped and put his hands out in supplication. "Of course I know who you are. You're Perdita Paxton. What the hell is going on here?"

"I'm Cordelia Ramsey," she told him, her voice cold as she faced him. "Bradfield killed my sister. Then he tried to kill me."

Jeffries stared at her, stunned.

"Did you lead him up here, Tom?" she asked. "So he could try again?"

"No," said a voice behind me, one that made no attempt to suppress its gloating tone. "I got that information from Colin Derrill."

I turned, slowly. Richard Bradfield stood in the doorway of Cliff House, looking quite pleased with himself.

In khaki pants, a work shirt, and a blue jacket, he was dressed far more casually than the old Richard Bradfield, the one who'd favored expensive blue pinstriped suits. His face looked much like the picture faxed to me earlier in the week. A little older, a little grayer, but the extra flesh at the jawline didn't disguise the arrogant tilt to his chin. What the picture hadn't shown were those eyes, which still held their blue fury. Right now the eyes held

297

something else, a glint of triumph. In his right hand he held a revolver.

"Colin?" Perdita said, the word hissing from her as she looked at Bradfield with loathing. Somehow she didn't seem surprised that he'd finally tracked her down. She'd been expecting it. "Colin would never—"

"Colin was attacked earlier this week." I moved my head slightly to the right, where Perdita stood, a few feet back. "He's in the hospital. Bradfield beat it out of him."

"Fucking faggot." Bradfield smiled contemptuously as he moved farther into the shelter. "I hit him a couple of times, with this gun, and he folded right up. Didn't even have to shoot him to get him to talk. You always did have lousy taste in men, Cordelia."

"It was my sister who had lousy taste in men," she snapped. "Starting with you."

Her words slid off him like water on a duck. He surveyed Jeffries, on my left, who still looked stunned at this twist in events. "So this is the latest one. Good to see you again, Tom. You were a big help."

"What are you talking about?" Jeffries shot back. "I only met you once, that day in Pebble Beach. I never helped you with anything."

"Oh, but you did. More than once, whether you knew it or not. At Pebble Beach . . . Well, we won't talk about Pebble Beach. Let's talk about what you've done for me lately."

Bradfield jiggled the barrel of the gun, as though he couldn't keep still. "When I got to Sam's apartment last January," he continued, "I discovered he kept in touch with his good friend Tom Jeffries. I read a few of your letters to Sam. You write a good description, Tom. That woman you met in Mendocino, the one you were so crazy about, she sounded a lot like Cordelia, even if the name was different. Of course I knew old Mike Paxton came from this neck of the woods. Sorry I didn't get up here sooner. But I had a few other things to take care of before I came calling."

"Such as killing Kacherian," I said. I took a step closer to Perdita, closer to the door. "Stealing his car, and all those others, so you could head up north to Berkeley and terrorize Vicki Vernon and her housemates."

"Stand still, where I can see you." I stopped. Bradfield turned the corners of his mouth upward, in what was an unpleasant grimace rather than a smile.

"Very perceptive, Ms. Jeri Howard. I thought you were too smart for your own good. Back then, when you and Seville pulled the rug out from under me. And now. I spent all that time in prison planning how I was going to get back at all of you. Such a run of luck I've had."

He smiled again, jiggling the gun. "I recognized Vicki last summer, working in that dental office, when I was swabbing out shitters as a janitor. She looks just like her old man, the hotshot Detective Vernon. He thought he was so damned smart. Him and that old war horse Kelso. But they couldn't pin anything on me. So . . . Little Miss Vicki Vernon. What better way to get even with Detective Vernon. I heard her give her new address in Berkeley to the receptionist. Imagine my surprise—"

"When you got to Berkeley," I said, "and discovered that your daughter lived in the same house."

"My own dear Melissa. Fruit of my loins, who damned me to hell, and said she never wanted to see me again. See, another stroke of luck. So was Ted Macauley. I saw him that day he followed Vicki and Melissa on Telegraph Avenue. He looked useful. So I struck up a conversation with him later, at one of the coffeehouses. He was easy to manipulate. What a self-involved little prick he was."

Just like the one before me now, I thought. I noticed he

299

spoke of Macauley in the past tense. That didn't bode well for Ted.

"Macauley helped you harass Vicki and her friends. Who made the calls? Which of you threw the bomb?"

"Both of us made the calls. I delivered the bomb. Ted lost his nerve in the crunch."

"Did he help you get the gun?"

"This?" Bradfield's eyes flicked down at the weapon, then back at me. "You could say that. Ted liked to play with guns as well as bombs. I found this under the seat of his car. Yes, meeting up with Ted was a real stroke of luck."

"I would imagine, since he did some of your dirty work for you," I said conversationally. "Maybe he can even play fall guy, after this is all over. Where is Ted, by the way?"

"Somewhere he won't be found till I'm ready for him to be found."

Which meant Ted was probably dead, killed by this madman sometime after the bomb went through the window of the house on Garber Street. Maybe even before.

In the distance I heard a dog bark and remembered Vicki and Emily, out walking somewhere on the headland, with the Airedale terrier. Perdita had told me earlier that the younger women had gone on ahead, that they were all supposed to rendezvous at the main entrance to the gardens, which closed at five.

I stole a glance at my watch. Four-thirty. If Perdita and Jeffries didn't show up, would Vicki and Emily come looking for them? Had Sergeant Sullivan ever gotten my message? That looked doubtful. I'd have to do something, and soon.

It started to rain again, drops beating a tattoo against the plate glass of the overlook. The unlighted shelter darkened and the faces of the three people with me stood out white in the gloom. I gauged the distance between me and the others, looking around for something I could use as a means of defense. There was the railing in front of the window, if I could wrench it free. There was also that big rock over in the corner, where Perdita stood.

"I saw Andi Haskell the other day," I said conversationally. "She told me you killed your wife. And that she'd testify to that in court."

That was stretching the truth concerning my meeting with Andi. But Bradfield didn't know that. My words wiped the smile off his face. He took a step toward me.

"Where is she?" he demanded.

So he didn't know. Or he hadn't yet made the attempt to find her. Or maybe he figured she'd never talk.

"You think I'm going to tell you? So you can go after her too? Forget it, Bradfield."

He took another step toward me. I heard the dog bark again. This time it was closer, and there were voices in the distance. Perdita heard it too. I felt her alarm.

"I'm not going to tell you anything about Andi," I told Bradfield, goading him at the same time I was hoping he didn't shoot me. But if he shot me, I couldn't tell him where Andi Haskell was.

He moved toward me and I circled to the right, closer to the door. Behind him I saw Tom Jeffries take a step toward Perdita. Bradfield caught the movement from the corner of his eye. He shifted position, so that he could see all three of us, and leveled the gun at Jeffries.

"You I don't need," he told the older man. "Shall I kill him, Perdita, right here in front of you?"

She swore at him, raising her voice in desperate anger. They could have heard her all the way to Mendocino. As it was, I'm sure she was hoping whoever was outside Cliff House could hear her.

I heard a low growl, then the Airedale came boiling

301

through the doorway, launching herself at Bradfield's legs. He pointed the gun at the dog and squeezed the trigger.

The report echoed loudly around the room and a crack appeared in the window. Bradfield's shot had gone wild, probably because Tom Jeffries had leaped at him the same time Molly had. The room erupted in a chaos of noise as shouts came at me from all sides. Perdita had her hands on Bradfield, trying to wrench the gun away from him.

The gun went off again and she screamed. I wasn't sure if she'd been hit, but her scream was echoed by one of the young women outside. Emily appeared in the doorway. She tried to run into the room, but Vicki grabbed her arm and held her back.

"Let her in," Bradfield shouted, exultant. "I want her too."

He kicked at the dog, which was trying to savage his leg. She yelped, then lunged for him again, undeterred. I scooped up the big rock in the corner. Then I hurled it at Bradfield.

It hit him on the side of the head. He dropped the gun and reeled backward, over the railing and into the plate glass. The crack in the glass widened, then splintered and shattered as if in slow motion. Bradfield's momentum carried him through the glass and down, to the rocks and the pounding surf.

Forty-four

I DON'T KNOW WHETHER THE ROCK I THREW killed Bradfield, or if it was the rocks below. I probably never will.

By the time the Mendocino County search and rescue team recovered the body, it was in bad shape, smashed repeatedly against the rocky shore during the night as the storm front moved across the coast. I talked it over with Kaz later, when he got back from Paris. He said Bradfield was probably stunned when he went through the window, and died when he landed on the rocks.

Either way, I contributed to the man's death. Bradfield was a sociopath. No doubt he would have killed us all. I kept replaying the scene, like a videotape on automatic rewind, the shock and the sick feeling in my stomach returning every time I relived the rest of that evening, seeing the flashing red lights through the rain, there at the botanical gardens, and the white, brightly lighted hallways at the hospital in Fort Bragg.

Sergeant Sullivan had gotten my message, and he'd arrived at the gardens in time to hear the shots. Perdita had a flesh wound in her arm. It was healing. She and Molly were at home in Mendocino. I didn't know if she'd resume her relationship with Tom Jeffries. He'd collapsed there at Cliff House. The doctors said he'd had a mild heart attack. That was why he'd retired early from

Belston Enterprises, as it turned out. I decided he was telling the truth about not having helped Bradfield get a job. Whether Perdita would give him the benefit of the doubt had yet to be determined. The jury was still out on that one.

Emily was treated for shock, but she came out of it all right. After a few days on the coast, she was back in class at Berkeley, utilizing the university's resources to get some counseling, according to Vicki, to exorcise the demons left over from her mother's murder at the hands of her father.

"She never did talk it out with anyone before," Vicki said as we sipped lemonade on the deck of the Garber Street house. It was another Saturday morning, a month later. The March that had come in like a rainy, roaring lion left like a lamb, making way for sunny, balmy April. Vicki wore shorts and a sleeveless shirt, and she was stretched out on the bench on one side of the picnic table as she brought me up to date on Emily. "Finding her mother murdered like that, and having to live with her father afterward."

"Then there was the custody fight, and Bradfield stalked her aunt, threatening to kill her." I shook my head. "At least Colin Derrill's going to be all right. Wayne Hobart said Derrill came out of the coma a few days after it all went down. It was Bradfield who'd attacked him."

"He's luckier than Ted Macauley," Vicki said. "Not that I liked the guy, but . . . to die like that."

"I know." They'd found Macauley's body the following day, on Sunday, buried in a shallow grave in a lot up on Grizzly Peak Boulevard. He'd been shot with his own gun, the one the sheriff's people had recovered at the same time they brought Bradfield's body up the bluff.

Hard to say when Bradfield killed him, whether it was before or after the bomb came through the window.

The harassment complaint against Sid had gone through the Professional Standards Section, with recommendations going up and down the chain, resulting in an official no-cause outcome and an unofficial serious talking-to from Sid's lieutenant. Sid was back at his desk at the Oakland Police Department, he and Wayne working like a well-oiled team. Vicki said Sid was still dating Graciela Portillo. From the way Vicki wrinkled her nose, I could see that this wasn't to her taste.

"As potential stepmother material," Vicki said, "I like her a lot less than I like you. Not that Dad has said anything to indicate that he's thinking of getting married again. But I won't mess with his love life if he won't mess with mine."

"Oh? Do you have a love life?"

She grinned. "I've been going out with Nelson."

"Nelson? That's like dating your brother."

"I won't mess with your love life," she intoned, "if you won't mess with mine."

"Fine, fine." I chuckled. And I did have a love life again, now that Kaz was back. In fact, I was seeing him this evening.

The door of the garage apartment opened and Ben came out, barefoot and in blue jeans and a T-shirt, heading for the back steps and the kitchen. "Morning," he said.

I looked at my watch. "It's afternoon, actually."

"When you work nights, morning is whenever you start. Is there any coffee?"

"Emily made a pot before she went shopping," Vicki said, pouring herself another glass of lemonade from the pitcher she'd placed in the center of the table. "There should be some."

Ben opened the back door. He returned a few minutes later with a cup of coffee and a spoon in one hand, a heaping bowl of cereal in the other. He joined us at the picnic table. "I got the last cup. I made another pot."

"How are the studies going?" I asked him.

He nodded. "Good. I cut back my working hours and everyone here's tutoring me on some of my tough subjects. My grades are up and I'm not feeling so stressed."

"I'm glad to hear it."

The back door opened and Rachel came out onto the deck. "Hi, Jeri. Didn't know you were here. I was up in my room studying and was lured downstairs by the sound of voices. I need a break."

"How about some lemonade?"

"Looks good." She went back into the house and returned with a glass, which she filled from the pitcher. I scooted down on the bench so she could sit down. "Say, Jeri. You remember that guy you saw at the clinic, Wellette? He got arrested."

"Doesn't surprise me. There in Oakland?"

"No. Blocking the door of a clinic in Pleasant Hill."

A horn sounded from the street in front of the house. "They're back," Rachel said. "Sasha and Marisol. They went to pick up the furniture."

"Time to get to work." Ben finished his cereal and got up from the table. "I'll go find my shoes."

As we walked around to the street, Rachel and Vicki explained that Sasha's insurance company had come through with a check for the needed repairs to the living room. Sasha had been haunting furniture showrooms during the interim and had picked out a replacement sofa. She and Marisol, in a pickup truck borrowed from Marisol's cousin Ernesto, had gone to fetch the new furniture.

Marisol, at the wheel of the elderly Chevy, backed the

truck expertly into the driveway. I saw Sasha on the passenger side, with Martin in between. The new sofa was tied in the bed of the truck and covered with a tarp. Marisol cut the engine and opened the door as Ben hoisted himself into the truck and pulled back the tarp to reveal resplendent new upholstery, a contemporary sectional sofa in a pale butterscotch.

"Beautiful," I said. "Looks cushy."

"There's even a matching chair," Sasha told me. "This new sofa's much more comfortable than the old one. And I got a coffee table too."

"Where's Nelson?" Ben asked. "He said he was gonna help."

"Here I am." I turned my head and saw Nelson walking up the street with his usual take-out food sack in hand.

Emily was with him, looking a lot calmer than she'd been the last time I'd seen her. There was color in her face and she was smiling at something Nelson had said. She carried a big bouquet of spring flowers—iris, daffodils, tulips—which she handed to Sasha. "Here. In honor of the new living room."

Sasha thanked her with a hug. Then she handed the flowers to Martin and we set to work, transferring the new furniture from the pickup truck to the newly plastered and repainted living room. We all took turns testing out the new sofa and chair, pronouncing them a success. Martin and Sasha put Emily's bouquet in a glass pitcher and set it on the new glass-topped coffee table.

Then Martin tugged at my sleeve. "We have new kitties," he said. "Come see."

"Kittens?"

"Martin's been after me to get a cat," Sasha explained. "The woman who had Emily's room last year was allergic, so we couldn't. Now nobody here is allergic to cats. So we all went to the animal shelter." She rolled her eyes. "You can just imagine this crew."

I glanced around the room. "Yes, I can. The Five Stooges . . ." I ducked as Rachel tossed a sofa cushion at me. "And you got kittens, plural, as opposed to cat, singular."

"They're pretty singular," Marisol said. "These two, well, they were brother and sister and we didn't want to separate them."

I followed Martin into his room off the kitchen. The kittens, one a silvery gray tabby and the other black with white paws and a white nose, were curled up on his bed, sleeping. "They sleep a lot," he said.

"That's what cats do best. What're they called?"

"I named 'em Stan and Ollie. The gray one's Stan. And the black one's Ollie. Ollie's a girl." I complimented Martin on his choice of names. "Cats make a house better," he said.

"They do indeed," I told him.

I left the house on Garber Street to its own rhythms and went home to my own cats. As I came up the walk, I saw Abigail snoozing in her usual spot on the back of my sofa, where the window looked out at the flower bed. The lemon tree had been replaced by a rhododendron. I unlocked the door and walked into my home. Black Bart was stretched out in a spot of afternoon sun. He opened one eye, surveyed me, then closed it.

The phone rang. I answered it, expecting it to be Kaz, who was due to come over so I could run my hands through his hair.

Instead it was Cassie, calling to tell me she'd found the perfect wedding dress.